Praise for **THE VAN APFEL GIRLS ARE GONE**

'How do you escape your childhood, emotionally, actually? This compelling mystery by Felicity McLean has a rare depth of psychological and emotional truth. It will engage your heart.'

Delia Ephron

'A smart debut. Beautifully atmospheric with its great sense of time and place.'

Melina Marchetta, author of *On the Jellicoe Road*

'A smart, classy thriller that blazes with the heat of Australia and slowly reveals its many layers.'   Fiona Mozley, author of *Elmet*

'I deeply admire the languid, lived-in prose of Felicity McLean's lovely novel *The Van Apfel Girls Are Gone*. This is a story as much about forgiving ourselves our own childhoods, as it is about acknowledging and embracing the people we've become because of those adolescent (and sometimes life altering) choices.'

Hannah Pittard, author of *Visible Empire*

'Sharp, mysteriously moving and highly entertaining.'

Robert Drewe, author of *Shark Net*

'McLean expertly maintains an air of suspense as the tragedy unfolds. Tikka is an unforgettable, if not entirely reliable, narrator full of black humour, brutal honesty and naive curiosity. This novel is one that will haunt readers long after they have turned the last page.'

Bookseller + Publisher Five Star Review

'Engrossing and goosebumpy from start to finish, this novel about three young sisters who vanish all together one night has the chilling feel of true events that are stranger than fiction, and the stuff of nightmares. But the magic of McLean's art is not just her gift for evoking, in almost hallucinogenic detail, her haunted narrator's childhood – a time and place linked to Australia's notorious true-life story of a baby dragged off in the night by a wild animal – but to do so in the most charming and irresistible of narrative voices. The result is a novel that is as delightful as it is terrifying, and just scary good.'

Tim Johnston, bestselling author of *Descent*

THE VAN APFEL GIRLS ARE GONE

FELICITY McLEAN

POINT
BLANK

A Point Blank Book

First published in Great Britain by Point Blank,
an imprint of Oneworld Publications, 2019

ISBN 978-1-78607-607-6
ISBN 978-1-78607-608-3 (ebook)

Printed and bound in Great Britain by Clays Ltd, Elcograf S.p.A.

Oneworld Publications
10 Bloomsbury Street
London WC1B 3SR
England

MIX
Paper from
responsible sources
FSC
www.fsc.org   FSC® C018072

For my parents.

And for Andy, of course.

PROLOGUE

The ghost turned up in time for breakfast, summoned by the death rattle of Cornflakes in their box.

She arrived on foot. *Bare feet.* Barelegged and white-knuckled, in a pale cotton nightie that clung to her calves and slipped off one shoulder as jaunty as a hat. Her hair was damp with sleep sweat – whose wasn't that summer? – and stiff strands of it fenced in her thirteen-year-old face like blinkers strapped to a colt.

By the time we got there she was already halfway across the cul-de-sac. Her unseeing eyes, her stop-me shuffle, they'd taken her as far as that and she might have made it further too, if it wasn't for the car that sat idling at a ninety-degree angle to her path. A right angle made from her wrongs.

The driver's elbow pointed accusingly out of the window and he leaned out and shouted to each neighbour as they arrived on the scene: 'She came from nowhere!' as if *that* was her crime. This girl who appeared from thin air.

We came running when we heard shouting. We ran into the street and that's when we saw her, illuminated against the heat haze and the headlights that hadn't helped and that weren't needed anyway now the sun had sat up.

'Cordie! It's Cordie Van Apfel!'

'Jesus Christ. Is she *sleepwalking*?'

'Can she hear us? Can she see us, you reckon?'

Then Mr Van Apfel appeared, stepping forward with his arms outstretched and his palms to the sky as if coming in from the Lord's outfield. In that instant he blocked the sun. Then he took another step closer and the eclipse was over and the sunshine streamed back in just as sinister as before.

'Nothing to see here, folks,' he declared in his lay-preacher's soothe. 'Nothing to see here.'

CHAPTER ONE

Dusk. That limbo land. And the world blurred by Baltimore rain. The windows of the cab were smudged with grime and muck mixed with the misting rain so that each time the wipers flicked over the glass they made a greasy arc like a smeary sunrise. The driver smelled of smoke and spearmint Tic Tacs, and when I'd got in his cab he'd asked me if I was feeling better.

'Better than what?'

'Than before?'

We were both confused now.

He must have mistaken me for someone else – the sort of someone who could be cured.

'But the hospital,' he said and pointed past the gilt crucifix that hung from his rear-vision mirror, towards the tower of dazzling azure glass that stood by the curb in the rain. 'You came from the hospital.'

'Working,' I explained. 'I work in a lab. At the hospital.'

I held up a pile of papers now damp and softening in my hands. But the driver was looking past me. He was staring at the tower, which was lit up so that a light burned in practically every window and the whole thing – the shiny blue tower, the grid of illuminated windows – looked like a gas flame, despite all the rain.

The trip downtown was slow and wet, and the air in the cab was humid. We crawled along the expressway behind a yellow school bus, its tyres sending up spray. Inside, the bus was devoid of life apart from a driver I couldn't quite see. Our cab turned left onto the avenue and into more traffic. Three lanes inching along. Outside Burger King a fight was breaking out, but you could tell, even from this distance, that their hearts weren't in it.

Past Subway. Past the pawnbroker (*We buy Gold! 411-733-CASH!*). Past the abandoned mini-mart. Past the Union Temple Baptist Church with its arches and its turrets and its torn-in-two sign, ripped clean between the 'l' and the 'c'. Once upon a time that sign must have encouraged sinners to feel 'Welcome'; now it simply commanded they 'come'. Past red-brick behemoths and abandoned car yards. Wrecks turning to rust in the rain. Past row houses in candy colours and past the Candy Bazaar, which stood white as a mausoleum.

And that's where I saw her.

There. *There*. Bag swinging. Coat billowing. Long hair loose like a kite. The past sashayed down North Avenue (west) caught up in the peak-hour push for the station. (The 'metro' they call it here. Only tourists and Australians go all the way to Maryland and ask directions to Penn-North *subway*.) Yes, there. She was caught up in the crush surging to Penn-North station, but also not caught up at all. Because she walked just the same after all these long years. As though hovering slightly above the earth.

'Pull over!'

The driver looked at me, startled.

'Here? You want me to —'

'Please! Pull over!'

It was the first time we'd spoken since we hit North Avenue and he said nothing more as he yanked the steering wheel towards the curb. The crucifix swung wildly from its mirror and threatened to take out someone's eye.

'It's a wet walk,' he warned, though the drizzle had stopped. Had vanished with the last of the grey day. I paid and then slipped out of the cab, scanning the pavement for her.

Only, in the time it had taken us to pull over, I'd lost sight of her in the crowd. I tried not to panic, tried to keep my breathing calm. On my left traffic roared, on my right – industrial blocks. I fell into step with two men in cheap suits fast-walking in the direction of the station and complaining about someone who worked in their office.

'She's a fake.'

'You're right,' his friend agreed. 'Total fake. She acts like she wouldn't but when it comes down to it? She's no better than all the rest.'

I could see the station up ahead. Its blue metro signs were the same shade as the hospital: regulation Baltimore blue. We crossed a side street together, the cheap suits and I.

And just like that I saw her again, maybe ten people ahead. She cut along the path beside North and Woodbrook Park, scaring the crows. Sending them up in a black fume above the trees. My heart lurched.

'Cordie!' I called. 'Cordie! It's me!'

She didn't hear me. Couldn't have heard because she never looked back.

'Cordie!' I yelled again. '*Cordelia!*'

She crossed the road ahead of me and walked quickly across the small paved square before she disappeared inside the blue-lipped mouth of the station. I broke into a run, crossing the street and then the square, before following her into the metro.

Inside I glimpsed her briefly, then she was swallowed up. Swept out and over the abyss of the escalator.

'Cordie! Cordelia!'

I pushed past crowds of people.

'Cordie!'

'Freakin' shut up,' someone muttered.

Down on the platform: wet floor, wet wall tiles. Vast overhead beams dripped. Commuters stood shoulder to shoulder while the departures board counted down. I had two minutes, now one, left to find her.

'Sorry, sorry,' I shuffled along the platform on the wrong side of the fierce yellow line. 'Sorry. Excuse me, I just need to —'

And then there she was. Leaning against a pillar at the far end of the platform. Coat no longer billowing. Hair rain-darkened and shrouding her face. She held her bag under her arm.

'Cordie!' I shouted, and I reached out to touch her. In that same instant the train rushed into the station. A hot wind blasted my back, propelling me forward. I flung myself at her and she turned to me in surprise.

'Sorry,' I stammered. 'Wrong person. Oh God, sorry.'

She waved dismissively – *no big deal* – then she picked up her umbrella, closed it, edged around me and walked to the train doors as they hissed opened.

She disappeared inside the carriage without looking back.

'I thought you were someone I haven't seen —' I called after her, but my words fell short and they landed in the crevice between the train and the platform.

'Someone I haven't seen for a while,' I finished.

Actually, it was twenty years ago that week.

* * *

I'd seen so many Cordies over the years that it became a nervous tic. Seeing the back of her head. Spotting her in a crowd. I saw her in the line at the supermarket checkout, buying petrol, at the dentist. She surfaced in the lane next to me at the pool, her stroke inefficient but beautiful to watch.

I was unnerved at first. As a kid, I was spooked. But as I got older I found it comforting. It calmed me somehow, and I felt disappointed if too much time elapsed between sightings. On my way to exams and job interviews, blind dates arranged by friends, I'd settle my nerves by trying to find Cordie.

And it was Cordie, always Cordie. Never Hannah or Ruth. Cordie was the one that came back. Who appeared and then evaporated before my eyes. Often it would be nothing more than a flash of eyes set ever so slightly too far apart. A wisp of stringy blonde hair. But that would be enough for my brain to make the leap, and I'd reach out and ask and she'd turn and face me, puzzled. *Do I know you? Can I help you? Have we met?*

And when she turned around, the illusion would shatter in an instant. *Sorry, wrong person*, I'd mutter. And she'd smile and shrug and melt back into the day, and I'd be left standing on the street, wondering where she learned such a trick.

* * *

I lived in a rundown row house in Baltimore. Red brick, white window frames. It leaned on its neighbours like crutches. It had rained so hard and so often during the time I had lived there that some days I expected to come home from work and find the whole row had spilled into the gutters and sluiced down the hill into Chesapeake Bay.

Not that I would have been home to see it happen. I was at the lab every weekday between eight-thirty and six and on more weekends than I liked to admit. There I watched the world through the glass eye of my microscope, pinning things under my focus. I worked as an assistant lab technician at a medical research centre, coaxing cells into existence and then towards survival. *Lactobacillus acidophilus*, *Bifidobacterium lactis*, *Streptococcus thermophilus*. I grew them in tubes of sterile milk, baptised them in water baths, and once they'd turned into curd I streaked them out onto agar plates to check for purity.

On a good day I could get through around a hundred and twenty plates. Standing with one hip hard against the lab bench, one foot forward, the other behind, streaking out cells. Standing and ignoring the dull ache in my Achilles, the twinges of fire at the backs of my knees. Standing because – despite what Detective Senior Constable Mundy instructed all those years ago – I never got the hang of sitting. ('Sit tight,' he told us after the disappearance of the girls. 'Sit tight and we'll find your friends.' Sit tight he'd said, and we'd more or less done as asked. Had done nothing else for twenty years.)

It took forty-eight hours to incubate each plate in the lab. From there they were suspended in sterile milk and transferred to tiny cryotubes that were stacked, packed and frozen – thousands of tiny vials like bricks in a wall – and shipped off to bigger labs elsewhere on campus. They went to other parts of the research centre where people investigated the effect of various strains on chronic medical disorders. Where those same people wrote papers, presented symposiums. Slept with their PhD students. Where they came up with answers to critical questions. While all I ever learned was how to get good at waiting. Streaking out life onto tiny agar plates while my own slipped quietly away.

But those were the good days. On a bad day – and there were a few – I'd be distracted. My mind would wander. On those days, dropped curd would puddle on the floor, flecked with shards of smashed glass.

Each December the bad days outnumbered the good. The anniversary of the disappearance always left me unsettled. There were days in December when it seemed like more cells got slopped on the floor than ever made it safely into cryotubes.

Sometimes I could go for days, even weeks without thinking about the Van Apfel girls – though even that made me anxious at first. As if I was scared of letting myself off the hook. But

I soon learned that I didn't need to worry. The sorrow, the shame – I could conjure them in an instant, as sure and as real as growing bacteria in a lab. *Escherichia coli* and a lifetime of remorse. I could streak them out onto agar plates to prove their purity. I could pile them high in their tiny vials.

Things had got worse six months ago, at the start of the Maryland summer. Tuesday 12 June 2012 – I have the clipping stuck to my fridge. That was when the Chamberlain case was in the news again, this time because the coroner had ruled the death certificate be changed to acknowledge what everyone knew: that a dingo had snatched and killed nine-week-old Azaria Chamberlain more than thirty years ago. And as the coroner pointed out, that meant it was more than thirty years, too, since the baby's mother, Lindy Chamberlain, had been wrongly convicted of murder. Since she had been sentenced to life in prison and had served three years in a Northern Territory jail cell, before the baby's jacket was discovered outside a dingo lair. That was when Lindy Chamberlain had finally had her conviction overturned.

The most notorious court case in Australian history, they reckoned. The Chamberlain case was the background to my entire childhood. Outside, we had smiling *Safety House* signs screwed to each letterbox in the street. Every house safe. Every house a refuge. While inside, the court case of a mother alleged to have murdered her child played out each night, in prime time, in the lounge room.

And even though Azaria Chamberlain disappeared twelve years before the Van Apfel girls did, and almost three thousand kilometres away, even though the Chamberlain case was resolved, while what happened to Hannah, Cordie and Ruth is still a mystery, the two things are tied so tightly together in my mind that I can't think about one without fixating on the other.

And so, ever since I'd walked past an electronics store six months ago and seen a wall of Lindy Chamberlains looking back at me (still wearing those dark glasses, still wearing her hair short, though it was lighter and spikier now), ever since then I'd had that old familiar feeling of dread.

It never stayed buried for long.

CHAPTER TWO

It was dark when I flew into Sydney. Starless and flawless and dark. I almost missed the overpass driving to Mum and Dad's from the airport. That bridge hadn't existed when I'd left for Baltimore; somehow, while I was gone, it had surfaced, sleek and confident and geometrically satisfying, from the sludge of the valley floor. It hung forty metres in the air, connecting our ridge to the rest of the world with a wide inverted grin.

As I checked in the rear-view mirror of the hire car, as I fumbled, one hand on the wheel, the other feeling around for the indicator, the bridge curved on behind me into the distance like the tail of some terrible thing.

We used to joke about tails. And teeth and claws and eyes. Hot breath on the back of your neck. We used to try to scare one another with stories about wild things that lived in the valley. *A panther. A python. A river bunyip that pulls people under and disembowels them as easy as peeling prawns.* (As if the things we dreamed up in our thin backyard tents could be worse than what lurked down there.)

People saw things too. Every few years the local newspaper would report a big-cat sighting and publish a photo of a polypheme paw print in the dirt with a cigarette lighter next to it for scale. Or there'd be a bull shark scare at the river. Once half a mutilated dog washed up in the mangroves, and the newspaper claimed a shark was responsible. At the time I thought it should have been easy to prove because, whatever it was, it had swallowed the microchipped half of the dog. But Dad had explained: no, microchipping didn't mean we could track the thing down. Just that if we had the chip, we could learn the name and address of the dog.

Another time the paper ran a series of night-vision photos proving the existence of a panther. Darks smears with pellucid eyes peered out from the front page, but by the time the newspaper had been printed, folded and flopped out of a car window by the Tooleys, who did the paper deliveries each Tuesday after lunch, it was impossible to tell what was a big cat and what was sandwich-grease stain.

When I arrived the house was lit up like a hotel minibar. It looked smaller, flimsier than I remembered. In the driveway the huge angophora overhanging the garage shook its leaves at me. Scent of eucalyptus like a punch in the gut.

'You're here!' Mum threw her arms around me on the doorstep. 'She's here, Graham! She's here – Tikka's home!' She slipped the bag off my shoulder and took another out of my hand, and then she hustled me down the hallway with her hip and into the yellow kitchen.

'How was your flight?' Mum wanted to know. 'Have you eaten anything? Sit down and I'll make you a cup of tea. Dad will get your things out of the car. What, just these bags? Is that all? How long are you staying for?

'We've been at the Heddinglys' all afternoon,' she told me. 'Did you hear Jade Heddingly is getting married? And the Van Apfel house has been sold again. Mrs McCausley can tell you the price.'

She rattled through the list of the things she would have been willing herself not to mention. *How long was I staying? Another wedding. The Van Apfels.* On the kitchen table an ancient *Women's Weekly* cookbook lay dog-eared in anticipation.

Dad wandered in then and wrapped me up in a hug.

'Good to see you, Tik.' He ruffled my hair.

The kettle complained on the bench.

'Flight okay?' Dad settled himself at the kitchen table, arms crossed, glasses gently cockeyed. 'I was following it using Flight Tracker.'

Flight Tracker was Dad's favourite app these days.

'You took off a bit late,' he told me, as if I hadn't been on board, 'but you made up the time over the Pacific.'

'That's when they asked us to lean on the seat in front. To go faster,' I explained.

'Cheeky bugger.'

'It's a fuel-economy policy.'

'That why your flight was so cheap?' he said drolly.

Because it might have been my idea to come home to see Laura, but Mum and Dad had to subsidise my flight.

'Something like that,' I said sheepishly.

Mum carried three mugs of tea over to the table and placed them on cork coasters. After they'd retired, Mum and Dad had bought a lightweight caravan, and each coaster on the table had been collected from a different tourist attraction around the state. *The Big Banana! The Big Bull! The Big Merino!* those coasters shouted.

'Big tour for a little caravan,' I noted.

'Drink that.' Mum ignored me and nodded towards the hot tea she'd placed in front of me. The mug was heavy and unfashionable. The tea was just how I like it.

'I'll make you some toast, Tik,' she said. 'You look like you haven't eaten in months.'

We all stared at my baggy hoodie, my faded black tights, at my feet in mismatched flight socks. I blew steam off the surface of my tea.

'Where's Laura?'

'Asleep,' Mum said.

'She gets tired,' Dad explained.

'How is she?' I asked tentatively.

Mum sat down opposite me and drew in a long breath. Dad placed his hand on her knee and then he surprised me by starting to cry.

'What? Is it worse? It's worse, isn't it? Dad? What haven't you told me?'

'We've told you everything, Tik,' Mum said. 'Chemo starts soon and the prognosis is good. Thank God the thing hasn't spread.'

Dad wiped his eyes with the edge of his hand. Replaced his glasses, lifted his chin from his chest. 'You expect it at our age,' he said. 'You expect your friends to get sick, maybe get crook yourself. But it shouldn't ever happen to your *child* —' He stopped as his voice cracked again.

And Mum swept one arm across the tablecloth, smoothing invisible creases. The back of her hand was marked with age spots.

'Lovely Laura,' she sighed.

* * *

Laura had phoned, just over a week ago, to tell me that it was cancer. *Nodular sclerosis Hodgkin lymphoma.* She'd been clinical, somehow, even when talking about herself, and I'd pictured her wearing her nurse's scrubs while she spoke to me on the phone.

'I'm coming home,' I told her. 'I'll book a flight today.'

'Why?' she said. 'There's nothing you can do.'

'I'm coming anyway. I want to see you.'

'I might not look too great,' she warned.

I was on the train when she phoned. On my way to the lab. Outside the carriage window: red brick buildings as relentless as the rain on the glass. My sister never phoned me at that time of the morning – just past midnight at home – so I knew, even before she spoke, that something was very wrong.

'My reception might drop out. I'm on the train,' I explained.

'My life just dropped out,' she replied.

* * *

When I saw her for the first time, that night I arrived from the airport, she wandered into the kitchen wearing a tired blue

16

bathrobe and an expression to match. She poked through my bag I'd left lying on the table. 'Ooh, duty free,' she said.

I abandoned my tea on the table and threw my arms around her, burying my face in her neck, breathing her in.

'Oh Lor.'

'You shouldn't have come back,' she said gruffly. 'You didn't have to do that.'

'Yes I did,' I said, and I smoothed down the part in her hair where it was mussed up from her sleep. In response, she leaned over and tucked in the tag that was poking out from the back of my hoodie.

'We're like chimpanzees,' I said, 'grooming one another.'

'*You* might be,' she said archly. 'You've got the face for it.'

'Ape-breath.'

'Face-ache.'

I grinned and pressed my cheek against hers.

* * *

It would be another week before either of us mentioned the disappearance of the Van Apfel girls, and even then we'd both be cagey.

'Have you told anyone?' My sister would say it casually, like she didn't care about my answer. Like I couldn't see her holding her breath.

'Have *you*?'

'I asked first,' she'd insist, becoming fourteen years old again. Making me forever eleven.

CHAPTER THREE

We lost all three girls that summer. Let them slip away like the words of some half-remembered song, and when one came back, she wasn't the one we were trying to recall to begin with.

Spring slunk off too. Skulked away into the scrub and there, standing in its place, was a summer that scorched the air and burned our nostrils and sealed in the stink. Like the lids on our Tupperware lunchboxes.

'Jade Heddingly says if it gets hot enough your shadow will spontaneously rust,' I reported.

'It's spontaneously *combust!*' my sister crowed. 'Jade Heddingly is an idiot and so are you, and anyway your shadow can't combust or rust or nothing. Your shadow is always there, dummy.'

'Not in the dark.'

Mum was right: you can't see your shadow in the dark. She stood at the kitchen sink ripping the heads off bottlebrush stems. *Flitch, flitch, flitch.* She snapped the dead blooms off at the neck and dropped them into the sink, where their fine spiky hairs were the same ferrous red as the scabs we picked off our knees. It was the year the Cold War ended. The year they stopped making Atari 2600s forever. I was eleven and one-sixth, but it wasn't enough. By then we'd learned shadows vanished in the dark.

'What else did Jade tell you?' Laura said.

She waited until Mum went into the laundry before she asked the question, so that the two of us were left alone at the kitchen table where we were pretending to do our homework.

'About shadows?'

'About anything. Go on, what else did Jade say?'

Jade Heddingly was fourteen, which meant she was old enough to wear braces on her teeth but not so old that she used those teeth and her tongue and the rest of her mean mouth to stop saying 'arks' instead of 'ask'. Jade kept saying it wrong long after the rest of us had left behind 'hostibul' and 'lellow' and all those other word jumbles we said when we were little kids. 'Why didn't you arks my opinion?' she would whine. As if that would ever make you change your mind.

'What else did Jade say?' I echoed.

'Yeah.'

I leaned in before answering: 'She told me that to hide a dead body you bury it six feet underground and then bury a dog three feet above that.'

'Why?'

'So that the police sniffer dogs will only dig as far as the dead dog, and they won't find the body below.'

'That's gross!' my sister squealed.

'Well, you arksed.'

'Is it true?'

'I don't know,' I admitted.

'Did she say anything else? You know, anything about – you know.'

'Nothing.'

'You sure?'

'Yeah, I'm sure,' I said defensively.

'Jade doesn't know anything about it,' I added.

She didn't know nothing about nothing.

What we *all* knew – even as far back as that – was that the valley stank. Jeez, it reeked. It smelled like a sore. Like something bad had been dug out before the sky was stitched back over, low-slung and bruised and suffocating.

They never did work out why.

It wasn't Ruth's fault, but. That valley had smelled bad long before any of the Van Apfel girls ever went missing there. Even from our house high on the western rim, the stench would waft up the gully and smack us in the face on a hot dry day, and they were all hot dry days once the Cold War had ended.

That summer was the hottest on record.

Back in those days the valley had only been developed in pockets. It was dissected by a cutting where a skinny, two-lane road wound down and around and across the river and then slithered up and out again, but the real excavation work had been done long ago by something much more primitive than us. The valley was deep and wide. Trees covered both walls. Spindly, stunted she-oaks spewed from the basin, swallowing the sunlight and smothering the tide with their needles. Higher up there were paperbarks, and tea-trees with their camphorous lemon smell. Then hairpin banksias, river dogroses and gums of every kind – woollybutts, blackbutts, bloodwoods and Craven grey boxes, right up to the anaemic angophoras that stood twisted and mangled all along the ridge line.

At school we called the valley the 'bum crack'.

We steered clear of the Pryders and the Callum boys and the rest of that handful of kids who lived in the shanty-style shacks in clumps along the valley. But the strangest thing about the place wasn't the kids who lived there. It wasn't the silence, or the way the sunlight sloped in late in the morning and slid out again as soon as it could in the afternoon. No, the awful part was the *shape* of the thing. Those terrible, fall-able cliffs. The valley wasn't V-shaped like normal river valleys; instead the whole canyon was a hollowed-out 'U'. It was almost as wide at the bottom as it was at the top, as if an enormous rock had been chiselled out but somehow we'd gone and lost that too. It was a fat gap. A void.

Even now its geography is only worth mentioning because of what's not there.

I used to spend hours down there on my own. I'd go when I was bored – when my sister was at Hannah's – and when the wind was blowing the right way for a change and the stink wasn't so awful. I'd pick fuchsia heath flowers and suck the nectar out of their tiny pink throats and then I'd pretend they were poisonous and that I was going to die. Back then dying was nothing to be afraid of. At least, that's what Hannah once said her dad said, and her dad was told it by God. But then Hannah's dad had never actually died and so *I* said: 'What would your dad know?'

What none of us knew – what we'll never know – is what happened to Hannah and Cordie that December.

We knew about Ruth because she came back, her lip curled in a whine like she'd lost her lunch money, not got lost in the bush all alone. (Or worse: *not alone*. What if she wasn't alone?)

When they found her she was poking out of a deep crack in one of the boulders by the river. She was stuffed right down, shoved into the fissure as if she'd been trying to jump in feet first but the gorge had choked on her at the last minute. Had tried to spit her back out.

Wade Nevrakis told us that when the police found her there were so many flies crawling over the surface of Ruth's rock that it looked like it was spinning. But Wade Nevrakis's parents ran the deli near our school so I don't know why Wade thought we'd believe his parents were anywhere near it. (But when Kelly Ashwood spread it that Ruth was alive enough to say: 'C'niva Rainbow Paddle Pop if I say my throat hurts?' well then, you could almost believe it because everyone knew Kelly Ashwood was a dobber, and also that Ruth was a pig.)

It took thirteen detectives, two special analysts from the city, forensics, plus all the local area command and the SES – State Emergency Service – volunteers to find Ruth in the rock that day. Them *and* the black cockatoos that circled in the sky above. They shouldn't have been there, those cockatoos. Not in numbers like that and not during breeding time, and yet there they were, going around and around, over and over, like a record getting stuck on a scratch.

When they discovered Ruth her eyes were squeezed shut as if she'd seen enough. Like she couldn't bear to look. And except for a smear of dirt running the length of her left cheek and a few dead pine needles sticking out of her plait, she appeared untouched, and as though she was praying.

Her parents would've liked that.

We all heard the wail of the siren that day as it wound jerkily up the bends and out of the valley, which by that stage of the early afternoon was already creeping with shadows. The noise of the siren rose and fell with each turn. Louder then fainter as the drivers negotiated each bend. Mrs Van Apfel was at the police command post at the time, waiting for Detective Senior Constable Mundy, and they say she froze when she heard the siren because the news about Ruth hadn't reached them yet. Mrs McCausley, who lived on the corner of our cul-de-sac, was at the command post making tea for the searchers. She said Mrs Van Apfel swung her head towards the sound, like a dog that heard its owner's whistle.

Each rise and fall of that siren's song, Mrs McCausley told us, 'was as if God himself was opening and closing the door on that poor woman's pain'.

Mrs McCausley had been 'Tuppered'. Least, that's what she told me.

'She's been what?' Mum said when I reported it back to her. 'There's no such word.' Mum was a librarian so she knew all about words. Words and overdue notices.

'*Is*,' I insisted. 'Mrs McCausley told it to me.'

But it took several back-and-forths to work out what she'd meant, and it wasn't until I explained how Mrs McCausley's life had changed for the better when she'd learned Tupperware products were guaranteed against chipping, cracking, breaking or peeling for the whole lifetime of the product, that Mum really understood where she was coming from.

'Bloody *Tuppered*,' I heard her say to Dad that night as I hung over the bannister eavesdropping on their conversation. 'Selling Tupperware to our kids now.'

And she sounded cranky, and so did Dad, even though I hadn't bought anything.

Mrs McCausley sold Tupperware, though it was more a hobby than a job.

'Just enough to keep me out of trouble,' she said.

Though anyone could see Mrs McCausley's door-to-door Tupperware visits were more about unearthing strife than trying to stay out of its way.

* * *

The Van Apfels didn't sell Tupperware – they didn't sell anything as far as we could tell – but they bought right into Jesus Christ. Yeah, Jesus was their rock. (And round here, didn't that make your family an island.)

Mr Van Apfel was a big man with big hands. Thick shoulders and neck. He had the goggle-eyed stare of a child. And when he painted the drainpipes or pressure-hosed the drive he wore thick plastic safety glasses, which made the whole effect worse.

Mr Van Apfel cared about that house with the same kind of devotion he showed his relationship with the Lord.

'That right?' I said when he told me that once. It was a Saturday morning and I sat melting over the handlebars of my bike, watching as Mr Van Apfel stooped down and shook pellets the size of rabbit poo in lines across the grass. *Shoosh-shooosh-shoosh.* They fell from the box in lovely neat rows.

'Is that for the birds?' I asked him.

There were kookaburras in the tree above and the three of us – the two kookas and I – watched him work.

'Because the kookas eat meat,' I added helpfully. Eat meat. *Eeet meet. Shoosh-shooosh-shoosh.* The sounds soft-shoe-shuffled in my head.

But Mr Van Apfel said, 'No. It's good for the grass.'

That's when he told me the bit about God.

And I was impressed that he could grow grass at the same time he grew his relationship with the Lord. And that the rabbit poo worked for both.

'Almost empty,' he said, standing up straight so that his wide shoulders, his thick neck filled my view. He shook the box for my benefit and a couple of loose pellets rattled around.

'Mrs Van Apfel will have more,' he assured me, even though I hadn't been worried.

It was true Mrs Van Apfel was organised like that. I'd seen for myself her kitchen calendar full of violent warnings. Each item on the calendar was written in red capitals so it was clear what she should steel herself for next. That's the sort of person Mrs Van Apfel was: she treated social engagements as emergencies. She read book dedications looking for evidence.

Most of all, though, Mrs Van Apfel was the sort of person who lived in dread of the dangers that surged through her daughters' days just as sure as that stinking river surged below.

I guess now she could say: 'I told you so.' That must have brought her some solace.

CHAPTER FOUR

On the Saturday night after the Van Apfels vanished we held a vigil in Coronation Park. It had been eight days by then since they first disappeared (but still twenty-four hours before Ruth would come back).

'Insanity,' sniffed Mrs McCausley. 'What would make *anyone* visit the scene of the crime while some maniac is still on the loose?'

But Mrs McCausley never missed a chance to stare down her nose at the rest of us, the way her house stared down from the rise of the nearest crossroad, and so she was there on Saturday night just like everyone else.

The whole suburb showed up in support. Just like they'd been showing up all week to volunteer in the search and had been cooking meals Mr and Mrs Van Apfel couldn't stomach. For a whole week I'd watched our neighbours deliver casseroles and pasta bakes to the Van Apfel front doorstep, laying their colour-coordinated Tupperware on the doormat.

Mrs McCausley would have approved of all that Tupperware – she'd sold almost all of it to us.

The vigil was run by Mrs Lantana, who was secretary of the school council. As well as the council, Mrs Lantana was in charge of the canteen roster and the annual spring fair and the uniform shop (open the third Friday of the month). Mrs Lantana liked attention to detail so the vigil was right up her street. And so, in those long, dreadful days while the rest of us were out searching for Hannah and Cordie and Ruth, or waiting for our parents who were out searching for Hannah and Cordie and Ruth, it was Mrs Lantana who stockpiled five thousand virgin white candles for us to cling to at the vigil.

The Senior Girls and Boys Choir sang 'I am Australian' as they'd done the week before at the Showstopper concert. They'd been rehearsing it for seven months without a single excuse to sing it and now they'd performed it twice in eight days. When they stood up to sing it, Mrs Walliams, the choir teacher, assured us they chose it especially for the vigil. But that was a lie because everyone knew the only other song the choir knew was 'Bound for Botany Bay'. And 'Bound for Botany Bay' was not right for the night. Not with everyone so dreadfully distraught. Not with all those toorali-oorali-additys in the chorus.

But in the end it didn't matter what song the choir sang because the search helicopter had returned by that stage due to the fading light. It *chkkt-chkkt*ed overhead the whole time they sang and the clipped rhythm of its rotors showed up the choir as being out of time. They finished the last verse half a beat too soon.

Mr Davidson from the Rotary Club spoke, and when he was finished we raised our candles in the air and chanted: 'Bring our girls home.' We were strong during a crisis, that's what Mr Davidson said. Strong when it counted the most.

'How are you holding up, Tikka?' Mum asked when Mr Davidson had finished speaking.

'Strong,' I replied, even though, honestly, my arm was getting tired from holding my candle all that time. Mr Davidson spoke for ages and my candle was drippy. It was hard not to spill wax on the picnic blanket.

Later, when my candle was just a stub and all that was left of the vigil was the scent of burned matches and singed hair, I asked Dad if the police had dusted for prints like I'd seen them do on TV.

'What? Dust the whole valley? Every single tree?' Laura said. And for the first time in more than a week my sister found a hole in her grief that was large enough for her to poke a snigger through.

Dad told her to bugger off.

'They're doing everything they can,' he assured me. 'The police, the searchers, they're all doing their best.'

And I guessed they were, whatever that meant. But on the day they disappeared Hannah, Cordelia and Ruth had been wearing twenty-one items of clothing between them. Two pairs of Converse sneakers (with socks); one pair of pink jelly shoes; three pairs of knickers; two bralettes (Ruth didn't wear one yet, though she probably needed to more than her sisters did); two T-shirts; one skirt (and belt); one dress; and one pair of Daisy Dukes (Cordie's). They wore three signet rings; five bangles; one friendship band (Hannah's, which she'd exchanged with my sister); two hair elastics; plus Cordelia was wearing an oval locket around her neck that Sara Addison swore contained a lock of Troy Murphy's hair (though I think it was probably Madonna the cat's). They had six femurs, ninety-nine vertebrae, three skulls and thirty fingernails. Six kneecaps, forty-eight carpal bones, and more than three million strands of blonde hair, all tinged alien-green by the chlorine in their pool, which, up until the day they went missing, we'd swum in almost every single day that summer.

And yet all these things vanished – just evaporated in the heat. Not a single sign was left for us.

No sign, that is, until the day one pair of pink jellies and one dress and one pair of knickers and one signet ring and one hair elastic and two curved cheeks (one dirt-smeared, one not) and two fat knees (one grazed and one not) and one harelip were spat back out of that stinking valley and into the burning air.

* * *

The Van Apfels had lived in our neighbourhood since a time when blocks of bushland could be bought for $13,000 and an hour spent in the company of a chain-smoking real estate agent. And starting with Mrs McCausley's at number one, up there on the corner, our cul-de-sac sloped stubbornly downwards in the direction of the valley like a spoon tipping towards a gullet.

It was a ganglion, Macedon Close. *A ganglion.* (I got 'ganglion' from our extension spelling list in week five of term two, back when we did 'The Human Body'.) That's what our cul-de-sac was: a lump that grows in some place it shouldn't and nobody's really sure why.

Our lump was swollen with quarter-acre blocks and backyards and carports and decks and pergolas and fishponds. No fences, though. No one around here built fences. At least, not front ones, and not back ones either. Just the thin kind that ran down the sides of our houses, made from chicken wire or brushwood or timber with missing slats. Leaky dividers. So that everything flowed easily from one house to the next. So that nothing could ever be contained.

Some of the families in our street had been there for more than a generation, and the Van Apfel family was one of them. It was Mr Van Apfel's father who had built the house on the corner opposite Mrs McCausley. Strictly speaking, the Van Apfel house was on the adjoining street, facing outwards to the rest of the suburb, giving Macedon Close the cold shoulder. But we didn't mind; we still included the Van Apfels in everything we did. Still invited them to our street barbecue each Christmas.

'A mole on the neighbourhood's blonde-brick skin' was what Mrs McCausley called the Van Apfel house, referring to its dark-coloured bricks and dark crosshatched windows. The pristine black tiles on its roof. That house was kept in immaculate condition but even that didn't mollify Mrs McCausley. 'Exhibitionist' was the word she'd used.

Then inside, that gloomy spiral staircase winding all the way to the top. Its steel centre pole like a stake trying to pin the house to the earth. As if it might rise straight up to heaven if it wasn't pegged to our cul-de-sac.

Mr Van Apfel Senior lived on his own in the house until, some time early in their marriage, Mr Van Apfel Senior's son and his new wife arrived and began filling up the dark house with pink girls. First Hannah, then Cordelia and, just when it was starting to look like you couldn't squeeze in any more cots or trikes or Cabbage Patch dolls or Space Hoppers, or hang any more nappies on the line like little white flags of surrender blowing in the breeze, Mr Van Apfel's father curled up his toes and died, leaving room for one more: Ruth.

But before he could die, and before Ruth arrived, Mrs Van Apfel led her young family like shrieking, squabbling magpies to the Hope Revival Centre across the valley. With its cavernous hall and its immaculate paintwork, its glossy whitewash repelling the heat, the Hope Revival Centre was a shiny silo rising from the dust on the eastern ridge.

God had blessed the Revivalists with an 850 square metre block in the new estate across the valley. The church looked out over the valley, over swathes of bushland and over the river that ran through the gully. (Although the church building itself was surrounded by felled trees and blank lots marked out with fluorescent tape. By the stumps of barely built homes. The roads were unsurfaced in the new estate in those days and the loose gravel baked in the sun while it waited for someone to return with the kerbs and gutters and the white road markings that were needed to hold things in place.)

It was along these roads that Mr and Mrs Van Apfel carefully negotiated their blue station wagon each Sunday morning, with their two small daughters strapped into the back seat, headed for the Rise Up service at eight. And several months later they added a baby capsule to the back seat in preparation for Ruth's arrival. Then, while Mr Van Apfel looked on, singing 'Lord, Mould Me in Your Image', complete with hand claps, Ruth was dragged, bloodied and ball-fisted, from Mrs Van Apfel's tight womb, her tiny cleft lip glistening in the hospital's bright glare.

That was seven years ago.

Seven days of creation, seven days Noah waited for the flood, seven solemn words Christ spoke from the cross. Seven hundred mentions of the number seven in the Bible (including fifty-four times in Revelations alone, which talks of seven churches, seven angels, seven trumpets and seven stars).

For seven years Mr Van Apfel had three daughters. Now, through some trick of mathematics, his three had become one and no number of prayers could solve that for him.

* * *

The final time we ever went inside the Van Apfel house was when we babysat the girls. ('Hannah and I are the babysitters – *you're a babysittee*,' my sister corrected me when I tried out that line at the time.)

The two of us *thwack-thwack*ed our way up to the dark house at the top of the cul-de-sac, the bitumen sticking to our thin thongs as we walked. Laura was fourteen years old and three grades ahead of me at school – the same as Hannah Van Apfel – but for the two of them to think that they were in charge was just the pair of them being stuck up. And anyway the whole world knew it was Cordie who ruled. Cordelia Van Apfel: the middle one. With her wide-set eyes and her violet lips. The air hummed when Cordie walked across the front lawn. As if you were letting out a breath you didn't know you were holding: Cordeli. *Aaah.*

Everyone had something to say about Cordelia Van Apfel.

Like the time the Van Apfel girls were angels in Mrs Blunt's nativity play and someone started the rumour that Cordie wasn't wearing any knickers under her costume. I was the narrator of the nativity so I had to open and close the play by reciting a poem I'd written. (*That* was the reason I was included in the production back when I was only in Mr Simpson's Year Three class at the time.) My poem was good – it got me into the play – but it wasn't that good it earned me a costume. Instead the narrator had to wear their plain old school uniform and the label of mine read ~~Laura~~ ~~Cordelia~~ Tikka and would probably soon include *Ruth*, as our clothes were passed back and forth between our two houses.

But on stage stood those Van Apfel girls. (Steps on a ladder. Ducks in a row.) They were wearing white bedsheet shrouds and Cordie had tried to hem hers so that it was shorter than her sisters' – a crazy staple smile looping along the fold. She was part Wood's *American Gothic*, part Kylie Minogue. (But no Botticelli angel, that's for sure.)

And from where I stood on the side of the stage, you couldn't say for certain if she had her knickers on.

Then there was the time we saw Cordie coming out of the school office on the first day of the school year. She was holding her mum's hand. (Though even from this distance you could see that it was Mrs Van Apfel who was doing all the holding. Cordie was so singular, so completely Cordie, that she didn't seem to need to touch anyone else.)

We'd been playing Chinese Whispers in the playground but when Cordie appeared hands dropped from mouths, and mouths fell to silence as if to continue with passing it on might shatter the sight. It wasn't just the hand–holding that had everyone stumped. No, the thing was that Cordie was supposed to start high school. She'd finished primary school at the end of last year and yet here she was, in the same uniform as us, even though she had turned thirteen.

Across the playground, skipping ropes were reverentially released, balls bounced out of bounds and nobody bothered to chase them. We watched while the two of them walked across the playground towards the Year Six classroom, connected only by their hands.

'Is Cordie *repeating* Year Six?'

'Why would they make her do that?'

There was no reason we knew of for the Van Apfels to hold Cordie back from high school (though you wouldn't put it past them), yet the idea she might repeat seemed familiar to us the instant it crossed our minds. She knew more, *she sensed more.* Cordie kept strange, private things curled up in her carelessness that were too tight for the rest of us to unravel. Of course she'd come back to flaunt that in our faces. It seemed so obvious afterwards.

On that first day back at school, though, as Mrs Van Apfel walked her daughter towards the Year Six classroom in the corner of the playground, Cordie gave no sign she'd noticed us staring. Gave no sign she'd noticed us at all. She held her head up seeking some unseeable spot on the horizon. We returned to Chinese whispers.

'Let's start the game again,' Melanie Firth commanded. 'I'll go first.' She flicked her eyes meaningfully at me. She was determined to wrest back control of things and so she made a big show of pouring her message into the next ear in line and then she smiled sweetly at me. Whatever was coming around the circle was coming for my benefit. But by the time Melanie's message had got two-thirds of the way around, it seemed to have almost dissolved. Next to me, Jodi McNally was having trouble deciphering what it meant.

'Say it again?' she asked but the girl on her left shook her head.

'Can't say it twice. That's the rules.'

'Fine,' said Jodi. She leaned in and whispered, her breath hot and thick. It prickled the inside of my ear.

'Isla gaudy do-si-do,' she slurred. I looked at her desperately for a clue.

Melanie shrieked. 'Say it out loud! You say it out loud.'

'But it hasn't been all the way around the circle,' I protested.

'Who cares? Just say it out loud. What's the message? Say it now!'

'Fine. *I love gaudy do-si-do*,' I muttered.

'Say it again!'

'I love gaudy do-si-do.' I raised my chin and said it louder this time.

'You love Cordie!' said Melanie. 'You admitted it! That was the message and you said it out loud: *I love Cordie, don't you know.*'

I folded my arms. 'Cordie's *a girl*. Your message doesn't make sense.'

And Melanie shrugged. 'It's just a game,' she said defensively, though we both knew she didn't mean that.

By now Cordie and Mrs Van Apfel had reached the Year Six classroom on the far side of the playground. Cordie never turned her head to acknowledge us. But as they rounded the corner to the entrance of the room, she raised her free hand and held it high behind her back. Then she flicked her middle finger at us.

* * *

We swam in the pool that day we babysat. The Van Apfels' pool was an in-ground one that swallowed half their backyard. It was all pebblecrete and landscaped bushes. A violent blue vinyl lining to give it that 'tropical feel'. That's what Mr Van Apfel told us when he first laid the pool brochure on the kitchen table in a way that reminded me of the Van Apfels' cat when she arranged possum carcasses on the doormat and then sat back and waited for praise.

We ran elaborate underwater handstand competitions in the Van Apfel pool that day. First round, second round, best of the best. Our skinny legs stabbing at the sky like the bows of some demented orchestra.

'Tikka cheated,' Ruth complained.

She appealed to Cordie, the judge on the side of the pool.

'How?' I asked. 'How do you even cheat at underwater handstands?'

But Hannah and Cordie were too busy talking about getting their ears pierced to care what Ruth had to say.

Later we lay on the grass under the peppercorn tree, our faces split into jigsaws by its shade. Madonna wandered over and sniffed us half-heartedly, and Cordelia put out a lazy forearm – her good arm – and let the cat rub her fur against Cordie's own peach fuzz. The girls had named the ginger after their idol (and let their parents think they meant Jesus's mum). Laura and Hannah lay on their backs, each with one hand resting across their stomachs and the other arm stretched out so that they were linked, pinkie finger to pinkie finger, while Cordelia was propped up on her side so that one round hip held up the sky.

Ruth had arranged her towel closest to mine and then sat cross-legged on it, hunched over, stabbing at ants with a stick.

'Whaddayawanna do?' Laura said.

'I dunno. Whadda *you* wanna do?' I said.

'I asked first,' my sister said flatly.

'Get a canoe?' Hannah suggested.

From the boatshed, she meant, down by the river. It was two dollars to hire one but we never had two dollars. Or it was too hot. Or Laura didn't feel like it.

'Yeah! Canoes!' I said.

Ruth shook her head.

'"Two in a canoe,"' she reminded us about the hand-painted sign that had hung by the boatshed for as long as I could remember.

Ruth counted us out: Laura–Hannah; Tikka–Cordie.

She thumbed her own pink chest. 'Two in a canoe but what about me?'

We never got canoes anyway.

Ruth hunched over again and went back to stabbing her ants.

'If you were a Buddhist you could come back as an ant,' my sister said.

'If I was a Buddhist I would burn in hell,' Ruth replied automatically.

Somewhere in a neighbouring yard a lawnmower started to moan and Madonna looked disdainfully towards the noise.

'Mr Avery said there is no hell,' said Cordie.

'When did he say that?' Hannah wanted to know.

'I've never heard him say that,' I said helpfully, and Cordie clucked her tongue sympathetically at me as if to say that was my dead loss, not hers.

'Is *that* where you go when you're sleepwalking?' Laura teased Cordie. 'To see Mr Avery, to talk to him about hell?'

But Hannah didn't like that. She didn't like it one bit.

'You're a moll, Cordie,' she said. She raised her head as far off the ground as she could without expending any actual effort and she looked disapprovingly at her sister.

'That's what Jade said too,' I confirmed.

Because Jade *had* said that. She called Cordie a moll at swimming club one day when Cordie hadn't bothered to go into the changing rooms to get into her cossie. Instead she got changed on the pool deck in front of the boys.

'What did the boys do?' my sister wanted to know.

So I told her how they waited poolside the whole afternoon in case she got changed in full view after her swim.

'And did you?' Laura asked Cordie.

'Nah, I went home in my cossie.' Cordie smirked.

But Hannah was more interested in what Jade Heddingly had to say.

'*I'm* the only one who can call my sister a moll. You tell Jade Heddingly that from me,' Hannah said warningly.

But then Ruth began complaining that she wanted an iceblock and so she was dispatched – as the youngest and therefore our slave, and as the one whose idea it was anyway – to go to the garage to get five Sunnyboys. She would have to dig them out of the chest freezer where Mrs Van Apfel kept great slabs of cut-price meat. The Sunnyboys and the slabs of meat were buried in the freezer together. So we waited for Ruth to separate the iceblocks out, and after that we sat and listened to the lawnmower whine while we ate our Sunnyboys, and Mr Avery and his hell-free existence were forgotten.

We drifted inside after that. Up the steps and onto the verandah and then into the entrance hall with its brown and yellow tiles. Its doormat warning *Love Lies Here*. The smell of cut grass followed us in. It seeped through closed windows and past the heavy front door. Snaked round the downstairs lounge room.

Upstairs the house smelled of mildew and also of bleach and you could just see Mrs Van Apfel on her knees on Saturday afternoon, scouring cupboards where enemy spores had sprung up during the week. Casting out mould-ridden sins.

We circled the kitchen then settled at the table. On top of the table, ready for Mrs Van Apfel to arrive home and start serving up tea, were five lots of cutlery, five amber glass tumblers, and a squeezy bottle of tomato sauce that had stood all day in the sun. There were five plastic placemats too, each one revealing pictures of foods still too exotic to be seen in Macedon Close. Eggplants, artichokes, ruby pomegranates. Every item had its name spelled out for us by a foreign cursive hand.

'What are the mice doing up here?' I said, noticing the tank sitting on the breakfast bar.

Normally the mice lived in the laundry downstairs and not on the kitchen bench. The cast-off aquarium had four squirmy white bodies inside. Pink tails, red eyes. A mouse for each girl plus a spare. (Cordie said Mrs Van Apfel did that in case one of them died. The mice that is, not the girls.)

'I'm teaching them to count,' Cordie said but then she didn't bother to explain what that meant. Didn't say how she was doing that, or why.

Outside the lawnmower gave one last whine and then stopped, and in that moment the world was quiet until there came the unearthly shriek of a lyrebird that must have been digging up Mrs Tierney's runner beans again, two doors up from us.

'Sounds like a human baby,' Hannah said.

Next to her at the table my sister checked the tip of her ponytail for signs her hair had grown overnight. Ruth rested her cheek against the tabletop.

We were still sitting there moments later when Mr Van Apfel pulled into the drive in his faded blue station wagon the colour of the rainless sky. We heard one car door slam, then another as he lifted his briefcase off the passenger seat. He took the steps of the verandah two at a time, as if to waste a moment on the odd ones would be an insult to the Lord, then he barged inside, conquered the spiral staircase and emerged in the kitchen doorway like a black blotch on your retina after looking at the sun too long.

Despite his bulk and his shock of blond hair, you got the feeling Mr Van Apfel was struggling to be seen.

'Ladies! This is the day that the Lord has made! Why are you sitting around doing nothing?'

But it hadn't occurred to us that we were.

'Is your mother home?'

Ruth shook her head without bothering to lift it off the table and the movement first squashed her cheek and then stretched her mouth into a forced kind of smile.

'Enough time then,' Mr Van Apfel reasoned as he moved around the kitchen, bumping a vase of plastic pansies, yanking the fridge door open to stare hopefully inside, 'for a family Bible study before dinner.'

My sister gave me the stink eye.

'Actually, we'd better get going or Mum'll be mad.'

As Laura spoke she flipped her index finger back and forth between the two of us as if to indicate exactly which of the bare-armed bodies draped around his kitchen table Mr Van Apfel should excuse.

'I just came over to help Hannah watch the others while you and Mrs Van Apfel were out,' Laura said. 'And so, you know, if there's an adult at home now ...' She trailed off.

I couldn't believe she was sticking to her story about her and Hannah being babysitters, but Mr Van Apfel seemed to swallow the whole thing.

'I see,' he said sagely.

He walked over to a small table near the doorway and picked up a Bible from where it sat next to the telephone like a second line to God, and then he came back and thudded it down on the kitchen table.

'But even babysitters need God's word, surely?' he said. *'All Scripture is God-breathed and is useful for teaching, rebuking, correcting and training in righteousness.'*

I thought Hannah and Laura didn't need any more training in righteousness just then – not from the Lord, not from anybody – but Mr Van Apfel seemed to think otherwise and he patted the air in front of him with flat palms, pressing us into our seats.

'Besides, it's Ezekiel 36 today, ladies,' he said. 'You don't want to miss this.'

Cordie rocked back in her chair, hanging in space between the table and the wall behind her, daring the universe to let her fall.

'You mean 37,' Ruth said without lifting her head off the table. 'We did 36 yesterday.'

'Yeah,' said Cordie sarcastically.

She rocked forward and planted her chair on the floorboards with a crack, and then she laid her cheek down on the table like Ruth, as if this one short syllable had just about worn her out.

'We did too!' Mr Van Apfel said in wonderment. 'My mistake, ladies. Ezekiel 37.'

'Sure, Mr Van Apfel,' I said, 'we can stay for a bit.'

'Suck-up,' my sister hissed at me, but she said it so low only I could hear.

'Wonderful,' Mr Van Apfel said. He flipped open his Bible and began to read its strange and magical words.

'*The hand of the Lord was on me, Ezekiel, and he brought me out by the Spirit of the Lord and set me in the middle of a valley; it was full of bones. He led me back and forth among them, and I saw a great many bones on the floor of the valley, bones that were very dry.*

'*Then he said to me, "Prophesy to these bones and say to them, 'Dry bones, hear the word of the Lord! This is what the Sovereign Lord says to these bones: I will make breath enter you, and you will come to life. I will attach tendons to you and make flesh come upon you and cover you with skin; I will put breath in you, and you will come to life …'"*'

I shivered as I thought of all those bones. But Mr Van Apfel had more.

'*So I prophesied as I was commanded. And … there was a noise, a rattling sound, and the bones came together, bone to bone. I looked, and tendons and flesh appeared on them and skin covered them …*

'*This is what the Sovereign Lord says: "Behold, O My people, I will open your graves and cause you to come up from your graves, and bring you into the land of Israel. Then you shall know that I am the Lord, when I have opened your graves."*'

When Mr Van Apfel got to a point he seemed satisfied with he paused and looked at us expectantly, but the five of us sat and stared at the grain of the table. At our bare knees tucked underneath. We stared lower down, at our calves; we studied the skin on the backs of our heels and the way it was segmented like worms.

In the end it was Cordie who took pity on him. Inscrutable Cordie. With those alien eyes set so wide in her face, those lips that were verging on purple. The confusing one, who didn't look much like her mum, and not at all like her dad, and therefore must have been a true child of God. Gifted to Mr Van Apfel, for him to favour all he liked.

'Ezekiel brought the bones back to life,' Cordie said dully.

She crossed her arms and looked unimpressed about Ezekiel and his old bones – or possibly her father, it was difficult to say.

Jeez, wasn't Mr Van Apfel excited.

'Ezekiel *did* bring the bones back to life, Cordelia! That's right! Ezekiel was to tell the bones that they would be brought back to life. That's correct,' he said.

'But if we listen carefully to the end of that verse – who was listening? Anyone? Laura, can you tell me? No? Well, Ezekiel didn't put breath into the bones *himself*. Oh no – and this is important – Ezekiel got his power from the Lord! From Jehovah! The Almighty One!

'*It was only through the grace of God that those bones were brought back to life.*'

Mr Van Apfel was getting wound up now. He was really getting going.

'Ezekiel was carrying out the *Lord's* work when he talked about putting tendons and flesh on those bones, and about covering them with skin. They were the bones of the Lord's people but those people had been corrupt and idolatrous. They had gone astray. They had *ignored* the prophets that God had sent to warn them and they had *refused* to repent, and so it was God, through Nebuchadnezzar, who had destroyed them all, and now he was telling Ezekiel to bring them back to life in his name!

'What do you say to that?' he said.

But none of us knew what we should say to that, especially not Laura and me.

Mr Van Apfel went back to his Bible then, flipping the cigarette-paper pages, thrusting whole sections into tall peaks until they collapsed into plains.

'Ezekiel prophesised that God would make breath enter the bones in the same way he first breathed life into Adam,' Mr Van Apfel told us.

'In Genesis,' he clarified for Laura and me, the heathens from down the street.

He stopped thumbing through pages and he looked up at the two of us.

'Did you know the "Apfel" in Van Apfel means "apple"?' he said solemnly. 'From the Garden of Eden. *From the Tree of Knowledge.*'

'By eating the *malus*, Eve contracted *malum*,' he told us. 'That means: by eating the apple, Eve contracted evil.'

And I had a feeling we were getting to the part when it would all be Eve's fault.

'Okay, let's recap, ladies,' Mr Van Apfel said. 'What have we learned so far from Ezekiel 37?'

He spoke slowly and he smiled widely as he talked.

'That the bones would come back to life?' I volunteered.

'That the bones would come back to life,' Mr Van Apfel confirmed, nodding enthusiastically. 'Good, good.'

'And who would bring those bones back to life?' he asked. 'Who would put tendons and flesh and skin on the bones? *Who would raise them from the dead?*'

'Come on, ladies,' he said. 'You can do this.'

But his voice suggested he thought otherwise. Like maybe he'd have more luck getting the mice to count than getting girls to do anything as important as receiving God's word.

Finally Ruth spoke.

'Ezekiel.'

She spoke without lifting her head from the table, and then she changed her mind and raised her head regally and held it there, stiff-necked and awkward, while she waited for her praise. She knew she was right – she'd heard Cordie give that exact answer only moments ago. But Ruth should have known better than to try to compete with Cordie. Not when it came to Mr Van Apfel. Not before the Lord.

'What did you say?' Mr Van Apfel asked Ruth.

'Ezekiel?' Ruth repeated, but she sounded less certain this time. She was watching something that hovered in the air above the table. Something invisible to me.

'After everything we've discussed here today, after everything I've told you about Ezekiel getting his power from the Lord, about the Almighty One, about the grace of God, *after all of this* you still think it was *Ezekiel* who resurrected those bones?'

'Yes?' Ruth said cautiously.

Then she changed her mind. 'I mean, no,' she said quickly.

'Ezekiel.' Mr Van Apfel said it again, only this time it came out in a slow and terrible whisper.

He lowered his chin and squinted his eyes and you could practically hear the scrunch of his skin as it puckered at his eye sockets. He stood and leaned forward, cementing his shirtsleeves to the table on two balled fists. The fridge hummed, then lost its nerve and shifted down a note.

'Ezekiel? Our Lord and Saviour, Our Redeemer is *Ezekiel*?' Mr Van Apfel said slowly. 'Is that what you said? Is that what you mean? *Ezekiel* will bring the dead back to life?'

Ruth froze.

'The Almighty One: *Ezekiel*?'

Ruth said nothing.

'Lord Ezekiel, was he? Is that what you're telling me? Ezekiel? *Ezekiel*?'

He kept repeating that name until I wanted to shout: 'That's not it! That's not what she means! She's just confused, that's all.'

Mr Van Apfel was still standing, still leaning forward over the table. He was still whispering in that horrible voice when suddenly he stopped.

We waited.

'Blasphemy!' Mr Van Apfel shouted. He thumped the table. 'That's blasphemy. And it's a sin. And I will not have you sinning in my house.'

Ruth looked stunned, and no wonder. She'd thought she got the answer right, but what was right moments ago was now blasphemy and a sin and Ruth was going to pay.

'Do not use thy name in vain,' Mr Van Apfel muttered darkly. 'Do not use thy name in vain. Do not use thy name in vain.'

He said it over and over again and I wanted to lean across and ask Laura if by 'thy' he meant *God* or if he was referring to himself because I was starting to get confused and I was nervous that, if pushed to say what I thought, I might give a wrong answer like Ruth. But the look on Laura's face told me it could wait, that I should ask her later at home.

I was ready, I realised. I was ready to go. I'd had enough Bible study for today.

The muttering stopped after that and Mr Van Apfel sat down, scraping his chair across the floorboards and making them cry out. Ruth chewed on her lip in that way she had, and even now I don't know if it was the lip or the chewing that set Mr Van Apfel off again. Or if Ruth had had it coming all along.

Whatever it was, Mr Van Apfel stood and lurched towards Ruth's end of the table, and I was shocked that someone so big could move so terribly fast. He raised his arm and brought it down with a dull, flat sound across Ruth's cheek.

She bowed.

Then she fell, slumping sideways in her chair. Her body jolted as it banged against mine, then she righted herself, gripping the chair as if she'd turned a corner on the bus. And the force of her small, thick torso barging into my shoulder was the only way I could tell that any of it was real.

No one moved. Across the table my sister had moulded herself into her seat.

Mr Van Apfel returned to his seat. 'Where were we?' he said. Then more brightly: 'Let's talk to God.'

Around the table four Van Apfel heads dropped as though pulled by one string and Laura and I followed fast. But the world Mr Van Apfel had been trying so hard to conjure up for us – a world of white bones and dancing skeletons, of miraculous resurrection – had slipped through his fingers and he couldn't get it back.

'Almighty Jesus, Lamb of God, forgiver of sins, cleanser of souls ...'

He was still going minutes later when I heard Mum's voice floating up the twisty stairs.

'Yoo-hoo,' she called. 'Laura? Tikka? Are you girls all right?'

I glanced at Laura, who glanced at the doorway, but neither of us was game to move. I noticed that my hands were gripping the table and that the fingerprints I left were wet. Across from me Cordelia was drawing arcs on the floor with one bare toenail. Ruth cried softly and Hannah was deathly still.

Mr Van Apfel kept on praying.

Out in the stairwell Mum called up to us again and I felt relieved, and slightly squeamish too. Because you could hear her confusion, the creeping concern, but we were too scared to answer back.

'Laura! Can you hear me? Are you there?'

She called out to us a third time and Mr Van Apfel must have noticed the alarm in her voice too because he opened one eye and fixed it directly on me and, without pausing the flood of words that were tumbling from his mouth, he nodded once.

Permission to go.

'Tikka!' Mum said when I appeared at the top of the stairwell. 'Where have you been? I was calling you! Didn't you hear me calling?'

She continued to walk up the stairs as I started down but I waved my arms to stop her. I pointed to the ceiling.

'What? Where's Laura? I thought you girls were *never* coming home. Didn't you hear me —'

I kept moving as she talked and, when I reached her, I grabbed her elbow and rolled my eyes to the roof. Then I pressed my hands together and mimed along with Mr Van Apfel's prayer.

'What? Tikka, where have you been?' she said irritably. 'What are you doing with your mouth, you look like a fish.'

'Shhh, they're in the kitchen and the —'

'Tikka Malloy, I don't know what game you girls are —'

'They're praying,' I hissed.

That stopped her dead.

'Who are?'

'The Van Apfels. *They're praying up there.* They're doing family Bible study and Mr Van Apfel is praying.'

Mum lifted her chin and her eyebrows as well and, sure enough, she could hear Mr Van Apfel now.

'Oh. Right. Yes, so they are.'

She looked flummoxed.

'Well, it's time for you and Laura to come home.'

'Okay.'

'You've been over here for hours.'

I wanted to tell Mum, right then, that Ruth had got hit, but the words just dissolved in my mouth.

In the kitchen the praying petered out and for one awful moment I thought maybe Ruth was going to cop it again. Then Mr Van Apfel's voice seemed to stand up on its own and saunter down the spiral staircase to where Mum and I were standing.

'Mrs Malloy, we're having a little family prayer time together,' the voice said. 'Why don't you come up and join us?'

Mum didn't miss a beat.

'Thank you,' she called up to heaven, 'but I've got mince on the stove.'

'Laura, I'll wait outside,' she added, and the two of us descended together.

* * *

Laura and I held hands that day as we walked home across the cul-de-sac with Mum. Paper dolls against the blazing sky.

Later, when we tried to remember exactly what had happened that day, I said I reckoned Mr Van Apfel's hand had been flat when it smacked Ruth's cheek, but my sister insisted: no. She said I was wrong and that I hadn't seen properly, and that in the final airless instant before his hand came down, Mr Van Apfel had flexed his palm wide and then drawn it into a fist so that when he hit Ruth, it was a punch.

That's what Laura said.

Either way we never told Mum about it. The three of us walked home together in silence so that the only noise came from the bottleneck to our street where Mrs McCausley's sprinkler *pftzz-pftzz-pftzz*ed away like the twisting cap on a fizzy drink in the instant before it bursts.

CHAPTER FIVE

We saw more of those girls *after* they disappeared than we ever did before. Their noses no longer pressed against the flyscreen of our back door, their lips bleeding through the tiny wire squares as they called us over for a swim. They no longer took their heads out of the chest freezer at the milk bar when we met them in that concrete bunker to buy ice creams together.

But we still saw them everywhere.

In the distraught faces of our neighbours. On the TV news. Their satin school bows shiny, their smiles slick with spit. Those same smiles were stuffed into our letterbox on a flyer detailing the approximate time and date of their disappearance, and the number to call with information. They were wrapped around telegraph poles all along the main road like the foil around Easter eggs.

In the week after the disappearance the police received the first in a series of fake ransom notes. All in blue biro, and all written on the back of shopping dockets from a store that hadn't yet worked out how to put paid advertising on the back of its receipts. The receipts were for things like fly spray and canned corn (total: $4.80). Always insignificant amounts. While the notes themselves demanded $750,000 per girl.

Then there were the sightings. We were plagued by reports of sightings in the beginning. Three girls aged between seven and fourteen, all with blonde hair, were seen getting onto a south coast train with a male (Caucasian, approximately twenty-four years of age). Three girls were spotted wading in the river at dusk (though nobody would be caught dead swimming at that time of day, not with the bull sharks around). Three girls were seen hitchhiking from the crime scene. They were seen rowing a boat. They were seen several hours south, although that turned out to be a false lead when police worked out they were German backpackers working as fruit pickers and that they were at least ten years older than Hannah, the eldest Van Apfel.

Everyone, it seemed, had seen those girls.

It was as if the three of them were far more visible to us now than they ever were before they vanished.

* * *

In the hours after the girls disappeared the police established a command post at the picnic sheds at Coronation Park. The sheds, with their carmine-red roofs like smears of mercurochrome, were at the southern end of the picnic grounds near the car park. Detective Senior Constable Justin Mundy from the neighbouring district was in charge of the police from the local area command, and he arrived in his football clothes because Friday night was training night and the Minnows had been in the middle of their shuttle runs when Detective Mundy got the call.

Even without wasting time having a shower or getting changed, it took Detective Mundy the best part of twenty minutes to arrive. Still, it was reassuring for everyone under his command to see him dressed in his Minnows uniform. You could trust a bloke who fronted up for work wearing his football shorts.

Later we'd get Detective Senior Sergeant Craig Malone, who'd come in a suit, not in shorts, but who'd bring with him a team from the homicide squad in the city. After Senior Sergeant Malone would come the detectives from the sex crimes unit, the crime scene officers, and special investigations. The water police cruised in too. In the end we'd have thirteen detectives, two special analysts from the city, forensics, plus all of the local area command and the SES volunteers. They'd talk in code, with maps and lists, and with a collection of highlighter pens in colours I didn't even know existed, scouring the valley and finding no sign, even though we must have outnumbered those girls by more than a hundred to one.

But until then? Until then we just had Detective Senior Constable Justin Mundy in his football shorts with a picture of a baitfish on them.

My parents had to give witness statements on the night of the vanishing — everyone's parents did. Though that seemed like a funny thing to have to do when no one had witnessed a thing.

That was the problem, as far as I could see.

All of the cops (aside from Detective Mundy) wore navy-blue boilersuits that looked an awful lot like the tracksuits we wore for school sport each Friday. Everyone had to wear the sports uniform on Friday, whether you'd been picked to play in a representative team or not (our uniform code didn't discriminate between those kids who could catch a ball and the rest of us who couldn't). The fact that some kids were still wearing their sports uniform at the park that Friday night only added to the confusion. They wandered around in their navy tracksuits and matching caps like creepy, shrunken versions of the cops.

Detective Senior Constable Justin Mundy didn't match anyone though. He stood out, and not just because of his shorts. Detective Mundy was the boss and you could tell. He stayed very quiet while he listened to the information he was given, and then he shouted instructions and stood back and watched, his fingers laced at the back of his neck, as teams of cops and SES volunteers and our own mums and dads nodded and frowned and jogged off in the direction he indicated, beating the ground with sticks and calling through cupped hands.

There were the dogs too. Three bouncy black–and–white ones, and a mean-looking German shepherd.

'English springer spaniels,' one of the cops told me, pointing to the bouncy ones. 'High levels of enthusiasm and endurance.'

He could tell that I was interested in his dogs. I'd been watching them for a while.

'They come from the dog squad?' I asked.

'Cadaver dogs,' he said proudly. 'Can sniff out a decomposing body under running water.'

'They go underwater then?'

'What? Dead bodies? We find them everywhere, kiddo.' He shook his head gravely when he said it.

'No, the dogs, I mean. Can they go underwater?'

'Sure can,' he said. 'But actually they smell out the bodies from above the surface.'

I wondered how that would work with our river, which already stank like the dead.

'How do you train them then?'

'Blood. Bone. Teeth,' the cop said casually.

And I nodded knowingly as if I knew what he meant.

'What's this dog's name?' I asked.

One of the bouncy dogs was snuffling around near my right knee and I reached down to pat him but the cop shook his head.

'Name's Alligator,' he said. 'Watch out. He bites.'

I snatched my hand back as if it was on fire.

'Nah, just kidding. But you can't pat him while he's on his shift.'

'Why not?'

'He's a member of the force, isn't he. Like me. And you wouldn't try and pat me while I'm on me shift, would you?'

I wouldn't try and pat you in a million years, I thought.

'Why's he called Alligator?'

'You mean, why's he called that if he doesn't really bite?'

'Nah. Why's he called Alligator if he lives around here? We only have crocodiles in Australia. Saltwater ones *and* freshwater. But we don't have any alligators. Mrs Laguna taught us that.'

Mrs Laguna was my Year Five teacher.

'You know a lot about a lot, dontcha, kiddo?'

I knew that knowing things was showing off and it was safer not to say.

'I better go find Mum,' I mumbled. And I left the cop and his springy dogs and went to see if my parents had finished giving their witness statements.

* * *

'They're English springer spaniels,' I told Mum when I found her. She was standing with Laura, to the left of the picnic sheds, where the two of them had been keeping an eye on me the whole time I talked to the cop.

'The big one's a German shepherd like Mr Daniels's dog, Samson, but the bouncy ones are English springer spaniels,' I explained. 'They've come all the way from Cadaver.'

'From where?' Mum said absently. She was distracted and looking for Dad now that I was safely back within touching distance. She gazed past me and scanned the sheds for him.

'Where's your father *now*?' she said.

'Wasn't he in the sheds with you?' I asked.

'We've got enough people missing without him adding to the list,' she said, ignoring my question. 'And who was that police officer you were talking to, Tikka? I want you and you sister right here where I can see you.'

So I stood in the dirt with Mum and Laura, while we waited for Dad to appear.

* * *

On the Tuesday after the girls went missing, a psychic arrived and told us where we should search. The sky was the colour of cold tea that day, the river a mirror image.

'What's a psychic?'

'She's a bit like a fortune teller,' Mum said.

'She's a quack,' Dad informed me. 'A crackpot.'

But I didn't know what a 'quack' was – or a 'crackpot' either – so I was left with Mum's definition.

The psychic had hair that fell in wispy pale waves and looked like it had never been cut. It was so long and so fine that you couldn't quite see the ends; it petered out somewhere between the tops of her thighs and the backs of her knees, but it was impossible to put your finger on exactly where. Funny that it was her job to find missing things when she seemed to be dissolving herself.

She told police to pump the septic tank behind the toilet block, near the oval, so a huge silver tanker, the same size and shape as a petrol truck, was shunted along the hairpin bends and into the belly of the gorge. It took three men in jumpsuits almost an hour to remove the manhole cover and lay it on the grass like an enormous concrete coin. A tithe for what might be inside.

When they removed the cover the stink was like every single egg in the world had gone off, and even the men in jumpsuits, who must have done this a hundred times before, winced as they fed the hose down the hole. Then the pump started up and the roar ripped through the gully. Stuffed every crevice with its sad chugging sound.

My sister yelled at me to stand back from the hole.

'It's not safe! Get back behind me!'

We were waiting near the oval like everyone else, while our parents helped out with the search. And with Mum and Dad gone, Laura thought she was the boss. (Though technically, Mrs Lantana was in charge.)

'Stand back, Tikka!' she instructed.

I took a step backwards, then inched forward again. What my sister didn't understand was that I had to see it for myself. How else to say for certain that the girls weren't down there? The pump men might miss them among the sludge and the mess. But as I watched the hose being fed down the septic hole that day, my stomach disappeared along with it. It was a sickening, slack-muscled drop.

'Get back!' Laura barked again, and I half-turned towards her and pointed to my ears.

'What? I can't hear you,' I mouthed.

And Laura rolled her eyes and mimed: 'Wait till I tell Mum.'

Anyone could have lip-read *that*.

For a while nobody spoke because there wasn't much point. But nobody held out much hope either. Not that it was useless. Just that we were unsure what it was we should hope for by now. So we stood and let ourselves be filled with the noise as though it might plug up some of our loss. Then: 'Nothing!' came the shout, and the pump was switched off and the silence that followed was shocking. After that, just a lonely mechanical beep as the septic truck reversed out.

* * *

For the rest of the morning my sister and I and the other searchers' kids remained stubbornly stuck behind. We sat in the playground by the oval like we had yesterday, and the day before that, and every other day when our parents went out searching and wouldn't leave us at home unsupervised like they would've done only last week. Back then they wouldn't have thought twice about ducking up to the shops without us. Or leaving us to let ourselves into the house after school and eat cereal and watch cartoons and not do our homework for all those delicious hours until they got home from work.

But that was then and this was now, and now there was a psycho on the loose.

'Who says?' I challenged Laura.

'Jade Heddingly,' she admitted. 'And she was told it by Mrs McCausley.'

We sat among the woodchips underneath the swings, flicking bits of bark onto the grass and occasionally at one another, but even that was pretty half-hearted. Mum had left Laura with strict instructions not to let me out of her sight, and so far she hadn't, but we both knew that was only because her best friend was missing, and at least I was a better option than Jade.

'Jade told me a psycho must have abducted the girls.'

'How does she know?'

'She doesn't,' Laura said, then she paused. 'But it *could* be true. That's what psychos do, it's part of their psychosis.'

'Is it?'

'Yes,' she said.

Laura knew I had no idea what the word 'psychosis' meant and she took satisfaction from not explaining it now.

'Do the police know that —' I started to say.

'Know what?'

'That thing about psychosis. Maybe we should —'

'Maybe we should *nothing*,' Laura snapped. 'Maybe we should sit here just like we've been told and not say anything at all.'

'What about the toilet?'

'What toilet?'

'Can I at least go to the toilet?'

Ordinarily I would never defer to Laura like this – I was old enough to make my own decisions – but the rules had changed and Lor and I were in it together. Besides, I couldn't see Mrs Lantana to ask.

Laura granted permission with a resigned nod.

Then she called after me as I started to walk away: 'Don't disappear though, or else Mum will spew.'

But she didn't sound as tough as she was trying to be.

By then it was late morning and the sun sat high and mean. I stared at it for a moment, which you're not supposed to do (Brett Underwood told me my retinas would burn to a crisp). But that day the sun was so white that it actually looked cool and I had the urge to touch it. Sweat prickled uncomfortably at the backs of my knees and slunk down my calves when I walked.

I headed towards the oval and the toilet block beyond, grass crunching under my thongs. At the oval I tightrope-tiptoed along the line markings spray-painted onto the grass, treading slowly, watchfully along each line, and if I lost my balance I went back to the beginning and started that line again. You couldn't fall off: a crocodile could get you. Or maybe a snake.

Snakey, snakey on your back. Which finger did that?

At the third corner I hesitated. I was at the closest point to the toilet block now but I still had one side of the rectangle to go. It was only a short side but I was at the toilets. I would have to forget the last side.

I had just squared up my new course – valley wall on my right, river on my left, toilet block dead ahead – when something moved among the mangroves and the mudflats. I stopped and took a sharp breath.

'Hannah? *Cordie!*'

A koel cried out from somewhere in the mangroves. *Koo-ooo koo-ooo.* It was a mournful cry and one that could go on, unanswered, for hours.

'Cordie?' I called.

The thing moved again. But it was too dark, the mangroves were too twisted together for me to see what was hiding in there. I shielded my eyes with my hand to try to see better while I shifted uncertainly on the spot. I could nick to the toilet and then go down onto the sand to see what was there. I should look. *Should I look?* I wondered. What I should probably do was get a grown-up. After I'd done a wee though.

I took three quick steps towards the toilet block but the thing in the mangroves didn't like that. It moved faster this time. Crack. A low grunt. I stumbled back onto my white spray-paint line. I didn't want to upset the thing.

'Ruth? Is that you? I can see you,' I lied.

The thing in the mangroves laughed.

It was a hard laugh that wasn't Hannah's or Cordie's, and not Ruth's laugh either. It came from the maws of something much bigger. The koel reared up in the air in alarm and hovered for a moment, wings thrumming above the mangroves. Then it cried out once more – *koo-ooo koo-ooo* – before it rose higher and pulled away.

'Mr Avery?' I said, and I squinted into the spindly-armed darkness.

It was him all right. It was just Mr Avery. Relief and mangrove stink flooded my mouth.

'Are you yabbying down there or something?' I called.

'I believe we're looking for something a bit bigger than yabbies, Tikka.'

Mr Avery wasn't the only teacher who called me 'Tikka' instead of using my real name. They all did, except for Mrs Tonkin. She'd called me 'Tick-Tock' ever since I was in her class in Year Two, when we'd first learned how to read a clock. She'd looked like a colossus, her bottom spilling over the sides of a child-sized chair while she sat out the front and swirled time tantalisingly forwards and backwards with just the tip of her pointer finger.

But when Mr Avery called me Tikka my stomach bunched up in a way that I didn't like at all.

'Something bigger than yabbies? You mean the Van Apfel girls?' I said.

'Correct.'

'Well, sure,' I said. 'Thing is, you're not going to find them in the mangroves, though. Is that what you're doing down there? I can't really see you in the dark. The Cadaver dogs have been through the mangroves about a hundred times already. Did you know they brought special dogs out here? I thought they came all the way from Cadaver, but Mum said no, that wasn't quite right.

'I can tell you about them, if you like,' I went on. 'They're called Cadaver dogs. Not the big one – he's a German shepherd like Mr Daniels's dog, Samson. Do you know Mr Daniels's dog, Samson? He lives with Mr Daniels in the house next door to the tennis courts, and whenever you hit the ball over the fence you're not supposed to go and get it because Samson can bite, but once I saw Joel Evans sneak into Mr Daniels's backyard and throw a whole heap of old balls back over the fence and Samson didn't bite him once.'

I hesitated.

'Though he might not have been in the yard that day,' I conceded. 'Samson, I mean,' I added. 'Joel Evans was there, all right. I saw him with my own eyes.'

I had been walking towards the dark shape of Mr Avery as I spoke, stepping off the grassy ledge and onto the sand. I had things I had learned that I needed to tell him. Weeing would have to wait.

'The Cadaver dogs are the little black and white ones,' I explained. 'Hey, did you get any?' I inclined my head towards the river.

'Any what?'

'Any yabbies. Oh wait, you said you weren't doing that, didn't you. Did you say that? What are you doing down here then, Mr Avery? If you're not catching yabbies … It stinks real bad, you know. Can't you smell that? You'd be better off coming back when the tide's a bit higher, that's when it doesn't pong so much. My cousins have got yabbies. Three of them. One each. They keep them in a tank and they're called Nipper and Snap and Jean-Claw-Van-Dam. Vivian — that's my cousin — she wanted to call one of them Twilight Sparkle but the boys both voted for Jean-Claw-Van-Dam and there are two of them and only one of Vivian, and so Jean-Claw-Van-Dam won. They didn't catch them here, but. They didn't catch them anywhere. My Uncle Steve got them from the pet shop near his office.'

I had reached Mr Avery by now.

'Geez, no wonder I couldn't see you from up near the dunnies,' I said. 'It's like night-time in here. Nice and cool but.'

We stood in the darkness where the world was wet and viscid. And where it stank to high hell.

'I think you'll find yabbies like fresh water,' he said eventually. 'Have you done the vertebrate and invertebrate unit in Social Studies yet?'

I shook my head.

'Yabbies are crustaceans,' he said. 'They don't have a spine, and they prefer fresh water over tidal rivers like this one. I don't think you'll catch many around here.'

'I've never had much luck,' I admitted.

'Do you know how to catch a yabbie, Tikka?'

And I wanted to say then: *Could you please stop saying my name? Or use my real one if you have to use anything?* I toed the wet sand.

'Not exactly,' I said.

'Meat,' he replied. 'Yabbies like meat. Anything with blood will do. We used to use sheep's hearts as bait when we went yabbying.'

I stared bug-eyed. 'Sheep's hearts? Like actual hearts from sheeps? That is *gross*.'

'Singular. No "s",' he said absent-mindedly. 'It's gross but it works. Rockmelon too. You'll find they like sweet things.'

We both thought about that for a bit.

'I used to go yabbying all the time in Lake Eucumbene with my brothers when we weren't much older than you,' he told me.

'You had *brothers*?'

This was a revelation even greater than the sheep's hearts, and Mr Avery laughed.

'Still do,' he said. 'In fact, I have a mum and everything. I might even be a human being, just like you, Tikka.'

'What about a dad?'

'A dad?'

'Yeah. You got one of those, Mr Avery? You said a mum but not a dad. Haven't you got one of those?'

'I started out with one.'

I wondered where Mr Avery's dad had gone to, and why it made Mr Avery look so strange.

'I could show you,' he was saying then and I realised I'd stopped listening.

'If that was something you wanted, I could show you how to catch a yabbie.'

'But you said there *were* none,' I said suspiciously. My legs itched and I was worried it might be sandflies. My bladder ached. I would have to go soon.

'Oh, I mean I'd just show you how,' he said. 'We won't catch any real yabbies. You won't have anything to show your friends.'

'But if you come here like this —' He didn't move until I half-raised one arm in what we both took to be my consent, and then he stepped towards me.

I faced the river in the useless hope we might see a yabbie. As if the wind might pick up and the water might part and there, before us, might appear a riot of brilliant blue bodies.

But all that appeared was Mr Avery's breath on my cheek. He stood behind me, leaning down to my level.

'You need to feel the yabbie *pull*,' he told me, and he mimed throwing a line into the water, testing its tension, and then he placed the invisible rod into my hands. He stayed like that, arms over my arms, hands encasing my hands, watching and waiting for *the pull*.

He smelled foreign like the sausages in Wade Nevrakis's parents' deli. His arms were covered in dark hair – his whole body seemed to be because coils of it poked out of the tight 'V' of his shirt, as if reaching towards his beard. The hairs on his arms, however, weren't the usual springy kind. They lay flat against his skin like fur. He noticed me looking at them and he tugged his shirtsleeves lower, trying to cover up the carpet on his arms.

I couldn't make sense of Mr Avery. This man with fur, this teacher with brothers.

'There's no pull,' I said eventually.

'No, no pull,' he said dully.

He released us from our imaginary hunt.

'Everyone is probably wondering where I am,' I said after a moment.

'Do they know you're down here?' he said, and I was surprised by the urgency in his voice.

'No?' I said hesitantly. I would have given the right answer, if only I knew what it was. Just like I would have caught a yabbie if it were possible to do so.

'Laura knows – I told her.' It was only a half-lie. 'But the others don't know where I am.'

As I said this I began gathering myself to go. The sun was directly overhead and in places it pierced the lid of the mangroves so that shards of sunlight lay on the sand in patches and made me think of those Cadaver dogs with their salt and pepper shag.

'Where are you going?' Mr Avery asked.

I was moving now, picking my way back towards the oval.

'Back to the others,' I said over my shoulder.

As I spoke I misstepped and my foot came down hard on a snapped-off mangrove skeleton sticking up out of the sand. The stump punctured my thong then went into my foot, piercing the skin near my arch.

For an instant the branch became part of my foot. Bone of my bone, flesh of my flesh. Then I yanked my foot away and my thong snapped in two. *Pop.* The sound was almost comical.

The rubber straps of my thong still clung to my foot, while the pink pearl base stayed impaled on the branch. I gasped in shock. At my thong. At my foot. At the stinging, which was fierce and blossoming across the underside of my foot.

'Laura!' I shouted in panic.

Waves broke softly onto the sand to my right, pushing pine needles up the bank towards me.

'Laura!' I yelled again.

I began lurching, stumbling towards the oval. Heading for the grass and sunshine. The straps of my thong, now unanchored, slipped off somewhere and were lost in the mangroves and muck.

'Laura, help me!'

I tripped coming up the bank near the oval and crawled along the spiky grass on my knees. Then I stood again and limped awkwardly on.

'Laura!' I shouted. 'Laura!'

Over at the playground my sister stood and stiffened, then she cupped her palms around her ears as if trying to keep hold of what she thought she had heard. She was still the first person I called for.

'Laur-ra!'

I raised my arm like I was stuck in a rip and not standing in a sea of dead grass. Laura saw me and screamed. She came barrelling towards me and I limped clumsily to her.

In that same instant a group of searchers emerged from the scrub on the far side of the oval and began snaking their way towards the sheds. They were going to regroup and refuel. Make a cup of tea. Report on what it was they hadn't found. For one awful moment it looked like they might collide, my sister and the searchers, but the tail of the group broke away at the last second, allowing Laura to run through the gap and continue across the oval towards me. I saw my parents in the group, though they hadn't seen me, and I watched as they registered Laura's panic. Mum wore her gardening hat, and the back side of it waved shyly to me as the wind flipped it up at the brim.

'Mum!' I shouted and I let out a sob.

My parents whipped around as if spun by the breeze. They saw me, and Mum let out a cry.

'Mum!' I wailed as they ran towards me. 'Mum! I busted my thong!'

The wind blew off the mangroves in gusts and carried my words away.

'You what?' said my sister.

She was only a few metres away from me now and her eyes narrowed and she slowed her pace.

'Your *thong*?'

She was out of breath and the words ran together so that they came out of her mouth as: 'You're-wrong.'

They all arrived then. Even Mr Avery, climbing up and out of the mangrove shadows with my pink thong flap laid out on one palm.

'Tikka! What happened? Where have you been?' Mum rushed over. 'Where's Laura? I thought she was looking after you? Laura? Why weren't you looking after Tikka?'

My sister opened her mouth to speak, then frowned and pointed past my shoulder to Mr Avery.

'What's that?'

Pearly pink rubber now hung from his finger. One neat fingernail of his index finger poked through the hole in the thong.

Snakey, snakey on your back. Which finger did that?

'My thong,' I said. 'I told you I busted it.'

'I need to wee,' I added urgently to Mum. I was standing on one leg, holding my injured foot in the air.

'What happened to your foot?' she said.

'Why have you got Tikka's thong?' Dad asked Mr Avery.

'We were looking for yabbies. My foot is really hurting, you know. Do you think I'll need crutches?' I added hopefully.

One of the SES volunteers stepped away from the group and walked over to me. She knelt down in front of my foot.

'Can I see?' she asked. 'What went in there?'

'Mangrove stump.'

'Ouch,' said the lady. She inspected my foot gently. 'Looks like a clean cut. No bits left behind.'

'Yabbies?' Dad said mystified. 'You won't find any yabbies in there.'

Mr Avery's face was ashen.

'We didn't. There was no pull,' I confirmed. 'But we *were* using an invisible rod.'

Dad looked at Mr Avery but Mr Avery was super-interested, just at that second, in the piece of dead grass that his toe could flatten and then resurrect with a single flick of his foot.

'An invisible what?' Dad said.

He made a move in the direction of Mr Avery and Mr Avery saw him coming and started talking real fast.

'I was explaining to Tikka about vertebrates and invertebrates, from the unit the kids do in Social Studies. I was explaining that yabbies are crustaceans and that they prefer fresh water, not tidal rivers like this, and that I didn't think she'd catch many yabbies around here.

'Still, she wanted to give it a go so I was showing her the right way to cast a rod,' he said.

I frowned at that last bit because it wasn't exactly true.

Only nobody saw me because I had my nose to my foot where I was supervising the blood that oozed out.

'But you don't catch yabbies with a rod,' Dad said looking baffled.

'I might need crutches,' I suggested again.

The SES lady squatted down and tucked her arm underneath mine.

'Lean on me,' she said. 'We'd better take you over to first aid and fix you up a bit.'

'Can I go to the toilet first?' I asked shyly.

'Sure,' she said. 'Toilet first.'

Then she turned to the rest of the searchers: 'Can I get a hand on the other side?'

Mum looked up from where she'd been interrogating Laura and she called out to my dad. She sounded panicky.

'Graham. Go.'

Mr Avery and Dad were still talking, but at the sound of his name, and the tone of Mum's voice, Dad put his hand up and stopped Mr Avery midsentence.

'We all are, mate,' he said curtly to Mr Avery, then he walked over and stood beside me.

'Now, where are we carrying you to, Tik?' he asked.

'"We all are" what, Dad?' I said.

'If you stand there.' The SES lady directed him to a spot on my left-hand side.

'Here?'

'That's it.'

'"We all are" what?' I said again.

'And you put your arms underneath, we'll do a chair lift like this ...' They put their arms beneath me and gripped each other around the wrists so that they formed a cradle to carry me. I slung my arms around their shoulders for support.

'On the count of three we're going to lift,' she instructed. 'We're headed for the first-aid station —'

'But first the toilet,' I interrupted.

'But first the toilet,' she agreed.

'What did you say to Mr Avery, Dad?' I wanted to know. 'What was he telling you?'

'Which one's the first-aid station again?' Dad asked.

'At the far shed. Can you see it? The one at the back. That's it.'

They fumbled for a moment trying to get my weight even, while everyone stood and watched. Mr Avery was off to one side, looking like he wanted to help but also that he shouldn't offer.

'What did you mean "We all are"?' I asked Dad again. 'What did Mr Avery say?'

I wondered if he'd been telling Dad that I'd asked him about his family, about his parents, about the fact he had brothers. That wasn't rude, was it? Sometimes I said things I shouldn't, though I never knew it at the time. And I did ask a lot of questions.

But Dad said he couldn't remember and that it wasn't important. And also: how was it possible I was so heavy?

'What are your bones made of, Tikka? Cast iron?' he said.

'We'll walk with you,' Mum told the SES lady, 'in case you need a hand.'

She wasn't about to let me out of her sight. Though I'm not sure what she thought she and Laura might do to help. I only had two sides and they were already being held.

'Thanks,' the lady said.

And Mr Avery said nothing, just stood very still. Apart from his foot, which was still teasing the grass.

* * *

It wasn't until years later that I learned Dad *did* remember his conversation with Mr Avery that day. He remembered it and he relayed it word for word to the police, who filed it with the rest of their evidence.

The suspect claimed he was 'distressed' and 'couldn't think straight'.

That's what the police report said.

'"Distressed" is a strong word. That's how he described his state of mind?' the interviewing cop asked Dad.

'That's what he said,' Dad confirmed.

'And what did you say?'

'What did I say?'

'That's right. What did you say to him in reply?'

Dad sighed and rubbed his thumb and his forefinger along the bridge of his nose. 'I told him we all were. Who isn't gutted about those girls?'

* * *

That day by the mangroves, when Dad and the SES lady held me and my foot suspended in the air between them, when the searchers stood on the oval watching as if waiting for the umpire's whistle, a Cadaver dog came wandering over to see what was happening.

The dog snuffled at the steel-capped boots of one of the searchers and then he nosed the grass for a moment. Bits of his fur were wet with sweat and they lay slick against his hot body.

'Thommo's dog,' someone commented.

The dog glanced up at his owner's name. Then he paused and staggered sideways and his back legs collapsed in a way that almost looked playful.

'What the hell —' someone started saying.

The dog sat in the dirt looking astonished. His eyes were open and his pupils were dilated. The black centres almost swallowed the surrounding blue. He looked at his legs and he yawned in panic. Then his front paws scrabbled at the dirt as if he was trying to drag himself forward, trying to outrun some ghost. A series of tiny yellow bubbles trickled out from between his teeth, then he lurched forward and slammed his nose in the dust.

'Jesus Christ. He's dead!' said the man with the steel-capped boots, and he slid his toe out from under the dog's hot belly in horror.

Dad and the SES lady thudded me down.

'He's crook all right,' said someone else.

'Crook? He's bloody dead!' the first man said and he wiped the cap of his boot on the back of his leg.

'Are you sure?'

'Well he's not alive!'

'Holy shit. What do we do?'

'Snake got him, you reckon?'

'Bloody hell.'

'Is there a vet anywhere? Or a doctor'll do. Anyone here a doctor?'

'Look at the way his snout's swelling up. You're right – he's gone and kissed a snake.'

Everyone peered at the dog.

It was Alligator. The bouncy one; the one I'd seen earlier in the week. The one whose salt-and-pepper body had squirmed and wriggled while I told the cop everything I knew about crocs. The one who'd quivered and spun just by my right knee. Now he lay dead in the dirt. His body convulsed a couple of times. Small, sharp jerks like he meant to do it.

'Jesus, what do we do?' someone else said.

'Better get Thommo. Wait till he sees this.'

* * *

Later, after I'd been to the toilet and after I'd been to the first-aid station, I asked Dad what it felt like to die.

'I dunno, Tik, I reckon you'll pull through. First aid said you don't even need stitches,' Dad said.

No, Alligator I meant. When he saw that snake did he know he might die?

'Lucky bugger probably never knew what got him,' Dad said, trying to console me. 'Bet he never saw a thing.'

I didn't like to point out that Alligator had been bitten on the nose, so chances are he would have seen the snake. Sometimes Dad's feelings needed protecting as much as anyone else's, and so I let him believe Alligator was blind to what he had coming.

We thought we'd seen the worst when those girls disappeared. But seeing and not seeing is a funny old thing. Even now I don't know which is crueller in the end.

CHAPTER SIX

Really it began when Cordelia fell out of the tree. When she slipped out of its branches and fell back to earth, landing in the mess of roots and drupes underneath, breaking her arm in two places. That was when it really began. Long before those girls went missing.

We used to collect the peppercorns from that tree. We'd sweep them up and put them on the windowsills of our bedrooms and wait for them to turn from green to pink to purplish brown. Then when they were at their ripest – their darkest, toxic best – we would feed them to our hard-faced dolls until we spoiled their plastic pouts.

But Cordie wasn't collecting peppercorns that day. She wasn't doing anything much. Just sitting and watching while the witchy fingers of the tree sank into her skin until the instant they didn't. Until it was her *skin* doing the sinking. Her skin and her bones and her hair and her teeth. Her bare toes released by the crone.

That's when it started.

When Cordelia fell out of that tree.

* * *

Ruth said Dr Adiga did all the usual stuff at the hospital. Checked Cordie's head, shone a light in her ears. Pressed his cold palm against her stomach. Ruth had to go to the hospital with Cordie and Mrs Van Apfel because you couldn't exactly leave her at home on her own. Not if you wanted any food left in your fridge.

But it was handy having Ruth in the hospital contingent because it meant she could tell me what happened. (You'd never get that level of detail from Cordie.) Ruth could tell, for instance, how Dr Adiga had asked Cordie if she had any dizziness or a headache, or if her eyes felt blurry. She could remember how he asked Cordie if her stomach felt okay. And how Cordie said she didn't eat any of the peppercorns.

'Everyone knows they're poison,' she said. 'I'm not stupid, you know.'

And Dr Adiga said that he never thought she was stupid, but that actually he was more interested in whether or not she had concussion. And I could see how that would be a useful thing for a treating doctor to know.

Mrs Van Apfel was there too of course – she wasn't going to miss out on an emergency. And when Ruth said her mum said: 'It was the peppercorn tree in our backyard. I've told my husband a hundred times to trim it,' well then, you knew Ruth was telling the truth about things because that's just what Mrs

Van Apfel *would* say. Just like you could bet she'd have sat in that hospital waiting room reading back issues of *Watchtower* as if Moses himself carried them down from the Mount.

Dr Adiga was the only doctor who ever worked in the hospital back in those days, or so it seemed to us. He was my doctor when I had chickenpox and I got a fever in the middle of the night, when Dad took me to the hospital and wore his clothes over his pyjamas. Lor had Dr Adiga too. That time when she burned her hand on a bunger at cracker night after Carl Mannix double-dared her to touch it. (Lor was all right but Carl Mannix was not. He got grounded for a week for that.)

And even though Dr Adiga had to look after all of us kids, even though he had to fix up our fevers and our burned hands and a whole bunch of busted bones, he never acted like he minded. He was never in a hurry. (These days it's different. They've moved the hospital to a new site across the ridge. There it's bigger and whiter than ever before, and Dr Adiga has retired.)

But back when the hospital was on our side of the valley, back when it wasn't much more than an emergency room with a few beds out the back and the floors were covered with lino that squealed when you walked on it, back then Dr Adiga seemed to be the only doctor around.

'Dr Adiga said she broke her radius *and* ulna,' Ruth reported as the two of us walked to school the day after the fall. Cordie was at home resting, and Laura and Hannah were long gone. They left early to catch the bus to high school.

'He said she did a good job.'

'You mean a bad job.'

'He definitely said good.'

'Yeah, but a good job of a bad thing,' I said. 'He was being sarcastic.' She'd understand when she got to Year Five like me.

'What about Cordie's sleepwalking?' I asked.

'Still doing it, you mean?'

'Well, yeah. But do you think the sleepwalking's related? Did Dr Adiga ask her that?'

'Related? To her busted arm?'

'Yeah.'

'How?' Ruth was confused.

'I don't know. Just – did Dr Adiga mention it? Did he say the sleepwalking could be linked?'

'She didn't fall asleep in the tree, if that's what you're getting at,' she said.

But I wasn't exactly sure *what* I was getting at, so I could hardly explain it to Ruth.

'She is still doing it but,' Ruth admitted. 'She goes walking every few nights.'

'Out of the house?'

'Not usually. She only did that the morning everyone saw her in the street. Normally she gets about as far as the hallway. Once Mum found her in the bath. She was crouched inside, and when Mum woke her up, Cordie had no idea how she got there.'

It was hot as we walked and the sky seemed to sag. Everything looked ready to melt.

'Dr Adiga *did* want to know how she got the other bruise,' Ruth said.

'What other bruise?'

'The one around the top of her arm.'

'The arm she busted?'

'Yeah.'

'Cordie had a bruise around the top of the arm that she broke?' I repeated.

'Yeah.'

'Then she did it when she fell,' I said. You didn't need to be a doctor to work that one out. Dr Adiga must have been having an off day.

But Ruth was saying no, Dr Adiga didn't agree. How he'd questioned Cordie when he saw the bruise there.

'What did Cordie say?'

'Same as you. That she must have bumped the top part of her arm when she fell out of the tree, and Dr Adiga said, "Are you sure about that?" and "That bruise looks like it's been there a while."'

'Had it?'

'How should I know?'

'Well, did Cordie say where she got it?'

'I don't think she knew where she got it,' Ruth said. 'I don't know where she got it.'

'Yeah, but it's not your arm,' I pointed out. 'If it was, you'd know.'

'Kids get bruises all the time,' she said with authority. 'Doesn't mean they have to know where they came from.'

'If I had a bruise,' I said, 'then I would definitely know where it came from. Don't you think it's weird Cordie didn't know where she got her own bruise?'

But if she thought it was weird, Ruth didn't say. We walked in silence while she concentrated on the path. There was no breeze along the street that day.

'The bruise *was* very yellow,' Ruth said eventually. 'So it's not surprising Cordie couldn't remember where she got it from.'

I nodded.

'It's probably disappeared by now,' she added.

And the one person who was there couldn't tell us anything because he didn't see it happen, so he said. Trent Rainer was doing the edges of his yard next door the day Cordie fell from the tree. He was using his new four-stroke line trimmer which cut grass in half the time of his old star-tooth edger, but which made more than ten times the noise. That line trimmer meant Trent Rainer didn't hear the *whump* when Cordie landed on the lawn. A *whump* like a basketball filled with rainwater.

* * *

Cordelia was back at school on Monday, and when we saw her cast we just about died with jealousy.

'Can I touch it?'

'Can I sign it?'

'Does it hurt when I do this?'

We'd abandoned our game of Poison Letter and stood pressed around Cordie, jostling for position, hoping to soak up some of her suffering. We asked how many bandages Dr Adiga had used and whether it itched underneath her cast, and she handed out answers like she was sharing her lunch.

One or two kids still stuck with the game and they stood frozen, legs bent, fists balled, while they waited for us to come back and join in. But to be honest, we'd been growing bored with Poison Letter long before Cordie got her arm in a cast. It wasn't the same, standing around on the asphalt, waiting for someone to call out the letters of your name. Lots of our games and our playground rituals were beginning to feel alien to us by then. The teachers called it 'being too big for our boots' and told us that high school would sort us out – by 'high school' they meant the Year Eights – but even that didn't really explain it. Not fully. Not the sort of restlessness we felt. As if our boredom was a symptom of some bigger change, a dangerous shift in the earth's axis. Something bigger than our school shoes getting too tight.

And so each day that we walked across the playground in the same two straight lines, under the same sun, under the same paint-chipped pergola slowly being strangled by wisteria, you could practically smell the change that was coming our way as sure as that stink off the mangroves.

The day Cordie came back in a cast was no exception. We stayed huddled around her, admiring her arm, until the bell went and we moved off to our classrooms, and the playground was left empty except for a lone legionnaire hat left skewered on a garden stake like some kind of ancient warning.

* * *

Around this time two things happened, and even now I find it hard to separate them in my mind. The first thing was Cordie falling out of that tree. And the second? Thing number two was when Mr Avery turned up at school for the very first time.

He arrived on the same day Cordie came back with her arm in a plaster cast. When 6H walked into their classroom that morning, ready to get out their Maths books, ready for another week of being baffled by compound fractions, they instead learned that Mrs Harrow had left after sport on Friday, taking with her the Reading Corner beanbag and the butcher's paper mural of the First Fleet, and that there, in her place, was an enigma more mysterious, more complex than any mixed numbers. There in her place was Mr Avery.

He stood in the space where the missing mural had hung. Great continents of bare wall floated behind him. The maintenance men had been in since Friday afternoon and had painted the blackboard a sickly sea green – a perfect clean slate – and the effect of seeing him there, marooned between the blank wall and the repainted blackboard, was one of only hollowness.

He wore a short-sleeved shirt and tie, and his shoes were foreign-looking. Leather but without any laces. His beard was thick and dark, though very neatly trimmed. Its colour matched exactly the fur on his arms. Mr Avery was the only man our school had ever seen who wasn't the maintenance man or the principal. And when he arrived Cordie and the rest of Mrs Harrow's 6H class were instantly promoted to '6A'.

Mr Avery arrived the same day as Cordie's cast did, and so the two things are stuck together in my mind. So stuck that, even now, it's impossible to say for sure that Mr Avery wasn't the cause of Cordie's problems.

Or maybe he came as the cure.

Still, that's when it began. Late in November, when the sky burned and the jacarandas started rotting just as soon as they blossomed, and soldier beetles flung themselves against our classroom windows, preferring the blunt smash to the roasting heat.

That's when it started. As far back as that. When the summer had barely got going. Back in the days before Cordelia Van Apfel disappeared, when she was still real and soft and falling from trees.

* * *

'No, it didn't,' my sister said when I suggested this version to her twenty years later. We were shopping together at the new SupaCentre – the one that used to be the milk bar when we were kids. Now it had a deluxe car wash and a 'Handsfree Shopping Experience' and car park that stretched for miles.

'Mr Avery arrived *before* Cordie broke her arm,' Laura said. 'You're not remembering it right.'

As she spoke she steered a shopping trolley expertly down the pantry aisle using her left hand, and I considered how, if I tried the same thing, I would hit the simmer sauces for sure. But Laura could left-handedly steer while reading a shopping list while correcting my history at the same time.

'It's natural that I'd remember it better,' she shrugged. 'I am older after all.'

On the drive to the SupaCentre that morning the suburbs that rolled past my window had felt shrunken and strange. Roads that once stretched out in school-shoe-sized steps now skimmed past under the spin of Laura's tyres. A doll's house version of itself. Then walking across the car park I'd half-recognised faces but they were older, or greyer, or strained.

'How do *you* remember it then?' I asked.

Laura stopped the trolley and turned to me.

'He came first,' she said. 'Mr Avery was already here when Cordie fell out of the tree. He came at the start of term four, remember? And Cordie didn't break her arm until nearly two months later, just before Hayley Stinson's party in November.'

'How do you remember when Hayley Stinson's party was?' I said. 'That was twenty years ago.'

'Because Hayley Stinson was exactly six months older than me. She still is. I see her here at the SupaCentre all the time. She lives in the white house two doors down from the school now. You know the one, with the ugly front bit and the palm trees. She's just had twins.'

'Hayley Stinson's got twins?'

'Yeah. Can you reach the olive oil? No, next to it. The green one. We don't buy that brand,' she directed.

I put the green one in the shopping trolley like I was told. I'd been back at Macedon Close for almost a week by this stage. Long enough to remember what it was like, and for Laura to always be right.

'So Mr Avery came at the start of term four, and Cordie broke her arm near the end?' I said.

'Right.'

'Around the time of Hayley Stinson's sleepover?'

'Right. Hayley turned fifteen in the November, and I didn't turn fifteen until the following May. But we were still put in the same age division at swimming club and then everyone wondered why she always beat me.'

'Good to see you've let that go,' I said.

'I was disadvantaged.'

'You're proving my point.'

My sister's hair was almost impossibly blonde under the supermarket lights. It had always been lighter than mine but now, with that shade, she could have been a fourth Van Apfel sister.

'You colour your hair,' I said, thinking of my own mousy hair with some greys showing through.

'Yeah,' she said, looking at me strangely. 'Did you think it was natural?'

We made our way to the end of Laura's list and then she steered the trolley to the front of the store. At the checkout I lifted the groceries out of the trolley while Laura arranged them on the conveyor belt in the order she wanted them packed.

'Hey, do you remember we did a séance at that party? At Hayley's sleepover,' I said. 'Remember that? And —'

'*The cup moved!*' we said in unison.

The girl at the checkout looked at us warily and then went back to scanning our groceries.

'The cup moved onto Community Chest!' I added, and then wished I hadn't.

'Geez, Tik, how do you remember *that?*' Laura asked.

'I don't know,' I said. I lifted a bag of rice onto the counter, fiddled around with the packet. 'I guess I think about it sometimes.'

'You've got to find a way to live with it,' Laura had told me once, using her best bedside voice. 'I'm not saying forget. But you've got to find a way to get up in the morning and to go on. Work through it. Keep going.'

Get up and go on. Work through it. Keep going.

She made it sound like muscle exercises for her patients.

Now she looked at me with her face full of scepticism. *You think about it sometimes?* was what that look said.

We paid and pushed our trolley outside the SupaCentre, where the day was cloudless and hot. The strip that ran along the front of the centre was busy with shoppers, mostly pensioners and parents with prams, and at the bus stop an elderly woman was hunched over a tartan shopping cart, rearranging the contents. She wore a floral dress that was the same red as the tartan and ended just below her knees. One tan stocking sock had slipped down her leg and gathered like a holiday-coloured wrinkle around her calf.

'Oh, it's Mrs McCausley,' Laura said. She let her shoulders slump as if just the sight was exhausting.

'What? Where? I can't see her.'

Laura pointed towards the bus stop.

'*That's* Mrs McCausley?'

I know I said it loudly but she was four shopfronts away, and the strip was noisy, and there were cars roaring past.

'What?' I said. 'You don't need to shush me. There's no way Mrs McCausley could possibly have heard that.'

'She hears everything,' Laura admonished. She was annoyed I'd contradicted her.

'We're going to have to walk past her to get to the car,' she said, grimacing.

'That's okay, I'll do the talking,' I said.

I was curious to see Mrs McCausley after all this time. It was years since I'd spoken to her.

'Yeah, well just don't say anything to her about me being sick,' Laura instructed. 'I don't need her going around gossiping to everyone.'

'Okay.'

'It's not up to her,' she added. 'I'll tell who I want, when I want, and only when I'm ready. Okay? You got it?'

'Got it.'

Laura pushed the trolley along the shopping strip, being careful not to lean forward and rest on the handle. ('No one will assume you're an invalid if you do that,' I wanted to reassure her.)

'Mrs McCausley!' I called when we got close enough. 'It's me, Tikka! Tikka from down the road.'

I indicated to Laura who was hanging back, standing a safe distance away, behind our trolley. 'And you know Laura,' I said.

Mrs McCausley raised her grey head and looked at me shrewdly.

'I know who you are, Tikka Malloy,' she said sharply.

I laughed.

'Mrs McCausley,' I said, 'you haven't changed a bit.'

'*You* haven't changed,' she said to me, looking pointedly at my messy ponytail, my shapeless T-shirt. The Swatch Watch I got for my ninth birthday was still strapped to the wrong wrist – the way I wore it when I first received it all those birthdays ago.

'Touché,' I said.

'Hello, Laura,' she said, acknowledging my sister.

'Hi, Mrs McCausley, nice to see you.' Laura smiled but stayed where she was. Behind her, through the window of the newsagency, a queue was forming at the Powerball counter.

'Well, Tikka, what are you doing here?' Mrs McCausley said to me, cutting straight to the chase in her inimitable way. Honestly, it was like winding the clock back twenty years. Only, as she spoke, Mrs McCausley put her arm out and for one confused moment I thought she was offering me a hug. Instead she gripped my left arm while she steadied herself and I realised she was using me for balance.

'Family,' I said. 'I came back to see the family.'

'Long way to come for a visit,' she observed and she released my arm.

I shifted on the spot and looked sideways at Laura but her face was impassive. She wasn't going to help me out.

'It *is* a long way,' I conceded. 'But I don't mind the flight.'

'Travelling alone?'

'Yes.'

'Still living in America?'

'Yes, Baltimore these days.'

'Still working in science? What was it? Germs or something?' She laughed at herself.

'Basically,' I said, not bothering to elaborate. Assistant lab technician wasn't worth going into detail over.

'I bet your parents are pleased to see you back.'

I told her they were, and that Laura was too, and that I was pleased to see all of them.

'They'd be *more* pleased if you were staying for good,' she said slyly. No one left for very long around here, and if they did then they had a good reason.

'And how are *you*, Mrs McCausley?' I asked.

'My hip, you mean?'

I hadn't meant her hip, but her hip would do. Laura sighed audibly from behind the trolley.

'It's been such a *palaver*, Tikka,' Mrs McCausley said. She sat down on the bus-stop bench as if to settle in for the story, and I was left towering high above her.

'I've had the most dreadful time with it,' she said, and she proceeded to tell me and Laura about how she had waited thirteen months for surgery and then how, when she'd finally had her hip replaced, she dislocated it again only three weeks later ('Just popped right out of its socket'), and she had to go back into hospital all over again.

While she was speaking a bus blundered past, coming so close I could have touched it. I bumped down onto the bench next to Mrs McCausley just to feel like I was out of the bus's path.

'It's very rare that happens, you know,' she confided, and for a moment I thought she was talking about the bus. Then I realised she meant her hip palaver. Her *rare* Hippalaver. (It sounded like something that might bite.)

'I'm sorry to hear about your hip, Mrs McCausley,' I said. 'That's awful.'

'It *has* been awful,' she confirmed. 'Just awful.'

Not as awful as Hodgkin lymphoma, though I didn't say that to Mrs McCausley. Instead we sat in silence outside the

SupaCentre for a moment while she contemplated her awful hip and I fought off the urge to bend down and pull up her sunken stocking sock. On the far side of our shopping trolley Laura was now leaning heavily on the handle. I caught her eye and nodded. I understood: she was ready to leave.

'We should probably get going, Mrs McCausley,' I said after what I hoped was appropriate reverence for her hip. 'It was good to see you.'

'You'll come and see me before you fly out, won't you?' she said to me. 'Come for afternoon tea.'

'What, at your house?' I tried to think of the last time I had been at Mrs McCausley's house up there on the corner. I would have been in high school.

'That's very kind of you, Mrs McCausley,' I said, 'but you don't have to do that.'

'I know I don't *have* to,' she bristled. 'Come and see me Thursday afternoon, Tikka. But come before four. I give the kookaburras their dinner on the back deck at that time and they don't like it when I'm late.'

And I could imagine Mrs McCausley out there on her deck, handfeeding bits of sausage to the birds. Taking beef strips out of Tupperware tubs and laying them out on the railing. Say what you will about Mrs McCausley, her heart was in the right place.

'Okay, Mrs McCausley, I'll come up and see you on Thursday.'

'Before four.'

'Before four.'

'And Tikka —'

'Yes?'

'I've got something to tell you,' she said, and she looked meaningfully at me.

'You do?'

'Yes.'

I waited for her to say whatever it was, but she stared at me in silence.

'Oh, you mean on Thursday,' I realised. 'You've got something to tell me on Thursday?'

'Yes.'

By the trolley Laura was shifting from one foot to the other just in case I was in any doubt.

'Then I'm looking forward to hearing it on Thursday, Mrs McCausley,' I said. I stood up from the bus-stop bench and dusted down the back of my jeans.

'I know why you're back, Tikka,' she said.

'Oh?'

She leaned in, and when she started to speak her mouth was at the same height as my knees.

'It's all right, I *know* about Jade Heddingly's wedding,' she said. She glanced sideways to check who else might be listening and, satisfied that it was safe to speak, she leaned closer and carried on.

'The Heddinglys have asked me to do the catering,' she revealed.

'They have?'

I looked to Laura for guidance. Was Mrs McCausley cracking up? She'd seemed so lucid till this point.

'Yes. And Mrs Lantana's doing the flowers, did you hear?'

No, I hadn't heard that. But then I hadn't really paid attention whenever the wedding had been discussed at home.

'I'm glad you've come back for Jade's wedding,' she went on, 'the Heddinglys are really touched, you know.'

And I wanted to say to her then that Jade Heddingly's wedding was hardly a reason for a person to fly sixteen thousand kilometres across the globe, but then I didn't like to delude Mrs McCausley. No more than she already was.

I looked at her there with her tartan shopping trolley, her grey hair set and combed. Those slippery stocking socks that wouldn't stay where they should. She looked so ancient it was hard to believe that I'd thought she was old back when I was eleven.

I realised Mrs McCausley was looking at me, waiting for me to comment on Jade Heddingly's wedding. And in that second all I could think to say to her was: 'How did he propose again?'

'What? Her fiancé?' Mrs McCausley said.

'Yeah.'

'I suppose he got down on one knee,' she said. 'You'd have to ask Jade.'

'Sure,' I mumbled. I'd *arks* Jade sometime. I'd arks her how he arksed.

'Bye, Mrs McCausley,' Laura said, finally asserting her right as the eldest sister to cut off the conversation.

'Nice to see you,' I added. And Mrs McCausley nodded, yes, it had been nice for me to see her, and then she got back to the business of stacking and restacking the contents of her shopping cart.

Laura pushed the trolley and led me expertly past the deluxe car wash and the Handsfree Shopping Experience and straight to where she had parked our car an hour earlier, despite there being more than two dozen or so identical parking rows we could have mistaken for ours.

'I can never find my car in one of these places.'

'It's alphabetised,' she said, rolling her eyes. 'There's a system to it.'

At the car I tried to get Laura to sit in the passenger seat and rest while I packed the groceries into the boot. But she took this as a slight on her strength. Or a sign I was taking over, or I don't know what, but she didn't trust me to put the stuff in the boot without her supervision.

'Just let me look after you,' I said.

'I don't need looking after,' she replied flatly.

So we both stacked the groceries into the car and then she returned the trolley to its bay.

Driving home, Laura flicked impatiently through radio stations and eventually settled on silence.

'Mrs McCausley isn't really doing the catering for Jade Heddingly's wedding, is she?' I said after a while.

'No, Tikka.'

'Is she, you know —'

'Is she senile?' Laura supplied the question for me.

I nodded.

'Looks that way. It's been a while since I've spoken with her long enough to tell. Mum goes up there sometimes and has a chat. Checks she's okay. I guess she must be well into her eighties by now.'

That was good, I thought. Someone should go and check on Mrs McCausley.

Laura didn't say anything after that, just concentrated on the road. I wondered if she was thinking about Mrs McCausley getting old. And about whether she'd get to see her eighties herself. Getting doddery wasn't the worst thing in the world. Not when compared to getting cancer at thirty-four.

But then Laura spoke and broke my train of thought.

'Anyway,' she said, 'Mr Avery couldn't have arrived at school in the November when Cordie broke her arm.'

Was she serious? Our argument about Mr Avery and Cordie's broken arm from earlier wasn't finished?

'You should have been a lawyer.'

My sister ignored me.

'Okay, why couldn't he have arrived at school in November?' I asked.

'What teacher would start a new school in the middle of a term?' she replied.

She had a point. But what about the map and Mrs Harrow's Reading Corner beanbag? I could have sworn they vanished over a single weekend. I don't know, maybe she was right. Maybe Mr Avery arrived before Cordie fell out of the peppercorn tree. It hardly mattered now.

'And also,' Laura said as she negotiated the turn into the drive, 'another thing —'

She said it as if she was remembering something we forgot to pick up while we were at the SupaCentre. *Soy milk, avocados, oh and this.*

'Cordie didn't fall. She jumped.'

CHAPTER SEVEN

During that heatwave summer of 1992, every TV news bulletin reported the government was doing deals with the devil. Night after night the thing simmered. I watched, fascinated, as the Northern Territory Government paid compensation worth more than a million dollars, plus almost half a million in legal costs and $19,000 for a car that was dismantled for evidence and, along with the lives of all the people in that family, was never put back together.

The devil, I noted, was a woman with a bob and, more often than not, a strappy sundress.

'What's she getting money for if she's guilty, Dad?' I asked.

'She's not guilty, Tik. *That's* the point,' he said without turning his face from the screen. 'Lindy Chamberlain's not guilty, even though they locked her up. That's why she's being compensated now. Not that these grubs want us to think she's innocent. Disgusting the way they're carrying on.'

He sat watching the screen, one ankle resting on the opposing knee, making a triangle where he rested his newspaper. He liked to have the broadsheet open in front of him while he watched the headlines, as if he was playing along at home. He wore a short-sleeved shirt and long-legged shorts. He hadn't loosened his tie since he'd finished teaching and walked out of his classroom earlier that afternoon. He *had* taken his shoes and socks off, though, and his legs were white where his long socks had stretched to his knees. He was tanned in a band round the top.

Mum came in then, carrying two glasses of something with ice that clinked as she walked. She crossed the lounge room, handed one to Dad and held the other against her cheek while she stood, hand on hip, and watched the screen.

'She's too attractive for them,' she observed to no one in particular. 'Too sultry-looking. They can't handle it.'

'Who, Mum? Lindy Chamberlain?' I asked. 'Is that who you mean, Mum?'

'It's hardly a crime,' Dad said. 'Not a hanging offence.'

'Do you mean Lindy Chamberlain, Mum? Her, Mum? Is she the one that's too attractive?'

'Not a crime,' Dad repeated.

'Yeah? Well, you tell those blokes,' Mum said. She gestured towards the TV with her glass and, on the screen, a group of men in brown ties were standing outside a courthouse. 'They'd still have her locked up if it was their decision.'

'She walks like Cordie,' Laura commented. My sister lay on the couch in the corner with her legs dangling over the armrest.

'Take your feet off there,' Mum replied automatically, and I waited for Laura to say that it was her legs, not her feet, and why couldn't it be a leg rest? If it was good enough for arms, why wasn't it okay for other limbs?

But Laura was too busy watching TV. She slid her legs off the couch without shifting her eyes from the screen.

'Hey, Mum, it's the school Showstopper concert soon,' I said, remembering, 'and Miss Elith said I can do a skit. Everyone else will be doing a dance or playing an instrument or stuff like that, but I'm allowed to put on a skit.'

'Big deal.' Laura said it low enough that only I could hear. 'The Showstopper happens every year.'

'Yeah, but no one's ever done a skit before. Miss Elith said. Miss Elith said I was the first person ever to ask.'

'Do you know how to write a skit?' Laura said dubiously.

'Yes!' I said.

Though in truth I had some doubts. (But they were the kind of doubts you kept to yourself, and not the sort you'd admit to your sister.) And anyway, I'd written a play before called 'The Staff Meeting', where I copied down everything I eavesdropped from the teachers' staffroom. 'The Staff Meeting' was a comedy. And a good one, too, if it was even half as hilarious as the teachers seemed to find it.

Plus, I'd written the poem that got me chosen for the nativity play. (Though I couldn't take the credit for the plot.)

All in all, I was pretty sure I could write a Showstopper skit. I just had to find something to write about.

'Miss Elith thinks my skit will be very dramatic,' I said. Actually, I was the one who had promised drama, but Miss Elith had said she didn't doubt it.

We did Music and Performing Arts with Miss Elith every Thursday when we had to share one instrument between two. That worked okay if you got the castanets, because castanets come in pre-prepared pairs. But the triangle was only fun if you were the partner who got to use the dinger. Miss Elith had a hard time keeping everyone under control during Music and Performing Arts on Thursdays. 'Eyes to the left, eyes to the right, eyes to the front and eyes on me,' she'd say desperately, though that never seemed to make much difference. Because everyone went ahead and put their eyes wherever they felt like, and that mostly didn't include on Miss Elith.

'I'm going to have costumes for my skit too,' I said, because the judge on TV had reminded me. The way he walked towards the courthouse with his black robe billowing, a white horsehair wig in his hand.

'And I need two dollars for the bus, Mum. Mum, can I have two dollars? We're doing a dress rehearsal in the amphitheatre on the morning of the concert.'

'The amphitheatre?' Mum said.

'Yeah. At Coronation Park. You know, the amphitheatre in the valley?'

'Why are they doing the Showstopper in the amphitheatre this year? It's usually in the school hall.'

'You can fit more parents in the amphitheatre,' my sister said cynically. 'More parents means more money for the school.'

'Oh, is it a fundraiser?'

'Can you lot keep it down?' Dad said, which was funny, because the only time he ever raised *his* voice with us was to tell us to keep ours down during the news. He smoothed the pages of the paper in his lap.

'Yeah, Mum, it's a fundraiser,' I said. 'It's on a Friday night, after work, so you and Dad can come and watch.'

'At the amphitheatre?'

'At the amphitheatre. In the valley.'

The amphitheatre was the only place you could hold an outdoor concert around here, and even then we hardly ever used it. It had a mottled-concrete stage that stared out into a set of shallow mottled-concrete steps. On one side of the stage were the public toilets, and on the other a gravel car park.

The real mystery about the amphitheatre was the Gothic archway that stretched over the footpath from the car park and served as a gateway to the stage. The arch was made of concrete and twisted metal that was rusty with age, and no one knew where the arch had come from or how long it had been there. We couldn't remember a time without it. That arch wasn't joined to anything, wasn't part of any wall, it just stood among the grass and the gravel. As if it were a prop from an entirely different play.

But we left the arch there because, aside from the stage itself, it was the only thing to signify you'd left the car park and were now standing in a place of culture.

'At the Showstopper —' I started saying.

'Shhh,' Dad said, and he pointed to the screen where the image of the judge had been replaced by a shot of a baby's dress. The dress was black cotton, puff-sleeved, dark lace frothing at the neck. Red satin ribbon dribbled the length of the yoke.

'Gross,' said Laura. 'Who dresses a baby in black? That's just creepy.'

'Laura —'

'Admit it, you think it's creepy, Mum.'

But all Mum said was: 'Laura, get your legs off that couch. I won't ask you again.'

'What does the dress have to do with it?' I asked.

And Dad answered me even though he didn't like talking during the news, because he liked misinformation even less.

'Tikka,' he said, 'these clowns think that because she dressed her child like that, because her family look a certain way, and because they think a bit differently to everyone else, it automatically makes her a killer.'

'Oh.'

'And that the child couldn't possibly have been taken by a dingo, even though that's the most plausible scenario.'

'Oh.'

They *did* look different, the Chamberlains, when I saw them on the news. The mum with her strappy sundresses. The dad the Seventh-day Adventist pastor with his sideburns and his tie. Those Chamberlains looked much more glamorous than anyone who lived around here. I couldn't imagine either of the Chamberlain parents camping in the outback. Putting up tents among the spinifex and red dust. (But then I guess they could never imagine losing their daughter to a dingo either.)

'You see, Tikka, not everyone agrees with the court's decision —' Mum started saying.

'A royal commission finding is a royal commission finding, Suze. It's not up for debate,' Dad spoke without moving his eyes from the screen.

'I wasn't suggesting it was,' Mum said. 'I was just explaining to Tikka the other side of the story.'

'The other side of the story *is not the truth*. It has bugger all to do with anything,' Dad said emphatically.

'Dad said "bugger"!' Laura called out helpfully from the couch, where her legs were dangling over the ravine of the armrest again.

But Mum was too glued to the TV to notice and we watched in silence until the bulletin was finished.

* * *

The next day we detoured to the milk bar after school. Cordie was with us, her arm covered in its cast and her cast covered in Texta doodles. Ruth was there, of course. And my sister and Hannah, straight off the bus from high school and talking and laughing about names I didn't recognise. Swishing their hair like ponies.

'Hey, Hannah,' I said, 'Hannah, did Cordie tell you about the Showstopper? Cordie, did you tell her? The Showstopper is on again, Hannah, and I'm going to write a skit!'

'Yeah?' Hannah said.

She was watching my sister, who had one hip pressed against the chest freezer, holding the lid open, and in each hand she dangled an ice cream in its wrapper like dead fish hanging on hooks. Hannah pointed at the Bubble O'Bill and Laura nodded solemnly and dropped the reject back in the chest.

'Because you get ice cream *and* a bubblegum nose,' Laura agreed.

She picked out a Bubble O'Bill to match Hannah's.

I'd already chosen my ice cream and I jigged about impatiently near the cash register, where the boy behind the counter looked bored.

'Did Mum give you money?' Laura asked me.

'Yeah.'

'Enough for two?'

'Yeah.' I sighed.

I put my hand out to receive her ice cream and Laura placed it in my palm and then she smiled winningly at me. Laura had a job now. She'd started working on the supermarket checkout on Saturday afternoons, and she had a uniform and everything, which meant she was impossibly grown-up. But not *so* grown-up she'd buy her Bubble O'Bill.

'What do they call it when the summer comes early?' Hannah asked Laura while I paid for our ice creams. 'An Indian summer? Is that it?'

'That's when it stays late,' I said authoritatively. 'When summer lasts into autumn, that's when they call it an Indian one.'

'Well, what do they call it when it comes early? Like now. In spring.'

'Just a heatwave?' Laura suggested. 'I don't think there's a special name.'

'There should be,' Hannah said. 'What's the opposite of India?'

'Geographically?' I asked.

'Yeah,' Hannah said.

'Mexico,' I said, and no one questioned my answer.

'Then this is a "Mexican summer",' Hannah decided. 'That's what we call it from now on.'

Ruth sidled up to me once we'd all paid for our ice creams and were headed for the doorway.

'Can I be in your skit?' she said. She had an ice cream in one hand and a scuffed drink bottle in the other, and when she sucked on the bottle it made a long kissy sound.

'Nope, sorry.' I shook my head regretfully. 'Infants aren't allowed in the Showstopper – Miss Elith said.'

'But *you* can be in it if you want,' I offered to Cordie.

Cordie was wearing her pink fisherman-style schoolbag across her front like a pregnant belly. She had both her arms fed through the straps – the good one and the broken one – and they rested on the canvas, which was decorated with hand-drawn black hearts shot through with pointed arrows.

'I'll think about it,' Cordie said noncommittally.

'What would she have to do?' Hannah asked suspiciously. She was always watching out for Cordie in a way she never bothered to do with Ruth, even though Ruth was the youngest.

'I'll let you know. I'm still putting the finishing touches to the script,' I lied. I pictured the mountain of dot-matrix paper I had stockpiled in my bedroom. All of it blank, all of it waiting for me to get started.

The five of us shuffled out of the milk bar after that and into the afternoon sun. My eyes had trouble adjusting to the glare, and I was still seeing black blotches when a bigger, darker shadow swam by.

The shadow gave a wave without raising its arm. Its hand waggling guiltily down by its thigh.

'Who was that?' Hannah demanded.

'Mr Avery,' said Cordie.

'*That's* Mr Avery?' Hannah said.

'Who's he?' my sister wanted to know.

'My teacher.'

'Your teacher since when?' Laura asked.

'Since Mrs Harrow left and Mr Avery is our new teacher,' Cordie said nonchalantly.

'That was weeks ago,' I supplied.

'Where'd Mrs Harrow go?' said Laura, ignoring me and asking Cordie.

'Dunno.'

'Why'd she leave?'

'Dunno.'

'What's *he* like?'

'S'okay.'

'You'll have lots of male teachers when you get to high school. We do,' Laura said sniffily. The inquisition was over.

We started walking home, legionnaire hats in one hand, melting ice creams in the other. Except for Ruth, who wore her hat and held her drink bottle and her ice cream and who trudged along bringing up the rear. Then, after our ice creams were gone, we chewed on the paddle-pop sticks, holding them in our mouths and twisting them until they snapped. The ends jutted out of our mouths like broken teeth and we walked along in silence, smoking the splintered stubs, gripping them between our sticky lips.

We were down past the tennis courts when a car sidled up. It slunk along beside us, keeping pace. The late-afternoon sunshine poured into its bronze paintwork. Then the driver's window sank into its sill.

'Like a lift home, girls?'

'Geez, haven't you ever heard of stranger danger, Mrs McCausley? You nearly gave us a heart attack!'

'*Stranger danger?*' she scoffed. 'You won't find any strangers around *here.*'

Not when she kept tabs on everyone like she did.

We piled onto the bench seat in the back of her boxy car, bums burning, legs scorched where they touched the cracked leather of the seat. All five of us squished in there. Bags on laps. Hats in hands. Paddle-pop stick fangs still drooping from our mouths.

'How was school, girls?' Mrs McCausley said. She patted her perm with her one free hand. Admired it in the rear-view mirror as she drove.

'Good,' we chorused.

'Isn't this heat dreadful?' she complained. 'Just revolting. Even my zinnias can't cope. The whole garden's *wilting*, and I'm wilting too.'

She laughed at herself, and glanced at us lined up along her bench seat.

'I might have an ice cream this evening myself,' she told us conspiratorially.

Mrs McCausley steered the car past cul-de-sac after cul-de-sac, each one looking deceptively like ours. She paused at an empty cross-street and then released the car on through and we coasted down the slope towards our street.

'How's that arm of yours, Cordelia?' Mrs McCausley asked.

'Fine,' Cordie said.

I pulled my stick from my mouth then and gave Mrs McCausley the whole story. About Cordie and how Dr Adiga said she'd done a good job of breaking her arm, about Mr Avery and how he was the new teacher at our school, and about how the Showstopper was being held in the valley and not in the school hall this year.

'But I can't be in it —' Ruth interrupted.

'Right, Ruth can't be in it because she's only in Year Two and the Showstopper is just for Year Threes to Year Sixes. *If* there are any Year Sixes who want to be in it ...' I said, looking meaningfully at Cordie.

The hot wind through the window whipped Cordie's hair across her cheeks. She parted it and peered benevolently through the curtains.

'I'll *think* about it,' she said to me.

'Mr Avery, did you say? Unusual name,' Mrs McCausley said. 'Is he married? Or single? Which school did he transfer from?'

'Shit a brick,' Cordie muttered, 'she asks a lot of questions.'

But to Mrs McCausley she said nothing.

'I dunno. Is he married, Cordie? Where did he come from? He teaches Cordie's 6A class,' I clarified for Mrs McCausley. 'They used to be 6H, but since Mr Avery they've turned into 6A.

'He's very hairy,' I added descriptively.

I guess Cordie didn't know if Mr Avery was married or not because she never bothered tell Mrs McCausley. Just like she didn't know the answer to any of Mrs McCausley's other questions about Mr Avery. Such as: which school did Mr Avery transfer from? And how old was he? Well, did he look older or younger than our parents? Was Mr Avery from around here?

'He just moved here, Mrs McCausley,' I said pointedly. 'How could he be from around here if he only just moved in?'

'I mean, Tikka,' she said, 'does he look like someone who might come from somewhere local, or could he have been *born overseas*?'

'Either,' I paused. 'Both, Mrs McCausley.' Because I couldn't tell what the difference was.

I appealed to Cordie for help, but she must have been busy thinking over the offer to be in my skit. Because she turned to me and said: 'You know the Showstopper, would it be a tragedy if I was in it?'

And for a moment I thought she was asking: would it be a problem if she was in the cast, then I realised she was talking about the *play* itself.

'A tragedy? Would my skit be a tragedy?'

'Yeah, would it be sad and could I die, and would everyone cry after I'd gone off stage?'

'Cordelia! What a morbid thing to say!' Mrs McCausley admonished.

But you had to admit: the idea was a good one. Cordie dying would get an audience reaction, all right. And if I made it a tragedy, I had a ready-made plot. All I had to do was watch the TV news.

* * *

We turned the corner into Macedon Close and Mrs McCausley let the car idle in front of her drive while we clambered out. I was behind Hannah and Laura, and I had to wait for the two of them to fix their hair before they'd move and release me. Cordie came last, her feet pushing against my backpack, her plaster cast clunking against the door.

'Thanks for the lift.'

'Yeah, thanks.'

'Thanks, Mrs McCausley.'

The Van Apfel girls crossed the cul-de-sac to their house on the opposite corner, Cordie walking alone mouthing some song to herself. Meanwhile, Hannah nicked Ruth's hat, held it just above her reach and led her sister home like a dog.

Mrs McCausley bunny-hopped her car into the carport and turned off the engine.

'You know,' I called to her through her open car window as the thought occurred to me. 'He was at the milk bar just before, Mrs McCausley. You only missed him by a few minutes.'

'Who was?'

'Mr Avery,' I said. 'If you'd come a bit sooner you could have seen him for yourself.'

And Mrs McCausley looked disappointed about that.

Laura and I went home to get changed, and then we walked straight back out the door and over to the Van Apfels' place for a swim. Afterwards the five of us arranged our towels in wide stripes crisscrossing the lawn. It was too hot to bake our legs in the sun so we lay under the peppercorn tree.

There were crows in the tree that afternoon – three crows – and their beaks flashed in the blazing sunshine, their black backs almost blue. The hackles at their throats wobbled as they cawed. *Ah-ah-ahhhh, ah-ah-ahhhh.*

'You wanna watch out,' Laura warned Cordie. Cordie had one of her pet mice on her towel, where it sniffed and ran in circles. 'Birds eat mice, you know. You wanna be careful the crows don't pick its eyes out.'

'Do they *really*?' I said. 'Pick out eyeballs, I mean.'

Everyone knew that birds ate mice but I'd never heard the eyeballs part.

'She's got more,' Ruth said pragmatically, thumbing towards the laundry door where Cordie had three more white mice in a tank.

'Don't listen to them,' Cordie cooed to the mouse that was in her palm now. She kissed his tufted fur, kissed his tail. Licked its tip.

'You'll be safe in here,' she said. Then she tipped the tiny body down the inside of her swimming costume where it made a lump the size of an apricot. The mouse panicked and struggled. Squirmed inside the shiny fabric. Cordie closed her eyes in delight.

'Don't tickle,' she commanded.

'Cordie, that's gross,' Hannah said. 'Get it out.'

'It's a sin!' Ruth shrilled, and she sat up straight on her towel.

'*It's a sin to put a mouse down your cossie?* Does the Bible actually say that?' My sister looked at Ruth sceptically.

'Do crows really pick out eyeballs?' I wanted to know and no one had bothered to say.

'Yeah, the Bible says it's gross and to stop being a weirdo,' Hannah said. 'C'mon, Cordie, what if Dad saw?'

'Why would I ever care what Dad said?' Cordie spoke savagely. 'Anyway, it won't matter soon.'

'Fine, don't listen to me. You never do,' snapped Hannah.

'Why won't it matter?' I asked. 'What's happening soon?'

Hannah glared at Cordie, who shrugged.

'Why won't it, Hannah? And do crows eat eyeballs? Why won't you tell me if you know?'

But nobody answered me, and Hannah and Laura exchanged the sort of look that said they were keeping secrets.

'What's going on?' I demanded. 'Laura, tell me! Cordie? Come on, why won't you tell me?'

But Cordie smiled coyly and ducked her chin. She looked satisfied having stirred up trouble. The mouse had settled now, and it was nestled in the centre of her chest so that the fabric of her swimming costume rose in a small mountain in the middle.

'Looks like I've got three boobs,' she said, and she patted the mouse affectionately through the fabric.

Above us, a crow cawed louder this time. *Ah-ah-ahhhh, ah-ah-ahhhh*, it groaned. It rose above the tree where it floated for a second, catching the breeze, before it went winging away.

'See?' Cordie said to her chest. 'You're safe in there. No crow can get you, can they? Besides, you could beat an old crow any day, couldn't you? Couldn't you,' she purred.

The mouse turned and started scrabbling downwards towards her stomach and Cordie wriggled to give it more room to move.

'A crow would win against a mouse,' I corrected Cordie scornfully. *How dare those older girls keep something from me? I*

113

looked at Cordie with disdain. 'A crow's much bigger. And it's *omnivorous*. A crow would beat a mouse, pants down.'

There was silence for a moment while everyone considered what I'd said.

'Did you just say "*pants* down"?' Hannah asked cautiously.

Then her stomach started to convulse and I could see she was struggling to hold in her laughter. Her eyes grew shiny with it, her mouth puckered and she turned her face away. Then Laura let out a whoop and I saw that she was laughing too, and the pair of them started hooting and thumping the ground.

'What?' I demanded. 'What are you laughing at? Stop it!'

They collapsed into each other, squeezing one another's shoulders, wiping their eyes. They'd just about get themselves under control and then they'd catch the other's eye and that was it, they'd set each another off again. Leaning together, shaking with laughter.

'Jesus, where'd you get that, Tik?' Laura said eventually.

'Yeah, where'd you hear that?' Hannah asked, drawing a breath.

'Did she get that from your friend Mr Avery?' Laura asked Cordie.

She and Hannah started laughing again.

'What? A crow *would* win,' I said huffily, and I hitched my cossie higher.

'Pants down!' Hannah and Laura shrieked in unison.

I turned my face away in disgust.

'It's *hands* down, Tik.' Hannah finally took pity on me and explained, and my cheeks burned with indignation.

'I don't know many crows who wear pants,' my sister said.

'*I* don't know many crows who have hands,' I shot back.

In the tree above us the crows (without pants, without hands) were stripping off leaves with their scissoring beaks. They cawed and flung bits of stick to the ground.

'Shoo!' Ruth said to them. 'Shoo, shoo! Get lost!'

And Laura was stirred, then, to put on her grown-up voice. 'I think we should all move away from the group of crows, now. Let's go inside and get something to eat.'

And as we stood up and gathered our towels in our hands, as Cordie scooped her hands gently under the mouse that was still hammocked inside her cossie, the crows gave up too and they rose up in one single dark flurry and then they wheeled away on the wind.

'And anyway,' I said, trying to claw back the older girls' respect and, at the same time, being too incensed to care. 'It's not called a *group*. When you see crows together like that, you're supposed to call it a *murder*.'

CHAPTER EIGHT

When I returned to the river all those years later, I arrived when the neap tide skinned the riverbanks, stripping back the shoreline and exposing the mangroves that clawed their way up through the silt.

And still it didn't stink.

That valley hadn't smelled bad for twenty years, as if it was appeased when we sacrificed those girls.

Now when I came back from Baltimore I would pick up a different scent. Wattle blossoms laced with cold air off the mountains in August. Cut grass and scaling jasmine in spring. Then in March, when the clouds massed and the sky cracked and the rain hammered down, the dirt would give off its wild petrichor.

Down at the river that day the sandflies rose up from the mudflats in near-invisible columns seeking out my exposed skin as I picked my way along the shore, slapping uselessly at my legs.

No-see-ums they call them in some parts of the States. As if the problem was there in their windowpane wings. Not the fact they won't leave me alone.

I walked as far as the bend in the river, and from there a whole new stretch of river appeared around the corner. A miraculous blue berth. I took several steps backwards and the view disappeared. I stepped forward and summoned it again.

At that bend I found a seat in the crooked vee of a mangrove tree where I could lean forward to make the view materialise whenever I wanted. But the tree was soft-skinned with rot and age – and I was heavier with both things too – and I snapped the branch clean off before I gave up and leaned against the trunk instead.

The tide was on its way out, so I stood and watched the waves retreat down the slope and back into the briny water. Then I gave up on the tide too, and I went and found a stick and wrote my name in the hard sand. *Tikka. Tik, Tik, Tik.* I wrote it like a countdown. Then I moved further along, to a stretch of fresh sand, and I wrote *Cordie, Cordie, Cordie*, as well.

Missing smell aside, that valley hadn't changed. Not really. Not enough. It was still tied together with that same skinny two-lane road that wound down and around and across the river. Although the flyover bridge did streak across the sky now like a correction across a page.

It took eighteen months to complete, that bridge. First they hacked back the trees along both sides of the ridge line to make way for the new expressway, and then they sent it out, slab by slab into the air so that now, instead of driving into the valley, you flew above it at eighty kilometres per hour.

Other than the new bridge, the valley still spurted turpentines and tea-trees with their acrid lemon scent. Spindly she-oaks still smothered the tide with their spines. And if you stood at my parents' place high on the western rim and gazed towards the east, then the heat haze in summer still made two horizons: the true one and its sister image.

That day at the river I decided to look for the place we used to go to as kids. Our spot was further up the river, to the south of the amphitheatre. It was a slash of cleared scrub – just a slit really. Where she-oaks stood rooted in soil and not sand, but where spangled dead fish sometimes washed up on the tide, their glassy eyes wide in surprise. Not mangrove, but not strictly bushland either. A trickier animal. A more in-between thing. And from every point in that clearing you could see the red roofs of the picnic sheds burning amber in the sunshine.

We used to go to the clearing to dig for artefacts. Crunching among the grit and the dirt we'd pick out mussel shells and whelks. Fish bones. Purple pipi shells. The thing was that all of them were missing some essential part. The pipis and mussels with their meaty middles gone. Fish bones missing their flesh. There must have been an Aboriginal midden somewhere nearby because, no matter how many times we dug up the dirt, there was always one more shell to find. One more bird bone buried just below the surface. It was our very own valley of dry bones.

It was in this clearing that Ruth hurt her hand once. She'd been trying to prise open a black mussel shell and somehow she pinched the soft webbing between her thumb and index finger and then howled as though she'd chopped them both off.

'Blood blister,' Hannah diagnosed dismissively.

'Blood blister?' Ruth perked right up once her injury had a name.

'Hey, Tikka, did you hear that? I've got a blood blister. Right here, a blood blister. Wanna see?'

'You know,' she said slowly as the thought occurred to her, 'if you got one too, then we could rub them together like they do on TV and then we'd be blood brothers forever.'

'Blood sisters,' I corrected.

'Yeah!'

'That's only if you're actually bleeding,' I pointed out.

But Ruth looked so disappointed that I pinched my skin too and I rubbed my hand against hers to make us blood sisters. Ruth and I: blood blisters for life.

The other thing about this clearing was that it was where the Van Apfel girls were supposed to meet my sister on the night they ran away. Laura always maintains she must have missed them by minutes. She was *insistent* about that. It wasn't her fault – she'd got to the spot at exactly the time they'd agreed. But somehow it was too late, and Hannah, Cordie and Ruth had already gone. Laura never saw them again.

And the irony wasn't that they disappeared from the very place they were supposed to appear. Or that the clearing was littered with empty shells and lonely bones – it was our clearing where things were *supposed* to go missing. No, the irony was that they vanished in full view of the picnic sheds where the police search centre would soon be set up.

CHAPTER NINE

The weatherman on the news said high-pressure systems in the Tasman were causing heatwaves all along the southeast of the state. He pointed to a chart, to a long mass in the shape of a gun with its magazine tracing the stretch of the coast, its muzzle pointing out to sea. The heat, he explained, was trapped close to the surface, where it was acting like kind of a lid. But even *that* didn't explain the claustrophobia that had settled over Macedon Close. ('Claustrophobia': extension spelling list, week nine. Also: 'foreboding', 'phantasmal' and 'pagan'. The Halloween-themed lists had dragged on long into November – the Van Apfels would not have approved.)

I walked to school with Ruth like always that day, though not with Cordie, because she stayed at home.

'Sick?' I asked.

'Pig's bum,' Ruth admonished. 'She doesn't look sick to me. Her arm's not hurting any more, so I don't know what excuse she's used.'

Ruth had lumbered out of the house alone, her legionnaire hat pulled down low. The sun was scorching, even at that time of morning, and the stink off the river was bad.

'Wish I had a peg for my nose,' I said.

'Wish I was allowed to stay at home like Cordie,' Ruth said bitterly.

She didn't seem to notice the smell.

'Carn, let's go,' I said, pushing off the signpost to our street. I'd been leaning against it while I waited for Ruth. But the signpost was old and the paintwork was faded and most of the letters to 'Macedon Close' had disappeared.

We started up the street in the direction of school. Ruth panted softly as we walked.

'What've you got to eat for recess?' she asked when we reached the first cross-street. As she said it she was already unwrapping something folded carefully in wax paper, which she'd pulled from that enormous backpack of hers. She examined it critically and then crammed it in her mouth, chewing mournfully, shedding crumbs as she walked.

'Nothing. Mum gave me money for the canteen,' I lied. Mum never gave me money to spend at the canteen. But I wasn't about to hand my morning tea over to Ruth. You wouldn't get change back from that.

We walked and Ruth concentrated on staving off hunger. That, and not overbalancing with her bag.

Then she had a thought that cheered her right up: 'Dad and Cordie had a massive fight last night.'

'Yeah?' I said. 'What about?'

'Because he won't let us go to Hayley's sleepover.'

'You're not going?' I was surprised.

Ruth shook her head. 'None of us are allowed.'

Hayley Stinson was in the same swimming club as me and Laura and the Van Apfel girls. We went every Saturday afternoon. And even though Hayley was turning fifteen (older, even, than Hannah and Laura), all the girls at swimming were invited to Hayley's sleepover.

'Not even Hannah's going?' I asked.

'Not even Hannah,' Ruth confirmed. 'Cordie says Dad's being mean.'

Actually, Laura and I were only going to Hayley Stinson's sleepover party for the evening part. We weren't staying the night because we had to go up the coast early the next morning for my nan's birthday. But I didn't know the Van Apfel girls couldn't go at all. I felt even worse for them than I did for Laura and me.

'What did your dad say, for why he wouldn't let you go?'

'We've got church the next morning. But Cordie says that's just an excuse. She said he and Mum could easily pick us up from Hayley's place on the way to church. It's not like it's too far to drive.'

That part was true. Nowhere was far to drive in our suburb.

'Is that when they had their fight then? Your dad and Cordie?' I asked. 'Did Cordie say that was just an excuse and that's when he got mad?'

Ruth nodded, and then remembered: 'Also, she said that Dad wasn't the boss of her.'

I whistled long and low.

No wonder the fight had been a massive one. Mr Van Apfel wouldn't have liked that.

'Anyway,' Ruth said, 'Dad's the one who's always saying God's the boss. He's the boss of everyone. Even Dad.'

To prove it to me she sang a few bars of a song I didn't recognise.

'But what happened to Cordie?' I wanted to know.

'Dunno,' Ruth said, chewing her cheek thoughtfully. 'Mum had sent me and Hannah to bed by then.'

'They've got a secret, you know,' she added.

'Who, your dad and Cordie?' I asked, though I already knew the answer.

'No, *Hannah* and Cordie. They're up to something. Ask Laura – she knows too. It's only you and me who are left out.'

'They don't have a secret,' I scoffed. 'You've got it wrong. They wouldn't keep a secret from us.'

When what I really meant to say was: *How come they haven't told me?*

* * *

We were getting closer to school, where the houses were larger and set further back from the road. They had deeper front yards here. Shadier trees. (Though their neat lawns still wilted under the relentless sun the same as everyone else's.) The trees along the nature strip were grander too, and we wove in and out of them as we walked. The heat was so thick that it made my skin crawl and I swatted at flies that weren't there.

Then suddenly something *was* there, something stung my bare skin. Something pinged past my ear, something else bit into my wrist.

'We're under attack!' Ruth bellowed.

She ducked her head low and started to run, her legs straining under the weight of her backpack, her arms pumping. She'd been several steps behind me when she'd picked up the pace and now, as she bumped past, she reached out and grabbed my hand and she dragged me along behind. Small, sharp pellets bounced off my body. They skimmed my arm, chipped my ankle. Hunted out soft parts of flesh.

I glanced back but there was only shadow and speckled sunlight behind us. Nothing stirred in the car-less street. Whatever had attacked us had vanished again. Melted back into the broiling heat.

And, oh boy, that heat. I still gripped Ruth's hand but we ran slower now. Just jogged along side by side. I could hear her laboured breathing, her soft grunts of effort. Sweat bled through the fabric of her dress.

Then, without warning, the pellets started firing again. Harder this time. Hard and fast. As though whatever great mouth they were being spat from was closing in on us. 'Run!' Ruth ordered, and I put my head down and ran, but as I did, something dark skidded past. It leapt and then landed in one liquid movement and Ruth and I both reared back like spooked horses.

The creature gave a blood-chilling cry – a holler of war – before it pointed its stick gun at me.

'Rack off, Jason Kenny!' shrilled Ruth.

He sneered. 'Rack off, Jason Kenny,' he mimicked and he flung a fistful of gumnut bullets at Ruth's face. They glanced off her cheeks, off her carefully ironed collar, and then pattered harmlessly onto the footpath. Jason Kenny was in Ruth's class at school and now she strode indignantly towards him. She opened her mouth, ready to shout out again, but Jason Kenny was too quick. He leaned forward casually and popped a gumnut in her open mouth. Ruth spluttered. Then spat it out onto the footpath.

'Yuck!' Ruth cried.

The gumnut landed in a divot and stayed wedged where it fell. Bullseye. Like she'd meant to do it. Like we'd been spitting watermelon seeds and Ruth had hit the target. You couldn't do it twice if you tried.

'Shut yer face, *Fish Lips!*' Jason Kenny said.

Fish Lips. The boys always called Ruth that. They'd call out in the playground whenever she walked past: 'Does a fish have lips? Does a fish have lips?' Or else they called her 'Roof' because her lip made it hard for her to say the 'th' bit of her name. 'Roof, Roof,' they'd shout, trying to sound like barking dogs. 'Roof, Roof' every time they saw her.

Ruth's eyes filled up and threatened to spill. She wiped her nose on the short sleeve of her dress. 'Leave her alone, Jason Kenny,' I said, towering over the both of them. Even then I spoke without Ruth's conviction.

And Jason Kenny must have sensed my hesitation because he tucked his stick rifle under his arm. Then he marched back and forth in front of the two of us, boldly blocking our path. As he marched he whistled the tune from the Cottee's Cordial ad on TV. Everybody knew that ad. And at the end of the refrain he stopped and he stood at ease and he rapped his stick against his flattened palm. *Whack-whack-whack.*

'Get lost, Jason Kenny!'

I said it louder this time and he stopped his marching. He lined me up in the sight of his rifle.

'You're a goner,' he told me.

'Well, you're going to hell because killing is a sin, don't you know!' Ruth huffed.

She wiped her nose on her forearm, which was at least drier than her sleeve, and then she barged past Jason Kenny, swinging her bum wildly at the last second so her backpack slammed into him, knocking him sideways. He stumbled and dropped his gun.

'Loser,' he said angrily, and he kicked his foot out to try to trip her. But Ruth wasn't about to fall down at that. She stepped over it grimly and then kept on walking.

'You're the loser,' I said, and I skittered around his outstretched leg.

I tugged my tunic lower as I hurried after Ruth and a spray of gumnuts thwacked against my backpack.

'Knock it off!' I shouted to the sky. Behind me I could hear him whacking his stick against a tree, assaulting invisible enemies while he sang to himself. He'd already lost interest in us.

I hurried to catch up with Ruth who'd found her rhythm again and was walking doggedly towards school. I snuck an admiring glance in her direction, but she was back to concentrating on not toppling over.

* * *

That afternoon I sat at the kitchen table and worked on writing my skit. Laura sat opposite doing algebra, which from where I was sitting looked a lot like drawing love-heart doodles in the grid boxes of her Maths book. Outside, pale blossoms reached towards the open window and their scent mingled with the stench from the river.

'What's that?' Laura asked, eyeing my writing.

'My skit for the Showstopper,' I said and I flipped back to the beginning of my book. 'Wanna hear it?'

'Nope.'

'I could do it for you now.'

'What, every person's part?' she said suspiciously.

So far there were six roles in my play, but I'd only been able to convince four other people to be involved. And that was *after* I'd tried recruiting using the most sure-fire method known: passing notes in class. 'Pass 'em on,' I had instructed Jai Fordham, who sat next to me in Mrs Laguna's 5L class. I gave him the handwritten duplicates, outlining my artistic vision. Jai read one and grunted in disgust. 'Don't worry, there's no parts for boys,' I said. 'Unless it turns out I need a murderer.' And at the word 'murderer' Jai sat higher in his seat. 'If the part opens up, I'll let you know,' I promised him. Jai would make a great murderer some day.

But I didn't need a murderer or, at least I didn't think so. I hadn't worked out all of the script. I hadn't worked out all the cast yet either, though Sharrin Helpman and Jodi McNally were in. Melanie Firth would be in it too, and her best friend Carly Sawtell, though the both of them hated my guts. But Melanie did drama lessons at a real studio after school and, in

5L you couldn't buy that kind of experience. Of course there'd be Cordie – she'd play the lead part. Just as soon as I saw her to tell her. But she'd been away from school so many days lately that I hadn't had the chance to say it.

'Why don't you do it as a monologue?' Miss Elith had suggested when I'd told her my casting problems. 'If Cordie's not interested in being in it, and if you're having trouble organising the other girls, then do it on your own.'

It wasn't, I explained, that Cordie wasn't *interested*. She just hadn't made a firm commitment yet.

'So try a monologue.'

'A mono-what?'

'A monologue. It's where you get to speak all of the lines yourself. Tell the story from your point of view.'

And I had to admit the idea was tempting. There'd be fewer arguments that way.

'No, you should do it in a group,' my sister decreed, and she turned back to her algebra.

Living with Laura was a monologue, all right. There was no room for anyone else's point of view.

Mum came bustling into the kitchen after that, in a cloud of white plastic shopping bags.

'Give us a hand, Tik?' she said as she dumped the bags on the bench. She went back to the car to unload more and for a moment I sat and looked longingly at my lovely workbook. Then I got up and went over to the bench and began to unpack grocery bags, heaving out sugar and instant coffee and tins of Golden Circle canned pineapple chunks. Lining them up in order.

'Give us a hand, Lor,' I said, mimicking Mum, but Laura shook her head and stared down at her doodles.

'Can't,' she said, 'this is really hard, Tik.'

I wished I was fourteen like her.

When Mum came back in ferrying more bags, the strap of her singlet had slipped off one shoulder.

'Ugh, this heat,' she said. 'Makes you crazy, waiting for the rain.'

She kicked off her shoes and left them lying on the tiles, then moved around the kitchen quickly and easily, and it felt good to watch her there. I leaned against the bench and began working on opening a packet of biscuits where they lay, hidden inside a shopping bag, so that Mum couldn't see what I was doing. Mum pulled out a packet of Weet-Bix and held it up.

'Remember what you used to call this when you were little, Tik?'

I'd heard this a hundred times but I played along anyway.

'Eat-Bricks.'

Mum smiled.

'Better name for it anyway,' I said. 'Tastes like eating bricks.'

She slid the box into the cupboard and carried on unpacking the rest of the shopping.

'I've been working on my skit for the Showstopper,' I told her.

'I can't wait to see it,' she said, opening cupboards and sliding things in. Rattling Tupperware like empty shells. 'What's it about again?'

'It's a mystery,' I said. Because right then it was. A mystery how I would finish it. 'A mysterious tragedy.'

'Righto,' Mum said as if that settled it. 'Well, your dad and I will be there.'

She pulled out a chopping board and began slicing up pumpkin with a knife that had a blade wider than my wrist.

'I saw Carol Van Apfel and Cordie at the shops,' Mum said. 'Cordie wasn't at school today.'

'Nup.' The biscuit wrapper crinkled suspiciously.

'Carol said she was sick, but Cordie looked okay when I saw her. I suppose it was her arm that was bothering her.' Mum would send Lor and me to school if we were missing a limb. No wonder she was puzzled.

'That's what Ruth reckoned too,' I reported to Mum. 'She said "pig's bum" when I asked her if Cordie was sick.'

'Anyway,' Mum said, as she flung open the fridge and began rummaging around the crisper drawer, 'I said we'd pick the girls up from Hayley's sleepover this weekend at the same time we pick up you and Lor. You know, in the evening before the sleepover part.'

'What? The Van Apfel girls?' I stopped what I was doing with the biscuits. 'But they're not going to Hayley's.'

'Mmm, that's what Carol told me. She said they had church the next morning but I told her we could pick the girls up when we go and get you and Laura. It's no trouble. It's not like we'd have to drive out of our way.'

'So that's what we're going to do. Pick you all up together. I told Carol we'd have the girls home by ten o'clock, so you and Laura had better be ready to go at that time.'

'Sure,' I agreed. But how had Mum talked Mrs Van Apfel

around? What about church? What about *Mr* Van Apfel? I wished I'd been there to see Cordie's face.

'Laura? Did you hear what I said?' Mum said. 'Ready to go by ten on the dot.'

Laura nodded without looking up from her doodles. 'Yeah.'

'And Tikka,' Mum said, nudging me with her bum to shoo me out of her way, 'stop ferreting around in those biscuits, I can see what you're doing. Leave them alone or you won't eat your tea.'

I left the biscuits and returned to the table. Got back to the business of my skit. I was still sitting there, moments later, when the Van Apfel girls appeared at the kitchen window. They were red-faced and out of breath.

'We've run —'

'All the way over —'

'There's a man —'

'A man!' Ruth confirmed hysterically.

Mum froze where she stood shaping rissoles at the kitchen bench, little worms of minced meat leaking through her fingers.

'What? What man?' she said urgently. 'You'd better come inside, girls.'

The three of them ran down the side of the house and then reappeared at the flyscreen door.

'Inside!' Mum said, and she threw the back door open, holding it ajar with her hip while she stood wiping minced meat from her fingers. She twisted the tea towel dexterously around each knuckle.

'Thanks-Mrs-Malloy-Thanks-Mrs-Malloy-Thanks-Mrs-Malloy.'

The door complained three times before Mum let it go. It creaked and banged to a stop.

'Here, sit down.' Mum motioned to the table where Laura and I were working. 'What's happened? Are you girls all right?'

'Yes.' Hannah spoke for all of them without checking.

Mum raised an eyebrow at Cordie and Ruth and they nodded. Yes, they were all right too. Hannah laid a hand protectively on Cordie's arm. Ruth sucked the tips of her hair.

'Where are your parents? Are they at home?'

'Mrs and Mrs Van Apfel aren't there on a Wednesday afternoo—' I started to say, but Mum held up her hand to silence me. She kept her eyes fixed on Hannah.

'They're not home,' Hannah said. 'Dad's at work and Mum's at Praise and Worship, so I'm in charge of the others.' She inclined her head towards Ruth and Cordie, who were now settled next to her at the table.

Ruth look stricken, her face was mottled with the effort of trying to run as fast as her older sisters. Cordie, on the other hand, looked faintly amused. As if she knew the end of the joke.

'All right,' Mum said. 'Now tell me what's happened? Who was this man?'

'We don't know —' Hannah began.

'Yes we do! He was coming to kill us!' Ruth interrupted.

'Actually, we don't know that for sure —'

Hannah looked slightly sheepish now she was in the safety of our kitchen. Outside the window a butcherbird perched lightly on a branch, its head cocked to one side as if it was sizing us up.

'We just thought, you know …' Hannah let her voice trail off.

'We *do* know,' Ruth corrected and then she started to recite. '1 John 5:19: *For* we *know that we are children of God, and the world is under the control of the evil one —*'

'I never said that!' Hannah snapped.

'Yes, you *did!*'

'Well, *you* weren't the one who answered the phone.'

Hannah was embarrassed and she studied the tablecloth now. Picked at embroidered yellow daisies with her finger. Then Cordie reached out and stopped Hannah's fidgeting.

'He *could've* been a murderer,' Cordie conceded.

'A murderer!' I shivered. Maybe I'd need Jai Fordham after all. This could be good for my skit.

On the stovetop something plopped in its pot and Mum glanced over at it. Then she turned back to Hannah and frowned.

'On the phone, you say?'

Hannah nodded. 'He rang us just then. *When we were home on our own.* I didn't recognise the voice when I picked up the phone. He sounded kinda weird. And he didn't tell me who he was.'

'What did he say?' Mum asked.

'Uh,' Hannah hesitated. 'He wanted to know what radio station we listen to.'

'Creepy,' Laura confirmed.

'2GB,' Mum replied. She said it without hesitation.

The thing on the stovetop plopped again impatiently.

'What?' Hannah was confused.

'The answer's 2GB,' Mum explained. 'It's a competition. Oh, girls,' she groaned. 'Nobody was coming to get you – the man on the phone was trying to give you a prize! You say that you listen to their radio station and then they send you a prize. What made you think it was a *murderer?*'

Outside, the butcherbird was still on its branch. It opened and closed its hooked beak rhythmically, moving it in time with the beat of the sun.

'We just thought, because you know —' Hannah petered out.

'We'd been watching scary movies,' she confessed.

'Not me!' Ruth protested.

'No, just Cordie and me,' Hannah said. 'We were watching M-rated stuff when we're not supposed to.'

'Even so —' Mum started saying, then she thought better of it.

'Scary movies can be quite convincing,' she agreed. She walked over to the stovetop and turned down the dial, then went back to her minced meat on the bench.

'They give you money, or sometimes a holiday or a car,' she explained. 'Did you tell him that your mum was busy? Did you ask him to ring back at another time?'

Hannah shook her head apologetically.

'I've been waiting years for them to call me!' Mum joked to Hannah, but Hannah didn't seem to find it funny. A prize? From a prank phone call? How was she supposed to know *that*? Hannah didn't know such things even existed. She thought she'd done the right thing bringing her sisters safely here. (She'd thought they were going to die.) No one told *her* that they could win a prize. Her parents didn't listen to commercial radio at home.

'You know, I thought it was probably something like that,' Cordie said lightly.

'No, you didn't!' Hannah said indignantly. Her face was flushed and she kicked at Cordie under the table. 'You thought it was a murderer too.'

'At least you're safe,' Mum said soothingly. 'Now, do you girls want to stay for dinner? There are plenty of rissoles. Why don't you wait here until your parents get home?'

'Yuck, rissoles,' Laura muttered. 'Stay and then you can eat mine.'

But Hannah said that they'd better go, that they had to be home by the time both their parents got back.

That night I crept out of bed and went to the kitchen for some water. While I was there I figured I might as well stay and listen to Mum and Dad for a bit. I liked hearing their voices drift up the stairwell, shot through with the sound of the TV. Liked hearing what they said when they thought we were in bed.

'Those girls were so upset today, Graham,' Mum was saying. 'You should have seen them. God knows what they're filling their heads with.'

'God,' Dad replied. 'That's what they're filling their heads with.'

'*The court warns it's a dangerous mix ...*' agreed the voiceover on TV.

'I don't know what the parents are telling them but those girls shouldn't be afraid like that,' Mum said. 'They're kids, for heaven's sake. What have they got to be fearful of? Movies wouldn't scare them *that* much.

'And Cordie didn't look very sick to me,' Mum said, remembering.

'Should she?'

'She wasn't at school today. Carol told me she was sick.'

'Maybe that arm of hers was giving her grief.'

'Maybe,' Mum said thoughtfully.

'Been sleepwalking again, you reckon?' Dad suggested.

'Who knows?' Mum said. 'In that house, who could say?'

CHAPTER TEN

Once the search was called off, my fire dreams began. Gusting through the flyscreen on the gritty wind. They tangled my shortie pyjamas and knotted the vines of my hair. Danced flame-licking into my sleep.

Fire dreams.

As if we might smoke those girls out.

When I had the dream as a kid I'd wake – mid-blaze – to find Mum or Dad, or sometimes Lor squatting there next to my bed. They'd be gripping my arm, saying my name. Pushing my hair off my face. 'Just a dream,' they'd murmur. 'Go back to sleep, Tik. Just a dream. It can't hurt you now.' Then they'd unclench the fingers on my right hand – my thumb, my pointer, my middle finger, all pinched together – gripping some invisible pen. And if it was Mum or Dad who'd come into my room to see me, they'd smooth the damp sheets and sit with me and stroke my hair. Talk me back off to thick sleep. (If it was Laura, she'd wait long enough to check I'd woken right up, but not so long I went back to sleep.)

For twenty years I'd been having that same dream. I saw eyeholes and claw marks. I walked across scorched earth that was raw as a skinned animal, and the world would smell of burning. Sometimes the river flowed through my dream, its spume pink and frothy like creaming soda, the water a dark cherry red. But it wasn't until I lived alone – not until Baltimore where there was no Mum or Dad or Laura or anyone else to wake me up when I thrashed in my sheets – it wasn't until then that I saw the dream end. Then I found I was holding the match.

CHAPTER ELEVEN

When Ruth first tried to tell me about her sisters' plan, I didn't want to hear about it. Neither did the bird-of-paradise flowers in the garden bed behind us. They stood in a row, their bright heads turned to look the other way. A disapproving corps de ballet.

'Tell me after,' I hissed.

'After first half?' Our school split lunchtimes into first and second halves – one for eating, one not. Like separating the white from the yolk.

'No, after school! Tell me on the way home.'

Ruth should have known better than to try to talk to me in the playground. She was only in Year Two, after all.

'But it's important,' she whined.

'So tell me after school.'

'Hannah and Cordie are running away and Laura is helping them go.' The words came out in a terrible rush like a spilt drink in the sun.

* * *

I have a photo of us that was taken around about that time. These days it's got watery-brown splotches on parts of it, as if something's seeped through from the other side. In the photo Hannah and Cordie are wearing matching dresses in different colours, which makes me think the dresses must have been on sale. Hannah's in hot pink, Cordie in fluorescent orange. Laura is wedged in between them, one arm slung across each of their shoulders. (Though she's lopsided where Cordie is shorter.)

Ruth is in the photo too, kneeling down, making her own front row. She has one hand resting on the grass for balance, while her other hand is raised, shielding her eyes from the sun, but whoever took the photo is casting a long shadow across her that wipes out most of her face.

Behind Ruth, to the left as you look at the picture, I'm standing and squinting into the sun. I look prettier (but sadder) than I am in my memory. When you look at the photo there's a gap between the three older girls and me that's big enough to fit another version of myself, and I'm leaning towards them, trying to be that person. But there's a valley of blue sky in between.

* * *

In the playground that day when Ruth told me about the plan, I dragged her off to the cleaner's store cupboard so she could tell me everything she knew. The store cupboard was barely a cubicle, full of Dettol and dustpans. No one ever went near the cleaner's store cupboard.

I pulled Ruth inside and rested up against the door, and then I made her repeat everything she'd overheard her sisters saying. *Whose idea was it? When were they planning to go? Where would they run to? How long would they stay away?*

The ceiling inside the cleaner's cubicle, like the rest of the toilet block, was spattered with welts of paper towel that had been wadded up, wetted and flung up there to stick. It had dried and turned to lumpy grey plaster. It must have been torture for the cleaner to have such a filthy store cupboard, or maybe the cleaner didn't care.

I stared at those welts while I listened to Ruth, while I pumped her for the details of their plan. I listened carefully but couldn't bring myself to ask the only thing I really wanted to know: *why hadn't they included me?*

Ruth explained that the idea was to do it on the night of the Showstopper when everyone was watching the show. It would be easy to disappear from down in the valley. Especially in summer. Especially at dusk. And especially when everyone they knew, including Mrs McCausley, who could spot you and report you back to your parents before you'd even made it to the top of the street, would be sitting in the one spot, facing the one direction. Eyes fixed on the amphitheatre stage.

It wasn't hard for a person to walk out of the valley. Not if they stuck to the road. There was plenty of scrub along both sides for cover. And once they were on the far side they could hitchhike easily. Or they could jump on a bus. Or it wasn't far to the train station. From there they could go anywhere. They could disappear south. Head down the coast. Interstate. Or go north and get lost in the city.

It was a good plan, I had to admit it. I couldn't have come up with better. And that stuck in my guts like wadded-up paper towel.

'Laura's giving them the cash.'

'What cash?'

Ruth shrugged. 'They'll need cash to go.'

From her job on the supermarket checkout on Saturday afternoons, I thought bitterly. No wonder she had no money for ice creams.

'You can't say anything but,' Ruth said, sounding panicky. She'd remembered she wasn't supposed to know. 'Don't say that I told you. Promise? *You promise?* Hannah and Cordie don't know I heard; they thought I was asleep.'

'But how can I help with the plan if I'm not supposed to know?'

Ruth looked at me. She was baffled.

'How could *you* help Hannah and Cordie? They're older than us, remember?'

'I could help,' I said sniffily.

'I could come up with an alibi or, better yet, a *diversion*! Buy them more time to run!' I was thinking of the news reports Dad watched on TV with their 'alibis' and their 'pending police investigations'. A diversion was what Hannah and Cordie would need. I would give them the cover to run.

Already my mind was racing towards my Showstopper skit. My skit could be vital to Cordie's getaway.

'My skit!' I said. 'They could run … while I … distracted … my skit!'

My brain was skipping ahead and my mouth couldn't keep up. Ruth looked at me like I was possessed.

'Cordie could be the star,' I talked while I planned it, 'and … and she could disappear straight from the side of the stage.'

'What about Hannah?' Ruth asked.

'Hannah?'

'Yeah, what about Hannah?'

'Hannah could be waiting for Cordie backstage,' I said. 'As a stagehand! She could be dressed in black and holding props as part of her disguise.'

'But Hannah doesn't even go to our school any more.' Ruth was suddenly indignant at the unfairness of it all.

'You're right,' I admitted. 'Maybe Hannah would wait in the audience and then she could sneak away and meet Cordie during the climax of my play?'

'Or maybe they could sneak off just like they planned in the first place at any old point in the night,' she said haughtily.

'If they did it during my play it would be better,' I explained. 'More guarantee that people won't notice.'

But Ruth was unimpressed.

'You shouldn't help them,' she warned. 'You shouldn't help and they shouldn't go. It's sinful. It's sinning, you know.'

But you could tell by the way she said it – by the way she dragged the back of her hand across her eyes, and by the way the trail it left was wet – that the real problem wasn't that her big sisters were going.

Only that they were leaving her behind.

'Have they packed?' I asked.

'I didn't hear that bit,' Ruth conceded.

'Have they even decided what they're going to take?'

Ruth hadn't heard that either.

I made a mental list of what I would choose. (A torch, a compass. My *Britannica Junior Encyclopaedia*, volume WXYZ *Atlas* because of the maps at the back.) But then I remembered: I wasn't going anywhere. I wasn't invited. I hadn't even been deemed special enough to know.

Outside, the Year Six girls were doing handstands against the wall of the cleaner's storeroom and their school shoes *smack-whacked* against the bricks. They scraped sideways down the wall when the momentum wore off, and I wondered if Cordie was out there with them, her shoes flinging upwards, her feet flying in the air like birds taking off. I wondered if she and Hannah were really going to go. If they would actually go through with it and run away from home, or if the momentum might wear off before then.

And it wasn't until years later that I realised the one thing I forgot to ask Ruth that day inside the cleaner's store cupboard. I was so distracted thinking about my skit and the runaway plan that I never thought to ask Ruth: *why?*

Why were Hannah and Cordie planning to run away from home? What had happened? What had made them go now? It seemed so obvious – *preordained* – that they would want to get away that I never thought to ask Ruth why.

* * *

On Saturday night Mum dropped the five of us off at Hayley Stinson's sleepover. There was Lor in the front, with Hannah squashed in next to her. (They might have been fourteen but their bodies didn't know it, four bum cheeks fitting easily in the front seat.) While Cordie, Ruth and I sat in the back with Cordie's cool cast resting against my leg.

'Dad'll pick you up,' Mum told us. 'And you lot better be ready to go the minute he arrives because if you're not home by ten, Mr and Mrs Van Apfel will have my guts for garters.'

We scrambled out of the car and onto the footpath outside Hayley's house, making promises to be ready when Dad arrived.

We cared about Mum's guts.

Hayley's party was in the backyard, where the Stinsons' pool stretched down one whole length of the yard. At the bottom of the yard was a chicken-wire fence that faced out onto the next street. Then a long trestle table, weighed down with party food, ran the length of the other side of the yard. A hot wind was blowing, and from a hook on the verandah a homemade *15* spun jerkily on its noose.

We swam and ate that afternoon at Hayley's party. Played Marco Polo in the pool. All except for Cordie, who sat on the edge, dangling her feet in the churning water but keeping her cast dry by wrapping it in a plastic shopping bag and laying it in her lap. We rolled our towels into crowns and we wore them with their terry-towelling tails hanging down our bare backs. Then we stood in a horseshoe to sing 'Happy Birthday' while Hayley's mum tried to get a decent photo. We sucked Redskins and ate popcorn that was every colour of the rainbow. We wore Cheezel rings on our fingers. Then we sat on the pavers under the coral tree with our limbs in a line and compared leg hairs and tan marks and moles. We played at being posh ladies, flipping our wet hair back from our faces in one fat curl, wearing the coral tree flowers like lips.

'Hello, I'm Pearl.'

'Hi, Pearl, I'm Shirl,' we said to one another.

We spoke like ventriloquists, our scarlet smiles unmoving until the flowers fell, bruised, to the floor. Then we got bored of that too and we wandered inside, where the twilight followed us in.

'Truth or Dare?' someone said hopefully.

We flopped onto couches, wearing our swimming costumes and turban towels. We were bare shoulders, soft midriffs. We slumped.

I sat on the floor, running my palms over the cork tiles, while in the corner Hannah and Cordie shared an armchair. Cordie sat in the centre, taking up all the space, while Hannah perched on the armrest like a conscience perched at her shoulder. The chair was orange and ugly and covered with thick corduroy-like material. That thing made me hot just to look at it.

'I've got one! I've got a Truth,' said Jade Heddingly. Jade was at the party because she went to swimming club; there was no other reason you'd invite her.

'Hey, Cordie,' she said, drawing out the words in a singsong way, 'is it true that you love Mr Avery?'

Cordie smiled and, without meaning to, I dug my nails into the cork, where they left tiny moon-shaped indents.

'Nah,' Cordie said, 'I don't love Mr Avery.'

'But I'd still do him,' she added. Then she folded her arms and tipped her chin up and dared us to say she *wouldn't*.

'Ew!' squealed Jade, and the older girls shrieked with laughter. 'She'd sleep with *a teacher*! Did you *hear* that? Cordie said she'd sleep with Mr Avery! *That's gross! He's so hairy!*' As if Jade Heddingly had anything to compare sleeping with Mr Avery to. As if any of us did.

'What?' Cordie said. 'Wouldn't you? Hairy's cute.'

She rubbed her cast nonchalantly and nobody spoke for a stunned moment.

'I heard he prefers boys,' Jade said.

'*I* heard he's been in jail,' Hayley said.

But nobody had any advances on that so we sat for a moment while we pondered Mr Avery's true identity and while we all watched Cordie, who was running her good hand up and down the surface of her cast. She paused and tickled the pads of her own fingertips as if the arm belonged to someone else.

'Aching?' Hannah asked her grudgingly. Hannah didn't approve of sleeping with teachers; not even joking about it.

'That means it's going to rain,' my sister said authoritatively. 'Broken bones always ache before it rains.'

'Nah,' said Cordie. 'I just banged it on the side of the pool.'

* * *

Somewhere between Marco Polo and Truth or Dare the wind had picked up. It had shifted south and down several degrees, and whenever gusts flung themselves through the open back door and circled the room they ruffled hair and raised goosebumps. There was music coming from a CD player in the corner – had been playing all evening so far – but a song came on now that Cordie approved of so she arched herself over the sunrise of her armchair to turn up the volume.

'You've gotta hear this,' she commanded.

Then she stood and let her towel fall away from where it had been wrapped around her head, and she sashayed across the room to switch off the lights. Her hip rolling was slight – just a suggestion – but coming from Cordie dressed only in a cossie the movement was almost obscene. The rest of us looked away.

The verandah light burned where no one had switched it off. A halo, hung from corrugated tin. Cordie danced towards it in the dark and positioned herself under its spotlight. She began to dance with more purpose, more intensity than before.

She moved slowly at first. She swayed and scuffed her feet. She gripped herself by the hips and then she slowly unfolded, stretching upwards, her good arm snaking around her cast shaft as she held her arms high above her head. She writhed and twirled, stomping her feet, reaching towards the dirty coin of light.

'Just ignore her,' Hannah instructed and she moved into the space Cordie had vacated on the armchair. 'She'll come back inside.'

And Cordie laughed at that, throwing her head back and opening her mouth wide to drink in the night, until she was filled to overflowing with dusk and cicada hiss and the scent of jasmine slowly strangling the fence. And in that instant a beam of light appeared among the murk and the chicken wire at the bottom of the backyard. It lighthoused across the rear of the house, illuminating Cordie for a split second – barely a heartbeat – before swinging off into the night.

'Did you see that?'

'See what?'

'What was it?'

'There's someone out there,' said Hayley, sounding panicky. 'Someone's in the street out the back, they had their high beams pointed at us.'

'How do you know?'

'What? A car?'

'Close the door, Cordie!'

'Cordie! Come back inside!'

Cordie laughed again. 'Who cares? Let them watch if they want.' She spun and stomped her feet.

'Come inside, Cordie!' Hannah urged. 'You have to come inside now!'

'Someone! Turn the lights on!'

You could feel the room getting frantic, feel the frenzy rising. Everyone was shouting now, but no one made any move to switch off the music or to turn on the lights. Everybody was transfixed.

'Cordie! Sit down!' Hannah yelled at her. 'Stop dancing! Now!'

But Cordie didn't stop. She was getting faster and faster, leaving the music behind. Spinning. Swirling. Spiralling. Stomping. Bare feet making the timber boards bounce. The chorus came on and Cordie mouthed the words to herself, her hands clamped to the sides of her head.

'Cordie! Stop it!'

It was Ruth shouting now, and something about her sister's voice made Hannah snap into action. She stood and ran out onto the verandah and lunged at Cordie, catching her by her good arm and pulling her towards the house, while someone else turned the music off and the whole night suddenly stopped.

The inside lights flicked on, flooding the weak verandah light in a sea of yellow.

'You're dead meat, Cordie, when Dad finds out about this,' Ruth said.

Mrs Stinson came in then carrying a bowl of popcorn. 'Do you girls want Mr Stinson to put the movie on yet or ...' she started saying, but she stopped when she saw Cordie standing there with Hannah still hanging off her arm.

'Everything okay, girls?' she asked.

'We're not ready for the movie yet,' Hayley said plaintively.

'Well, just let me know when you are,' Mrs Stinson said. 'I'll leave this here.' She put the bowl down on a table by the door, and backed out of the room.

Hayley turned to us after her mum had left. 'What do we do now?'

She could feel her party slipping away from her, and Cordie was to blame.

'What about the light?' someone asked. 'What if there's someone still out there?'

'It's probably nothing,' my sister said. 'Just someone doing a U-turn in the street. Anyway, we're safe inside.'

'Wanna go back in the pool?' someone suggested. 'Marco Polo?'

'Not again.'

'Not out there!'

'We could make prank calls?'

But Hayley shook her head anxiously at that idea.

'Dad'll be here soon anyway to come and pick us up,' Laura said. But that only made Hayley more upset. She wasn't ready for her birthday to be over.

Outside the wind flung bits of leaves and sticks and gumnuts onto the roof in place of rain. They pinged off the corrugated roof of the verandah without rhythm, silent one moment and then clattering fistfuls the next.

'Hey, let's do a séance!' someone said. It was one of the older girls – a friend of Hayley's who didn't go to swimming club with us, and so I didn't know her name. She was much bigger than the rest of us, with real bumps and curves in her swimming costume, but in exchange her eyelashes and eyebrows were so incredibly pale that they looked like they weren't there at all.

'It's easy. My cousin told me. All we need is a ouija board and an empty glass and we need to turn the lights off again.'

'No more lights off,' Hannah said.

The birthday girl narrowed her eyes suspiciously at her lashless friend. 'What is it called again, Nicole?' she asked.

'A séance! It's where you talk to dead people by asking them questions and things. And then they reply by moving a glass around the board to spell out the letters of their answer. You can ask them anything. Like what they're doing, or how they died … It'll be really fun!'

'You can talk to actual dead people?' I said incredulously. *How had I not heard of this before?*

Not that I pretended to know any dead people. No one I knew had ever died, except for Mrs McCausley's husband, Ralph. He'd 'passed', she always said, as if he'd passed an exam. As though Ralph really knew his stuff. But Ralph had gone and *passed* long before I was born, so I was guessing he didn't really count.

'Can you talk to *any* dead people?' I asked. 'Or just ones you know? Can you talk to famous ones? Like people from history? Or do they have to be related to you? And what about ones that don't speak English? How do you talk to them?'

I had so many questions, so it was lucky this older girl had plenty of answers as well.

'You can only talk to people you know,' she said firmly. 'And they have to speak the same language too. Plus, you can only try the same person three times, *that's it*. After three goes, you leave them alone.'

'Or what?'

'Or else.'

And Laura muttered to Hannah: 'Wonder who died and made *her* boss.'

Which was a bit rich coming from them.

Nicole went on to explain the ins and outs of ouija board etiquette, which sounded suspiciously like our classroom rules ('Raise your hand when it's your turn to talk'), and also a bit like Knock and Run ('Every man for himself once the door is opened'). But she knew so much about it, and I was entranced. This was definitely what I wanted to play.

'So, have you got one?' Nicole asked Hayley eventually.

'One what?' Hayley said.

'A board.' The older girl rolled her eyes. 'We need something like Scrabble tiles to use as the ouija board. Something with lots of letters.'

Hayley panicked. 'We don't have Scrabble. We used to, but Mum threw it out in the council clean-up. We've got Monopoly and Hungry, Hungry Hippos and that's it. She kept Hungry, Hungry Hippos for my younger cousins.'

My sister snorted. 'Hungry, Hungry Hippos! Yeah, we'll ask the dead people if they want to play Hungry, Hungry Hippos. Best of three.'

She and Hannah were pretending they weren't interested in the séance, even though the girl who suggested it was older than both of them.

'We could use Monopoly,' I suggested. 'Make it so the first letter of every property was the letter being spelled out by the dead person. Like Park Lane means "P" and Mayfair means "M".

'There's an "A" for "The Angel, Islington" and an "E" for "Euston Road". "A" and "E" are the letters we'll need the most,' I said, thinking aloud.

I really wanted this séance to work.

The older girl nodded approvingly. 'Right,' she said. 'That would work.'

And to Hayley she said: 'Go get Monopoly. We'll use that.'

Hayley went off, glancing over her shoulder at me, not knowing whether to be grateful or annoyed.

Before we could get started though, the Van Apfel girls had to excuse themselves from the game. At the mention of the word 'séance' Ruth's face had taken on a strained look and you got the feeling a séance was something they'd heard of before and, what's more, it was the kind of something that was a sin.

'We're not allowed to talk to dead people,' Hannah explained.

She was perched back in the ugly orange armchair by the back door. Cordie was next to her, within easy reach. And when Hannah spoke, Cordie's expression said it wasn't a big deal. Like talking to dead people wasn't the strangest thing to come up in conversation at the Van Apfel breakfast table.

'She's right,' Ruth confirmed.

Hayley returned with Monopoly then and we all sat in a circle around the board. Except for the Van Apfel girls, who were prohibited from bugging the dead. (The instant the board appeared, Ruth stood up and moved across the room to the safety of her sisters and she sat cross-legged beside Cordie's bare feet, her back hunched against the armchair's wooden leg.)

'We need a cup,' Nicole said.

A plastic cup was produced and it was handed to Nicole, who placed it ceremoniously on the board.

'Now what?' my sister said.

'Turn the lights off, stupid,' Nicole instructed.

And I was so shocked to hear someone giving orders to my sister (instead of the other way around) that it didn't occur to me that I should defend her. Laura must have been shocked too. Because she did what she was told without arguing, although she did switch on the reading lamp by the couch as a small act of rebellion. Through the doorway I could see branches moving in the tree next to the verandah. A possum poked its head out, then pulled it back in and ran along the branch that overhung the roof.

'How do we start?' I said.

We were lying flat on our stomachs around the board, legs fanned out, arms reaching forward, so that each girl had one finger on the upturned cup.

'Do we need to say something to bring the spirits out?' I asked. 'Like an incantation or something?'

'No inkan-nations,' Nicole said firmly, wresting back control. 'Local ghosts only. But everyone has to close their eyes while I say a spell to call up the dead spirits to see if they're willing to talk.'

I felt the queasy burn of embarrassment because she hadn't understood my word and I wriggled uncomfortably on the tiles.

'If Cordie closes her eyes now she'll fall asleep,' Lor whispered to me and I snuck a look in the direction of the armchair and there was Cordie, sullen and sleepy and curled in a 'C' like an animal trying to burrow into shallow dirt. She must have been worn out from all that dancing.

The Nicole-girl started to chant then and I was surprised by her voice, by the deep, guttural sound it made, and by the music of her words. She was talking about ravens and nightshades and spirits and death. She rhymed 'vermilion' with 'cotillion' when I didn't even know what a cotillion was. 'That's from *Beetlejuice*!' my sister said indignantly. But no one else heard her, or if they did they didn't care. Or maybe they just hadn't seen the movie like Lor had. Everyone seemed more interested in listening to Nicole as she instructed the dead to come to life.

For one moment after she uttered the words, the air around us seemed to swell almost to the point of splitting. I held my breath and waited, and listened to the *shush* of leaves sweeping against the verandah roof as the possum moved about in the tree. Hannah and Ruth had been drawn in, I noticed. They'd abandoned Cordie in the armchair and now peered over the back of the couch to watch the ouija board. Twin sets of eyes. Four chicken-wing arms splayed.

'Told you so,' Hannah muttered after several seconds of silence. 'See? Nothing.'

Ruth nodded and looked satisfied, and she turned her head away, but in the next instant the plastic cup moved. It skidded across the board and stopped hard on 'Community Chest'. We screamed. And the sound punched a hole in the dark.

Next came the noise of the body on the roof. The possum landed on the waves of corrugated iron with a beautiful, terrible *bang*. We screamed again – long and loud – and when we finally stopped we could make out a scrabbling sound across the roof, a *scritch-scratch* of sharp pointed nails, and we tripped over each other in our panic to get away. Someone bumped the reading lamp and its beam teetered drunkenly, and we screamed in horror, and our screams made us scream even more. The ouija board was knocked over and the box was tipped off the table. Monopoly money fluttered in the air like moths. Finally a man's voice called out sardonically from some deeper part of the house: 'Jesus Christ, haven't youse ever heard a possum on the roof?'

The lights came on then, flicked by Hannah's smooth hand, and we stood in its glare, not meeting one another's wild eyes.

'It moved! The cup moved!'

'Did it?' Ruth said. 'I didn't see it.'

'You weren't watching! It moved! All on its own!'

'You did it,' Hayley said, pointing at me. 'You moved it.'

Her birthday was not going how she planned.

'*I* didn't move it,' I protested.

'Yes, you did.'

'No, I didn't! Someone else must've done it!'

'A spirit,' the Nicole-girl said.

'There's no such thing as spirits,' Laura snapped.

'There is,' Ruth said quickly, and she looked set to quote a Bible verse at us but Laura cut her off: 'So what does it mean then? "Community Chest". "CC". What's that supposed to mean? What was the *spirit* trying to say?'

'Maybe "C" stands for a place or a name?' I suggested. 'Or maybe "see"? Like: "look see"? But look at *what*? What did it want us to look at? Something starting with "C"?'

Nobody knew, but everyone was getting tired.

'Look at this *mess*,' Hayley said, pointing at the Monopoly money that had scattered all over the tiles. Her mum would be in again in a minute and she'd be on at Hayley to tidy it up.

'That crap always takes ages to pack away,' Ruth said sagely.

CHAPTER TWELVE

We grew older and also younger at the party after that. We were scornful of our séance ('What ghost comes back to play Monopoly?' Laura scoffed), but we were spooked too. And I was adamant I wasn't the one who moved the cup, but then, so was everyone else.

It was a relief when Dad came to collect us shortly before ten o'clock. When he arrived Hayley's mum brought him to the doorway, where the two of them stood side by side, looking bemused while we crawled around on the cork tiles picking up paper money. While they watched us Dad told Hayley's mum all the things she already knew. (That my sister and I had to go up the coast early in the morning. That the Van Apfel girls had to go to church. And that he was sorry to knock on their door at almost ten o'clock at night but that he didn't reckon they'd be getting much sleep anyway.) And seeing Dad there and hearing his voice was the comfort I hadn't realised I needed. I could feel the fear of the past few minutes falling away until it lay there spooled at his feet.

'You lot ready?' he said.

Laura and I nodded.

'Ready, Mr Malloy,' Ruth said, standing up. She hauled Hannah up by the arm.

'Who's missing?' said Dad. 'Shouldn't I have five?'

'Where's Cordie?'

'Did Cordie do the séance?'

'What séance?' said Mrs Stinson, alarmed.

'Where's Cordie?'

'She was in the orange chair before.'

We all looked at the armchair that sat solitarily in the corner, its cushion sucked inwards like a rind. For several minutes there was confusion while we tried to work out whether Cordie was really missing.

'How can you not know?' Dad asked, mystified. 'What've you girls been doing?'

Someone thought she might be in the bathroom but that turned out to be Hayley's younger brother. 'No chicks in here,' he said sadly, exiting the bathroom.

'I'll get Mr Stinson to search outside,' Mrs Stinson said in a tight voice and she disappeared down the hallway.

'I'll go too,' Dad called after her. 'Have you got an outside light here somewhere?'

'You don't need a light,' a voice behind us announced. We wheeled around and there, standing in the doorway that led onto the verandah, stiff-necked and ashen-faced behind his dark beard, stood Mr Avery from 6A. He knocked awkwardly on the doorframe, even though the door was wide open. We'd never bothered to shut it the whole night. Next to him stood Cordie, who was still in her swimming costume. While he was fully clothed. He gripped his car keys like a badge and wore his laceless leather shoes. Her hair hung loose and limp and faintly chlorine green. And in the half-light of the doorway that sliced them front to back, the babyish swell of her stomach shone like a seal's.

'Can I come in?' Mr Avery said, but he made no move to.

'*Cordie!*' Hannah cried.

'I found her,' said Mr Avery, 'walking along the side of the road in the dark.'

'Which road?' Mrs Stinson said urgently. She was back now, along with her husband, and the two of them stood next to Dad in the centre of the room.

We all waited to hear Mr Avery's answer as if the name of the road was important. As if that was the detail that might clear things up.

'Blaxland Road,' he said and we nodded. We knew it. Blaxland Road was only a short walk away. It ran perpendicular to this street and it led to the local pool. We'd driven it a thousand times before tonight.

'She was sleepwalking,' Mr Avery said. 'At least, I think she was. She didn't seem to know how she got there, and I was a bit confused too. A bit thrown by the swimming costume, you know.' He turned red at having pointed out that Cordie was in her cossie. 'Because of – because of the pool. I thought maybe she was going to the pool on Blaxland Road ...'

We stared at Mr Avery then as if we hardly recognised him at all. *I heard he prefers boys. I heard he's been in jail.* He looked different, but no less formal, when he was wearing his weekend clothes. Maybe we'd never known him to begin with.

Dad spoke first. 'You thought she was going to the pool at ten o'clock at night? In the dark, all by herself?' he said incredulously. He stepped towards Mr Avery and they began to talk between themselves in that infuriating way adults do when things get interesting. But we girls got the giggles then anyway, and we laughed, half with shock, half with relief, at the punchline that stood in the doorway. *Sleepwalking! That was all. Cordie had sleepwalked away from us. There was nothing more sinister about it than that.* Only, Cordie didn't laugh. Her face stayed still and sullen for the entire time Mr Avery talked to Dad. 'It's none of my business what she was doing out there,' I heard Mr Avery say defensively. 'I was more worried about bringing her back!'

Mr Avery left after that and the five of us got ready to go home with Dad.

'I'll walk you out the front,' Mrs Stinson said.

'Actually, we're out the back,' Dad said. 'We're parked in the street behind.'

'Let me turn the outside light on for you then,' she said and she lit up the backyard for us.

We trailed Dad out the back door, past the pool and through the gate in the chicken-wire fence at the bottom of the yard. Hannah held tight to Cordie's hand the whole way. Then out in the street behind the Stinsons' place we saw Mr Avery getting into his little red hatchback. It seemed odd for such a hairy man to have such a dainty car. Dad patted the bonnet as we walked past as if to say: 'On your way.' But when I walked behind Dad and did the same thing, the engine of Mr Avery's car was cold to touch.

'Hey, that car's been sitting out here the whole time —' I started to say. But Dad bundled me into our car and we drove away.

'It *was* cold,' I protested as we sped through the dark. Each slice of pale light that fell from the streetlights got sucked under our wheels as we passed. 'I'm not making it up, I swear. You felt it, didn't you, Dad?'

But Dad had a bigger problem than Mr Avery and his cold engine.

'You won't say anything to our parents will you, Mr Malloy?' Hannah asked him anxiously. 'You won't tell Dad about Cordie's sleepwalking, will you? About her wandering off?'

Dad stared at the road like he was weighing it up, like he'd rather not say anything to the Van Apfels given the choice. Eventually he replied: 'You know I have to, Hannah. Why don't we explain it to your parents when I drop you off?

'I'm sure they'll understand,' he said unconvincingly.

* * *

When we pulled up at the Van Apfel house that night – with its crosshatched windows, those twisted spiral stairs – Mr Van Apfel appeared from underneath the rising garage door like a televangelist stepping onto the stage. He waved hugely. As though he was guiding our car along a runway and not into his flagstone drive.

'The return of the prodigals!' he announced to the night. And in the glow of the interior car light I saw Cordie roll her eyes.

'You better believe it,' Dad said under his breath, and he stepped out of the car to speak with Mr Van Apfel and the rest of us scrambled out after him so we could hear what he said.

On the drive there were two startlingly bright security lights fixed to the corners of the garage. Their beams angled together at a single point where Mr Van Apfel stood. Tiny insects buzzed around his head.

'Graham,' Mr Van Apfel pumped Dad's hand enthusiastically. 'Thanks for bringing the girls home. Carol and I hadn't planned to take them to the party – we've got the Rise Up service in the morning, you see. So if it weren't for you and Susan driving them there and picking them up afterwards, they wouldn't have got to go at all. Isn't that right, girls?'

The girls said nothing.

'It was no trouble. But look,' Dad started to say, 'tonight when I picked them up —'

But Mr Van Apfel wasn't finished.

'The Rise Up service used to start at eight-thirty but they've pushed it back slightly to nine,' he explained. 'Even then, do you think I can get these girls out of bed on time? I need to prise them out on a Sunday morning.'

He laughed and raked his fingers through his hair in mock anguish at his sleepy daughters. The insects scattered at the swipe of his hands, then immediately resumed their circling with more urgency than before.

Dad cleared his throat and looked ready to try again, when Ruth pushed past him and into the spotlight.

'Cordie sleepwalked away from the party!' she blurted. 'She disappeared and she only came back when that man-teacher returned her!'

'What?' Mr Van Apfel's eyes narrowed. 'What *man-teacher*? What are you talking about?'

The insect-circling got more violent.

'And what do you *mean* she sleepwalked away? I thought you weren't present for the sleepover part?' He spat out the words as if they were distasteful to him. As if all those 'P's were disgusting.

'Actually, that's what I need to talk to you about.' Dad spoke casually but there was an edge to his voice that I knew meant he was ready to be firm if he had to. It wasn't hard to imagine him handing out detention to his Year Nine students when they were acting like dills.

'Ruth's right,' Dad said.

Ruth blushed. It wasn't a phrase she was used to. She shot a smug smile at her sisters, but a death stare from Hannah was enough to set her straight and her smile slipped quickly to the ground.

'When I arrived to collect the girls tonight, it seems that Cordie had sleepwalked away from the party,' Dad said. 'Don't worry – she didn't get far. And Hayley's parents were both at the house for the party. They were made aware of Cordie's disappearance almost as soon as it happened.'

Mr Van Apfel looked stony.

'Anyway,' Dad went on, 'it turns out she'd wandered out the back and got herself onto Blaxland Road and then a passing car saw her and stopped and brought her back to the party —'

'It was Mr Avery,' I supplied.

'Thank you, Tikka,' Dad said.

'He's Cordie's teacher,' I said helpfully.

'Mr Van Apfel knows that, champ.'

'He replaced Mrs Harrow so 6H is now 6A. *And* he coaches the senior girls' tee-ball team.'

'All right,' Dad said. He placed his hand on my shoulder, which was his signal that I'd said enough. We practised it sometimes at home.

Mr Van Apfel listened to all of this with his fingers pressed together to form a tiny tent. His face was impassive.

'You're telling me that Cordelia's classroom teacher happened to be driving past at exactly the moment that she sleepwalked out of a party?'

He spoke slowly and enunciated every painful vowel, and it was like listening to a china plate crack. And the whole time he was talking to Dad, his eyes were fixed on Cordie. He held her there with his stare.

And Cordie said to Mr Van Apfel: 'I was wearing my cossie the whole time I sleepwalked away.' She said it casually as if daring Mr Van Apfel to disapprove.

And it was only then that I noticed she'd put a cotton dress over the top of her swimming costume to travel home. Its ruffled skirt snapped scornfully in the wind.

'I spoke with Mr Avery when he dropped Cordie back at the party,' Dad said. 'He didn't seem to have any prior knowledge of the party. Or about Cordie being out walking by herself at night.'

Mr Van Apfel visibly stiffened at this last part.

'He seemed genuinely worried about making sure Cordie was safe,' Dad said.

'Although,' Dad spoke with forced lightness now, 'I'd still report the incident to the Department if it were one of my two. Just for the record, you know?'

'To the Department?' I said. 'What Department, Dad? Is there a Department for Sleepwalking? *Really?*'

I pictured an office of cotton-wool clouds.

'The Department of Education,' Dad said gravely.

'But what about the car? And the headlights, *and the dancing!*' Ruth sounded slightly hysterical by now.

But Dad look confused.

'I don't know anything about that,' he said to Mr Van Apfel sincerely.

Then Dad said that it was time we got going. Had to be up early. Family thing in the morning. And Mr Van Apfel agreed it was late: 'We've got the Rise Up service ourselves.

'Time I got my Wandering Jew safely home,' he said cryptically. And that's when he put his hand on Cordie's neck and frogmarched her into the house.

* * *

'How long was Mr Avery's car there tonight, you reckon?' I asked Dad once we were inside our own garage at home. 'In that back lane, behind the party. How long, you reckon?'

I'd waited until Laura had gone into the house before I asked.

'Jeez, Tik, I don't know ...' Dad trailed off.

'What's your best guess?' I urged. 'Come on, Dad. *I'm eleven and one-sixth* and you don't tell me *anything*.'

And Dad yielded at that.

'My best guess? My feeling is he'd been there a while, Tik. At least an hour for his engine to cool down like that. Maybe two.' He looked thoughtful. 'Although, it was only a small car, so maybe it was less. Three cylinder that hatchback, you think?'

But even *one* hour meant Mr Avery had been parked there while Cordie danced on the verandah that night, and that the headlights that shone towards the house had been his. My stomach did a strange flip-flop.

'So the bit about him driving past and spotting Cordie sleepwalking along the side of the road ...' I said.

'Fiction as far as I'm concerned.'

'Why didn't you do anything?'

'What, to Mr Avery? Well, I spoke to him, Tik.' He scratched the back of his head thoughtfully. 'And I'll talk to your mum tonight too. See what she thinks about it.'

'See if she thinks you should report it to the Department?'

'Something like that,' he admitted.

'What about the Van Apfels?'

'Should we report the Van Apfels, too?' Dad smiled grimly at his own joke. I could tell he was trying to change the subject so he didn't have to tell me what was really going on.

'*No*,' I said. 'Why didn't you tell Mr Van Apfel about the car engine being cold.'

Dad looked flummoxed for an instant.

'I don't know, champ. Maybe I did the wrong thing.' He fiddled with his keys in his hand.

'The wrong thing?' I was stunned.

'The thing is, Tik, I was worried about getting those girls in trouble,' he said carefully. 'It's not always easy to know how their parents might react.'

* * *

The way Ruth reported it, it wasn't until later that night that the Lord visited Mr Van Apfel, who in turn came to Cordie when she was taking a bath. There he held her head under the shampoo-slick surface to cast away all of her sins. Swimming costume sins. Sleepwalking sins. (Cold–car–engines–in–red–hatchbacks sins.) He was careful to keep her cast arm dry, and it protruded like a plaster periscope. While the rest of her shameful body was submerged and washed clean. Baptism among the bath salts and the bubbles.

And when Mrs Van Apfel walked past putting the clean laundry away, she must have wondered what her husband was doing in the bathroom while their thirteen-year-old daughter was in the bath. But when she heard him talking in tongues, she knew it was the Lord's work. That he was building a temple to Jesus right there and then in the ensuite.

CHAPTER THIRTEEN

In the backyard with Mum the weekend after Hayley's
sleepover, the grass was dew damp and lush. I padded about
touching fern fronds and palms, plasticky camellia leaves. There
was a sheen to everything as if the hotter it got, the more things
here thrived. Our backyard felt wild and strange and remote.

Mum walked around the yard dropping little piles of sand,
and I trotted behind her keeping her company. 'What *is* that
stuff? It stinks worse than the river.' I watched a silty handful
slip through her fingers. A marker mound where we had done
good work.

'Blood and bone,' Mum said and she reached into the tub
for another sandy scoop. 'It's good for the garden.'

'I guess you can do it then,' I said grudgingly.

'Thank you,' Mum said. 'That's magnanimous of you.' She
didn't stop working to speak to me, just kept scooping and
depositing, bending and turning. I pressed my nose closer and
took a deep sniff.

'Peew-yooh! It *smells* like the river. Don't you think that's exactly the same smell as the river?'

Mum was looking around for her spade now and she answered without turning to face me. 'Mmm? Tikka-Likka, can you pass me that? No, next to you. That's it, ta. Funny, I hadn't noticed the river. Does it smell?'

I crouched down low next to the tub and read the label that was beginning to peel off it. 'Nitrogen, calcium, phosphorus.' It was like some kind of wonderful spell. We should have had *that* at Hayley Stinson's party – blood and bone would have brought the ghosts out.

'It says here "fish bones",' I read. 'That's why it smells fishy.'

'It's good fertiliser,' Mum said, seeing my wrinkled nose.

I sniffed again dubiously, and it got up my nose and I spluttered in surprise. It made my eyes smart and I pressed the heels of my hands into them to stop them from watering.

I moved off to sit in the shade then, squatting under the wattle tree. It was shedding dead blossoms like little burned bits of hair.

'You've got a good spot there,' Mum said. 'Nice and cool.'

But I was sweaty already, even in the shade.

Mum walked towards me a few minutes later with an armful of vines, green tendrils spilling over her arms. She dumped them in a pile near where I was sitting, then turned and headed back down the yard to cut back some more. Back and forth she went, cutting the thing back then carrying it up the yard. I twirled one of the leaves in my fingers and it was striped like a boiled lolly, with wide white strokes against the green. The next armful Mum dumped was dotted with flowers. Creamy white specks like fat in a chop.

'What is it?' I asked.

'Pain in the neck,' she answered, and as she headed back down the yard again I saw that a circle of sweat was beginning to bloom on the back of her shirt. I picked the flowers out of the heap and lined them up in a row, then changed my mind and arranged them in a flower pattern. Each individual flower was a perfect pyramid. Three prongs. Three tiny tear-shaped petals.

'Pretty,' Mum said when she returned with the next bundle. 'A flower made of flowers. I like it, Tik.'

'What do you call it?' I asked again, tucking one of the flowers behind my ear. But the flower was too tiny, and my ear was too big, and the thing disappeared behind the fuzzy shell of my ear and slid down inside my collar.

'Wandering Jew,' Mum said. 'It's such a curse. If you miss a bit then the whole thing grows back again.' Her pruning shears hung loose on a cord around her wrist, and the curved beak of them bumped against her bare skin as she walked back down the yard.

'Wandering Jew!' I said in surprise, but Mum was walking away, off to collect more armfuls. Wandering Jew was what Mr Van Apfel had called Cordie on the night of Hayley's sleepover party, and I'd looked it up in the dictionary afterwards. That was when I learned that the Wandering Jew had taunted Jesus, or maybe hit him, on his way to the cross. (The dictionary wasn't sure, on account of not having been there to see it.) But whichever one it was, what the Jew did was unforgivable. And his punishment was to wander the earth forever – no resting, no destination.

I'd shivered when I'd read it. And then I'd put the dictionary back on the sideboard where it was kept next to the dining-room table. It made me wonder what Cordie had done that was so bad, and why she wandered the earth in her sleep.

Mum came back then with another armful of vines and she dumped them on the pile.

'I've got a job for you, blossom,' she said, wiping her forehead with the back of her glove. 'Can you pop over to the Van Apfels for me and borrow my hose back? Mr Van Apfel was using it the other day to run sprinklers in the front and back yard at the same time.'

It sounded like the sort of big-deal thing he'd do. 'Why couldn't he use his hose and do them one at a time?' I asked.

'Not sure,' Mum said. 'Only, I need mine now, so can you nip over and pick it up for me?

'I'll make us some morning tea when you get back,' she added.

I stood and started to walk across the yard.

'But the Van Apfels won't be home,' I said, remembering. 'It's Sunday. They've got church this morning.'

'Damn,' Mum said, then she made a face. 'Sorry – not very holy of me. Can you just check if the hose is in their backyard, Tik? Or in the garage, if they've left it unlocked. Carol won't mind. I want to try and get all this finished this morning.'

She waved her hand across the backyard, where molehills of clippings littered the lawn.

'Okay.' I shrugged. And I turned and headed up the side path of the house and across the front lawn, and then out into the cul-de-sac.

There was no life in Macedon Close that morning. No one washed their car in their drive. There were no kids running under sprinkler archways. Even the cockatoos, pale and ghostly, took off when they saw me approach. I walked up the centre of the road, slicing the cul-de-sac up the belly.

At the Van Apfel house the curtains were pulled wide. Fresh lilies sat in a vase at the window. In fact, the only sign they'd all gone to Rise Up across the valley was Madonna, who sulked on the mat.

'Hell-ooo?' I called out. 'Cordie? Are ya home?'

Madonna looked at me with contempt.

In the front yard angel's trumpets hung heavy on their stems. There were stumpy canna lilies in violent orange rows, but nothing as interesting as Mrs McCausley's garden gnomes. And no hose either, as far as I could see. I wandered around the back to take a look.

There, the air pulsed with dry heat. The pool was disturbingly still. Except for patches where the sunshine hit the surface of the water and made it dazzle and dance. And in the shallow end an abandoned Aqua Duck butted forlornly against the steps, its crew having all walked the plank.

I hunted around in the bushes and checked along the verandah. Searched in the shade by the fence. But Mum's hose was nowhere and I was too hot. I decided to call it a day.

I was halfway along the side path of the house when I remembered what Mum had said about the garage. How I should check in there too, if it was unlocked. And that Carol wouldn't mind if I did. I eyed the side door suspiciously. It was thick and mission brown. There was a good chance it was open, even if the main roller door at the front was locked. But that wasn't the problem – the problem was Mr Van Apfel. I noticed Mum hadn't said anything about whether *he'd* care. And I wasn't going to risk getting into his bad books just so Mum could water her plants.

I walked past the door without trying the knob. Then I sidled back – it didn't have a keyhole. A door that couldn't lock. That couldn't *be* locked. Well, that was just perfect. Just what you'd expect from a street that didn't bother with fences.

For a long while I dithered. The doorknob was metal. It would be blazing hot from sitting all morning in full sun. Another good reason not to want to touch it. No, there was no way I was going into Mr Van Apfel's garage without getting his permission.

I retreated around to the front of the house and was most of the way over the crest of the drive, when I thought about Ruth meeting me out in the cul-de-sac in the mornings so we could walk to school together. I thought about the way she stood up to Jason Kenny when he ambushed the two of us the other day. Ruth, who the Lord blessed with that lip so she learned quick smart to survive (or so Mr Van Apfel assured us). *Roof.* Who backpack-slammed bullies, who spat gumnut pellets. Ruth, who could smash through her recess snack before you'd even left Macedon Close and was still willing to have a crack at yours.

Ruth wouldn't let a garage door defeat her.

I marched up the drive and back down the side path. Gripped the hot handle and twisted it hard. The door opened easily and I stumbled forward. Inside it was impossibly dark.

Once my eyes had adjusted, I found a light switch to the left of the doorframe. The bulb flickered, then it bloomed into a cool blue–white light that brought everything into focus. The Van Apfel car was missing of course. There was just a car-shaped clearing amongst the mess. Plus an oil stain the shape of North America but with the southern states missing. And crammed around the edges, resting against the garage walls, were tennis racquets and pink and purple bikes in ascending size. There were Christmas lights and a disassembled baby's bassinet. A discarded papier-mâché volcano, post-eruption. In one corner a rocking chair lay on its side where it was missing one curved wooden rocker. In another corner was the chest freezer, which Mrs Van Apfel kept stocked with meat cuts and iceblocks, and where we sent Ruth, as the youngest, to fetch our food. (That was why, I realised then, I'd never been in here before. I'd walked past this garage a thousand times or more but had never been inside. I'd never needed to. We always met the girls on the driveway, ready with our bikes.)

On the back wall there were tools of every description: hammers, pliers, saws. Each tool had its own little nail to hang from and a neat black outline showing where it should hang. Mr Van Apfel had set up a workbench there too – a simple timber worktop, covered in at the front with a piece of thin board. The bench was set far enough out from the wall for one person to fit. (It only took one man to keep the Van Apfel household running, after all.)

But when I walked back there now and stood behind Mr Van Apfel's bench, when I bent down to see if Mum's hose was on the ground, I found boxes of nails and screws, coiled cords, electrical tape. Plus a whole wall of Van Apfel girls under the bench.

The photos were taken at various stages. All showed blonde hair. Skinny limbs. Missing teeth. Some were posed, while others were more candid shots. Three daughters, frozen in an instant.

Riding a bike. Blowing out candles. Winning a ribbon. One photo was just a bare back turning away from the camera. All you could make out was a spaghetti strap and a lone strand of stringy fair hair.

I peered closer.

There was a picture of someone – was that Cordie? – balancing on a fence. Cordie waving. Cordie scowling. Cordie immortalised forever pinching an out-of-focus sister. Cordie asleep in the back of the car. There must have been fifty photos pinned to the plywood wall of that bench. But why would Mr Van Apfel hide them down there? And, wait – why did he only have photos of Cordie? There was none of Hannah or Ruth, except where they'd stumbled into a shot.

That whole board was devoted to Cordie.

I decided then that I'd seen enough. More than enough, more that I'd ever intended to see. I switched off the light and closed the garage door behind me and didn't stop running until I was home.

'Didn't see my hose then?' Mum asked when I got back. 'Never mind, I'll pop over later.'

CHAPTER FOURTEEN

'Do you still think we did the right thing?' I asked Laura.

'*You're* not doing the right thing,' she replied, and she pointed at the mugs lined up by the teapot. Black tea sat stewing in each mug. We were in the kitchen at Mum and Dad's and I had been back almost two weeks, but Laura still felt compelled to direct how I made the tea.

'Milk first,' she advised. 'Otherwise the milk heats unevenly.' In case I didn't know about whey protein denaturation. Like I didn't spend half of my life in a lab.

'Sure. Milk first,' I agreed, because what did I care if she made all the decisions? I emptied the tea into the sink and it whirlpooled darkly towards the plughole. I retrieved the milk from the fridge and then turned to face my sister with the carton in my hand. 'But do you, Lor? Do you still think we did the right thing not telling anyone Hannah and Cordie planned to run away? Don't you ever worry we might have got it wrong?'

It wasn't the first time we'd had this conversation – not by a long shot. Though it was the first time we'd had it since I'd been back. Invariably it was me who brought it up and my sister who shut it down, and then we'd both walk away feeling worse for having spoken.

'It wouldn't have made any difference if we said anything or not.' My sister spoke with precision. If we were going to have this conversation, then she wanted it over quickly. 'You know the ending to this one, Tik: they're not coming home. Nothing we did would have changed that.'

'How do you know it wouldn't?'

'How do you know it *would*?'

'The police should have had all the facts,' I said.

Laura shook her head decisively. 'It wouldn't have brought them back.'

On the table between us a packet of biscuits sat unopened. Summer sunshine streamed through the window.

'And what about Ruth?' I said.

'We didn't even know Ruth was going with them,' Laura said sharply. 'So you can't feel guilty about that.'

My sister's barometer for such things had always been two years older, two years superior to mine. And she was right of course, and at the same time she was wrong. I was responsible and not guilty. I was both things, and neither. Like the valley: a thing and a void.

I made Laura's tea the way she'd instructed. Then I stood blocking her view while I poured the hot water mutinously into my mug before I added the milk. I placed the two mugs on the table.

'Survivor's guilt, is that it? Is that what this is?' She looked pleased with herself, and with her diagnosis. 'You feel guilty you didn't disappear too.

'Anything could have happened to them that night,' she went on. 'Anything could, and anything *did*, but it's not your fault, Tik.' As she spoke I could imagine her patrolling the wards at work, keeping the dying alive. You wouldn't curl up your toes if my sister was on duty. You wouldn't dare.

'There was nothing we could have done,' she said.

Although of course there was plenty that we could have done. We could have told the police everything that we knew. We could have explained how Hannah and Cordie had planned to run away, I said, and how Mr Van Apfel was violent at home. We could have said something about Mr Avery. About the way he looked at Cordie, the way he always showed up at the same place she was. We should have told the police all that, and we should never have helped those girls try to run away in the first place. We shouldn't have encouraged them. Given them supplies.

'I didn't,' interrupted my sister.

'Fine, but you know what I mean,' I said. 'We tried to. We were wrong to speak about the plan like it was a good idea —'

'Wrong to have spoken to them at all.' Laura talked over me now. 'In fact, we should never have been friends with them in the first place, would that make it better, Tik? Would you feel exonerated then? Because that's what this is about, isn't it?'

'Don't be stupid,' I said.

On the table our mugs of tea sat stewing. The milk in my mug had separated when I added it to the boiling water and now small flecks of white swirled on the surface like floaters in front of your eyes. Maybe my sister was right about the tea. About the tea, and about everything else.

'You going to drink that or what?' she said after a while, nodding towards my mug. She spoke more gently now, and she held her head tilted slightly to one side as if she was talking to a child.

I gave a grimace and drank, and I imagined I could feel the milk clumps slide down the back of my throat.

'Really, Tik,' Laura said as I swallowed. 'It was so much bigger than us. It was beyond our control. Whole teams of police investigation units couldn't figure out where those girls went, and it's not like we could have solved that.'

Laura caught a drip running down the side of her mug.

'Anyway, what did they expect us to do?' she asked. 'We were only kids. And they were our friends.

'Mum said she and Dad lent you the money to fly back here,' she said, changing the subject. 'You broke?'

'No.'

'Need a loan?'

'No.' I shifted uncomfortably on my chair.

'Oh, Tikka,' she groaned. 'Have you quit your job?'

I hadn't quit, I told her. I hadn't done *anything*. I explained about the offer for promotion I'd deleted from my inbox before I flew out. About the conference opportunities, the research symposiums. About how I'd erased all those things when I trashed the email. As easy as hitting 'delete'.

'That new job would have got me nowhere,' I lied.

'So what are you going to do? Do you like working in the lab?'

'There are worse things,' I said defensively.

'You were the smart one, Tik,' she said. 'You could have done anything.'

'You sound like Mum and Dad.'

'Mum and Dad said you were the smart one?' she bristled.

'What? No. God, you're so competitive.'

She drank a mouthful of tea. 'You can still do anything, you know. You've got plenty of time.'

Unlike her was what she didn't say.

A breeze came through the kitchen window and in the lounge room I heard the Venetian blinds clatter. The southerly always came at this time of day. It was funny the things I remembered now that I was back. All the things you keep stored away.

'Do you ever wonder if they made it?' I asked her cautiously. 'You know, if somehow they survived?'

Laura gave me a look that said she was done, and I should save it for my therapist. 'Tikka, you're exhausting.'

'Do you, though?' I persisted. 'Do you ever think of looking for Hannah?'

I thought about the way I saw Cordie all the time. Like the other week, in the taxi going down North Avenue. I'd been so sure it was her. Right up until the instant I stood in front of the stranger on the platform at Penn-North station.

My sister surprised me then by telling me she'd tried searching for Hannah. 'I ran some ads in the personals, and in the classifieds in the *Herald*. But it was years afterwards and I never got a response.'

'Did you?' I was stunned.

She nodded. 'Cryptic ones. Silly stuff Hannah would understand.'

'Like what?' I wanted to know.

Laura thought for a moment. 'Like: "Seeking ginger-haired, female dance partner. Must be able to vogue better than the Virgin Mother. Please send photo."'

'Madonna!' I said laughing. 'That's Madonna.' I hadn't thought about the Van Apfels' cat in years.

'Did you get a reply?'

'Not from Hannah, I didn't. Plenty of weirdos got in touch, but.'

'What else?'

Laura smirked. '"Tix for sale (x2). Boxing match. Crow versus the Mouse, 8 rounds, super middleweights. See who would win *pants down*. Forward address for delivery."'

'That's not funny,' I said sulkily.

'Remember when you thought it was "pants down"?'

'Like you'd ever let me forget,' I said.

'What about the way Jade Heddingly always said "arks"?'

'And the way Ruth used to call herself "Roof".'

But the memory of Ruth sent me back into my guilt spiral and we sat in silence for a while.

'Do you remember when Ruth tried to drown me in the pool?'

Laura looked blankly at me.

'You do,' I said. 'You do remember.'

But she gave no sign that she did.

'That day, remember, when we stayed for Bible study? When Mr Van Apfel – you know, that day he hit Ruth?'

We'd swum in the pool beforehand, the five of us girls. Dreaming up synchronised swimming routines, trying to outlast one another at holding our breath. All except Cordie, who was in the water but who'd stayed firmly anchored to dry land, her cast arm resting on the edge of the pool while her legs kicked lazily in the water. Cordie was supposed to be judging our underwater handstand competition, but she wasn't even facing the right way.

'Tikka cheated,' Ruth complained when I surfaced from my turn. I blinked and pool water beaded on my lashes.

'Tikka cheated!' Ruth insisted, but no one paid any attention. 'She cheated! I saw her do it!'

I was still squinting into the milky light, still catching my breath, when Ruth reached out and pulled my head under the water. She dragged me down by my hair, one hand gripping my ponytail, the other palm smothering my face.

It never left me, the sight of the blue sky that day. Blazing between the gaps in Ruth's fingers. Blue sky in my eyes, in my ears. In my lungs. Blue sky and blue water. Iridescent as a fly.

'She did too,' my sister said now, as I reminded her of it all these years later. 'She held you under the water, that's right.' Laura swallowed the last mouthful of her tea with effort, and then went to the sink and rinsed out her mug. 'She was furious with you about something.'

'She thought I cheated. Remember?' I said. 'You had to pull her off me and drag me to the surface.'

Because Laura was the one who had wrenched me to the surface. Held my chin up while she kicked Ruth away.

'Did I?' Laura was surprised. She nudged the tap off with her elbow and shook the drips from her mug into the sink. 'I don't remember that part.'

'What, you don't remember saving me?'

She let the corners of her mouth droop while she thought about it. 'Nope.'

'Well, you did,' I said.

Laura had yelled at Ruth, telling her she could have drowned me. 'You don't hold someone's head under the water!' she'd said. 'Where'd you get a dumb idea like that?'

Ruth had been outraged. She'd swum a safe distance away, and then she'd spun and shouted back at Laura. 'But she cheated! And cheating's a sin!'

In the kitchen Laura put her mug upside down on the drying rack and faced me. Behind her, through the window, the day was impossibly bright.

'It wasn't your fault, Tik,' Laura said. 'What happened to Hannah and Cordie. It wasn't your fault. Not your fault about Ruth either. Despite what you think, none of it was because of you.'

'You're right,' I said, and in that moment I believed her.

'Sure, I'm right. So don't go blaming yourself. You're not *that* important,' she deadpanned.

But the tenderness in her voice had caught me off guard and I smiled at her with wet eyes. Twenty years had passed and I was still coming home so my sister could hold my chin up.

CHAPTER FIFTEEN

My skit was turning out to be an *unmitigated* disaster. (Extension spelling list, week six. Topic? Prefix 'un'.) For a tragedy it sure was looking grim, just not in any of the ways that I'd planned. For a start there were all the normal problems that came with writing and directing a play (uncooperative cast, unlearned lines, unavailable star). There were so many 'un's during those two weeks of rehearsals, I could have written that spelling list myself.

I thought it would be easy writing a play about a true story – one that already existed. And so as I sat down to watch the news each night at home, as Dad rustled his newspaper and Mum told Laura to get her feet off the couch, as angry courtroom scenes flashed across the TV screen, I sat with my 2B pencil and a blank piece of paper and simply transcribed each thing as it appeared.

It was four years since Lindy Chamberlain had been found innocent of killing her baby, Azaria, and had had her murder conviction quashed. Now the family was wading through a minefield of compensation.

'What's a coroner?' I asked Dad while we watched. I hadn't cast one of those in my play.

'It's a person who investigates the circumstances of someone's death. They weigh up all the evidence and then they work out how the person died. In this case, the coroner is trying to come up with an answer for how Azaria Chamberlain died.'

'What, they still don't know?'

I reckoned finding the baby's clothes near a dingo den was all the evidence anyone could ever need.

'Two inquests have been heard, Tik, but that was back before they discovered the baby's matinee jacket. That was new evidence. A lot's changed since then.'

'Like, Lindy Chamberlain's been released from prison?'

'That's right. She's been released and pardoned, but the Crown hasn't yet made a finding on who or what was responsible for the baby's death. As far as they're concerned, it's still a mystery.'

I was glad I didn't have to include all those inquests in my skit. My skit would mostly be about the night Azaria disappeared, about the dingo that stole her away.

I knew the Chamberlain story would have the right effect. Everyone in our house was *glued* to the TV whenever it came on the news. And if I wanted to give Hannah and Cordie the best chance at running away then, what better story to stage? I knew it was controversial but that was the point. I wanted to create a proper diversion.

I'd had to change it a bit so that Azaria Chamberlain was nine *years* old, instead of nine weeks old (I didn't know anyone who had a baby that small and, even if I did, you could bet they wouldn't lend her to me). I'd cast Melanie Firth in the role, even though Cordie was meant to be the lead. Cordie had the right star power for it. And she could have snuck off the stage during the disappearance in the play and no one would have suspected a thing. (It's not like the audience would have expected to see her again.)

Only *that* was the problem: we never saw Cordie. She was off sick from school so often lately. She'd been away so many days that I couldn't very well give her the lead role when she'd never been to a single rehearsal. She never even knew we were holding rehearsals, and the rest of my cast had turned up for three hopeless run-throughs at recess already.

At rehearsals we'd decided Carly Sawtell would be the dingo – we were relying on good costuming there. Sharrin Helpman and Jodi McNally would be police officers, while I read out the lines for the mum. In fact, I read out the lines for everybody's part because no one had bothered to learn them. Not even Melanie, who must have known about learning lines from her drama classes. You'd have thought she'd be more professional.

I didn't like cutting Cordie out of my play. Not even considering she hadn't known she was in it. It hurt to shove her copy of the script under my bed, with all those pink highlighted lines she never learned. But I'd hardly seen her since the night of Hayley's sleepover party, and whenever I did see her now, she was busy plotting with Hannah and Laura. Busy leaving Ruth and me out.

They were so busy *not* telling us about their runaway plan, we never got the chance to tell them we already knew.

Until the day before the Showstopper, that is. Then we got to say it all right. Only trouble was, we weren't expecting Mr Van Apfel to appear out of nowhere like that.

At first it was just Ruth and me, like always. We walked home from school together, bags heavy, hats pulled low. It was strangely silent for that time of the afternoon. The cicadas sat and quietly slow-roasted in the trees.

'I saw Mr Avery today at the bubblers,' Ruth said, and a small droplet of sweat slid out from under her legionnaire hat and worked its way down her face. I could imagine Mr Avery, there at the bubblers. Water beading on his thick beard.

'What, drinking?' I asked.

I took off my own hat and soaked it with the last of the water from my drink bottle and a deeper shade of blue bled across the cotton as it got wet. I wrung it once, then put it back on my head, and fingers of cool water pressed into my scalp.

'No, just standing,' Ruth said.

Fat beads of water clung to the brim of my hat, threatening to fall if I moved my head.

'He wanted to know why Cordie was away today,' Ruth went on, and I drew a sharp breath and the jewels of water tumbled off my hat.

'How did he know she was away?' I was aghast.

'Because she's in his class, that's why. It's his job to know who's at school and who's away.'

My cheeks burned at the indignity of being chastised by *Ruth*. Of course, if I'd thought about it for even a second I'd have known Mr Avery was Cordie's classroom teacher and so he would have marked a small cross next to her name on the roll. It was just he always acted so suspiciously, that's all.

'Anyway, why *was* Cordie away today?' I asked. 'She sick again?'

'She's a faker,' Ruth said.

We walked along in silence and two lorikeets went belting past. A flash of jungle green.

'I saw Mr Avery the other day at school too, you know,' Ruth said as we rounded the corner to Macedon Close. She spoke cautiously, warily, as if she wasn't sure she should be telling me but that we were so close to home now it might be safe to say. But I was wary now too, and I wasn't about to be outsmarted by a Year Two kid again.

'So what?' I replied. 'He works there, you know.'

But Ruth was trying to tell me something.

'No, I saw him *with* Cordie. The two of them were down beside your classroom. I saw them when we were in the playground, doing map-reading worksheets.'

My classroom stood away from the all the other classroom buildings, like a kid in the corner. In disgrace.

'What were they doing?' I wanted to know.

'Dunno. Just talking. Cordie didn't seem to be saying that much but she was laughing at him a lot.'

I thought about the two of them, down there, alone, by the rear brick pier of our classroom. Cordie, with her back leaning up against the pier, one leg raised, one sole pressed flat against the bricks. Cordie and Mr Avery. Out of sight from almost all of our school.

'Well, did you ask Cordie about it?'

Ruth shook her head. 'She'd never tell me anyway,' she said. 'It's not like they've told us about their runaway plan, and that's heaps more important than this.'

I had to admit, Ruth had a point. But that didn't mean it didn't sting.

'They'll tell us when they're ready,' I said defensively. 'They can't keep it a secret forever. They're just waiting for the right chance to say.'

Ruth looked unconvinced, but she said nothing as we crossed the top of Macedon Close together. I walked her to her drive and then turned to go home, when we heard voices drifting out of the backyard.

They were familiar voices. Plotting voices. Leaving-us-out-again voices. Ruth squared her shoulders and gripped the straps of her schoolbag.

'C'mon,' she said as she led me into battle.

I followed Ruth along the shady side passage of the house, across the roots of the peppercorn tree. When we emerged, all was sunshine and bare legs and that shimmering pool. A backyard arcadia spread before us.

There were Hannah and Laura lying side by side in the grass, discarded ice-cream wrappers beside them, their schoolbags propping up their heads like pillows, their eyes closed to the blistering sky. Cordie sat beside them. She wore a babydoll dress made of faded check cheesecloth, her brown legs stretching out long below the skirt. She wore a frangipani nicked from Mrs McCausley's yard behind one soft, tiny ear. Between her splayed legs, her pet mice played in the grass.

'What are youse doing?' Ruth announced our arrival. Her voice was accusatory and loud. Fury simmered not far below the surface. '*We* didn't know you were here together. *And you got ice creams.*'

'I didn't,' Cordie said carelessly. She raised her palms to show she was empty-handed.

But Ruth wasn't interested in Cordie's virtue now. It was too little, and it came far too late.

Ruth had been ignored and excluded. She'd been babied long enough. Missing ice cream was tantamount to sin.

She charged at the older girls, her school backpack swinging, her plait lashing like a scorpion's tail. She was headed for Cordie but then she swerved at the last instant and ran instead towards Hannah and Laura, yanking the schoolbag out from underneath Hannah's head so her skull crashed onto the grass. Hannah yelled and sat up, but Ruth ignored her. She held Hannah's bag high above her head. She swung it from side to side and then she upturned it savagely so its contents rained down on the lawn.

'Rope!' Ruth said triumphantly. 'A torch! Warm clothes! I *told* you they were running away.'

'Give it here …' yelled Hannah and she stood up and moved angrily towards Ruth.

'Give it here,' said another voice evenly. We swung around in surprise.

And Mr Van Apfel stood up from where he'd been crouched, in his red PVC gloves, scrubbing mould off his pavers.

We never heard him there, by the pool gate. Never heard the back-and-forth swish of his brush. The older girls must have known he was in the backyard, but then they'd been there before us.

Blood pulsed in my ears as he walked across the lawn, though the rest of the world fell silent. He swung an open bottle of Handy Andy original ammonia from his fingers and the smell was sickening.

'This,' he said, his face twisted in disgust as if he couldn't bear to look at us. 'This is how you treat me? *This* is your idea of "honour and obey"!'

His sleeves were rolled up for scrubbing and, emerging from his red rubber gloves, his forearms were an angry striated pink. He waved his free arm over the upturned backpack. Over its spilled guts on the lawn. Over the rope, the torch, the pile of fleecy clothes. Over the five of us. Petrified in the sunshine. Laura was still lying on her back on the grass, her head raised awkwardly in the air. Hannah was still reaching out to grab Ruth, who was busy cowering from her. Cordie sat cupping her mice in her hands, her legs still splayed in the sunshine.

Meanwhile I stood uselessly over to one side, my hat leaching water in warm trickles down my neck.

'Run?' he bellowed. '*Run?* You would *run!*'

The word sounded feebly small.

He, on the other hand, was so tall, so broad-shouldered. He loomed above us and caused an eclipse. His shadow slanted all the way across his zoysia grass and to the roots of the peppercorn tree.

Van Apfel. From the apple. From the tree of knowledge. *Mr Van Apfel knew*. He knew about the plan to try to run away, and all hell was about to break loose.

'Where did you think you would run away *to*?' His voice was dangerously low. 'Or hadn't you worked that part out yet? Go on. Tell me. Honestly, how far did you think you could get?'

For a moment no one spoke.

'I didn't think ...' Hannah started. 'I mean, we didn't want —'

He cut her off with the sweep of his hand. He wasn't interested in what Hannah had to say. His eyes were fixed on Cordie, whose eyes were fixed on her mice. She placed them down onto the grass.

'You'd never leave me,' he appealed to her.

Cordie said nothing. Either she was too scared or she wasn't sure what to say. Or maybe she never realised he was speaking to her because she never looked up from her pets.

'You won't leave,' he said again, looking directly at her. Willing her to agree. 'Say it. Say you won't leave. Go on, say it now.' He sounded hurt. Almost whiny. And the wounded tone that had crept into his voice was what frightened me most of all.

Between her legs, Cordie's mice crawled and sniffed at the grass. She had trained them to stay when she let them out of their cage. Even for pets, they were incredibly tame. Maybe *that's* what enraged Mr Van Apfel in the end.

The fact Cordie wouldn't say what he was asking of her. The fact she had more control over her mice than he had over his daughters. And when Cordie finally turned her face to him, she saw Mr Van Apfel upturn the bottle he'd been carrying and empty it over her pets.

Cordie screamed and propelled herself backwards on her hands, away from the falling liquid. Drops of ammonia splattered onto her legs. Beside her, her sisters stood wild-eyed in terror. One mouth gaping, the other clamped shut. On the grass there was squealing. High-pitched mewling. Blind mice panicked in the bright daylight. Except for one mouse, which fell still in a matter of seconds, its tiny body rigid, its legs taut. It was full stride like a carousel animal.

Cordie moaned and shook her head: 'No. No, no, no.'

She reached out and scooped up the remaining three mice. Tried to wipe them clean on her check dress. She cradled them to her chest, where the fabric started turning pink. Those mice weren't even three check-squares long.

Mr Van Apfel looked worn down by Cordie now. A grim sheen appeared on his upper lip. As if he was exhausted by her constant failure to satisfy what it was he was asking of her. He turned his bottle the right way up.

'Cordelia,' he said, 'I'll deal with you later.' Ammonia and disgust dripped from his red gloves.

'They're dead,' Cordie said dully, ignoring her dad. She uncupped her shaking hands and the three last mice lay silent and stiff, their dead bodies cutting a path across Cordie's open palms.

'I think,' Mr Van Apfel said in a voice that was at once recognisable as the one he normally used, and also shockingly calm, 'that it might be time for Laura and Tikka to go home.' Like it wasn't too late to make a start on our homework, maybe catch some cartoons on TV. And I wondered if the Van Apfel girls might like to do the same thing. To walk up the side of the house and across the drive, head down the slope of Macedon Close as though none of this had just happened. To let themselves believe that everyone's parents were violent like this and today was simply the day they'd grown bored of it.

Laura picked up her schoolbag and threw Hannah a look that said everything and nothing all at once. I was still carrying my bag – had never taken it off – and I went and took my place next to my sister.

'I'll walk you out, girls,' Mr Van Apfel announced. 'I'm headed for the garage myself.'

And nobody spoke as he retrieved his scrubbing brush from where he'd left it on the pavers. He carried it in the same hand as his bottle. And Laura and I followed him into the shade at the side of the house.

'I'll leave you here, girls,' Mr Van Apfel said as we reached the roller door to the garage, and we nodded dumbly and walked up the drive. And there, at the top, Dad's car swung into the cul-de-sac as if he'd been waiting around the corner for us all along.

'*Dad!*' I shouted with relief. I waved him over the curb. The car windows were wound down into their sills and the aluminum casting framed his face.

'Tikka-Likka,' he greeted me. He smiled at Laura. 'Like a ride?'

We slid into the back of the car.

'You two are quiet this afternoon. What's going on?' he joked. 'Cat got your tongues?'

In the back seat Laura placed her hand over mine. 'I won't tell,' I mouthed in defence. But Laura shook her head and I

195

realised she wasn't trying to silence me. Only that she wanted to hold my hand just as much as I needed her to.

Dad released the handbrake, ready to drive off, when Mr Van Apfel appeared at the top of the drive. He waved and for one moment I was worried he was going to come over.

'Graham!' he said to Dad, as if Dad was the very person he'd been hoping to see. His wide mouth broke into a comradely grin. Beside me, Laura shrank back in her seat.

'Thanks for having the girls,' Dad called out, then he paused and leaned further out of the car window. 'I take it they've just come from your place?'

Mr Van Apfel smiled worse than before.

'Impossible to keep track of, aren't they?' he commiserated.

Dad returned Mr Van Apfel's smile awkwardly. Then he waved and steered our car down the slope using his free hand, while Mr Van Apfel walked over the crest of his drive like the sun setting on another God-given day.

* * *

Lor and I never told anyone what we witnessed that day, so no one could be blamed for not knowing. (Though Mrs Van Apfel must have wondered why the aquarium in her laundry sat empty, and where Cordie's mice had got to.) I guess I figured if I never said the words out loud, then maybe the terrible things we saw never really happened. So we kept our mouths closed, like we squeezed our eyes shut.

Our family of four blind mice.

CHAPTER SIXTEEN

The day of the school Showstopper — like every other day — the sky was blue and clear. It had been windy in the night and the she-oaks had shaken off their needles. They lay on the ground like brown entrails we couldn't read.

I waited for Ruth, like always, at the signpost to our street. Where the letters of 'Macedon Close' grew more faded by the day, and where Ruth would show up and ask what I had for recess. But Ruth never showed and neither did Cordie, even though I waited for longer than usual. Then Mr Van Apfel emerged from the house on his own, and anyone could see that spelled trouble.

Mr Van Apfel was carrying things out to his car and loading them into the back. The station wagon was nose in, but whoever had parked it hadn't taken it flush up against the back wall of the garage, so its blue boot hung out onto the flagstone paving like a gut hanging over a belt.

'Morning, Tikka!' he waved to me. Then he leaned back against the car and swung one ankle over the other, folding his arms confidently across his chest. A sea of black bitumen floated between us.

'Waiting for my two?' he asked.

I was, I replied. For Cordie and Ruth (if Cordie was coming to school for a change).

'They're not feeling well, I'm afraid,' he called across to me. 'They're both going to stay home with Mrs Van Apfel today.'

He motioned for me to come over to his car. I glanced down the street but there was no one around, and I figured I didn't have much choice but to do what Mr Van Apfel said.

'Whatcha got in there?' I asked him warily as I approached the open boot of his car. He had the rear seats folded down and the whole back section of the car was piled high with junk. There were ring-binder folders and bundled-up brochures. A box overflowing with papers. Plus three long black bags zipped securely to the top.

'In here? You mean the bags?' Mr Van Apfel laughed and patted the bags. They caved easily under the weight of his hand. 'Those are Mrs Van Apfel's. She's donating old curtains for the concert so I'm dropping them off at the school.'

'For the Showstopper?'

'That's the one. The Showstopper concert. I hope your parents are going to be there?'

'Yeah,' I replied, and I thought about my skit. We had a lot to get through at today's rehearsal.

'Then your parents are in luck, Tikka!' He beamed at me. 'Because Mrs Van Apfel and I are bringing along some brochures to hand out tonight. They're for our upcoming *Salvation!* service at the Hope Revival Centre.' He picked up a pamphlet and fingered the embossed words on the front. A golden sun rose out of the deep 'v' in *Salvation!*. The rest of the card sat in black, matte-finish sin.

'Okay,' I said uncertainly.

The girls were still going to the Showstopper then, if Mr and Mrs Van Apfel would both be there. They would hardly trust them to stay home on their own now, all things considered.

'We're holding the *Salvation!* service in the worship hall next week.'

'Okay.'

'You'll make sure you tell your mum and dad, won't you?'

'Okay.'

'*Salvation!* service. You got that, Tikka? Do you want to write it down so you don't forget?'

I had it, I assured him. I was good at remembering. I never forgot when it was important.

'Well then, have a good day, Tikka,' he said. 'Ruth and Cordie will be back at school on Monday.'

'What about tonight? They going to the Showstopper, too?'

I shouldn't have asked; I knew as soon as I said it. Laura was always telling me I gave things away. (That was probably why they didn't tell me about the Showstopper Runaway Plan in the first place. That, and they were just being mean.)

But Mr Van Apfel didn't flinch.

'They'll be there, Tikka. My girls have got some repenting to do,' he said. 'They can hand out pamphlets for me at the show.'

He smiled. Then he turned back to his boot and started rearranging his brochures, whistling contentedly to himself.

It was the only time during our conversation that Mr Van Apfel gave any sign yesterday afternoon had happened. The mice, the ammonia. *The runaway plan.*

I headed over the crest of the drive. I would walk to school on my own.

'They'll be walking out the door at the Showstopper tonight!' he called to my back and for one awful instant I thought he was talking about his girls.

I turned.

'The brochures,' he said, and he held one up for my benefit. 'The brochures will be walking out the door.'

'*Salvation!* service,' I promised. 'I've got it, Mr Van Apfel.'

He nodded approvingly as I crossed the street.

* * *

We had a dress rehearsal the morning of the show and we paid our two-dollar toll to ride the bus to the pit of the valley. I sat behind Melanie Firth and watched her ponytail bounce. The road got rougher the closer we got to the river. I'd made a prop for my skit from cut-up cardboard boxes that I'd got out of Mrs McCausley's recycling bin. It was supposed to represent The Australian Bush, where my tragedy would take place. So I'd painted it lime green and stuck crepe-paper leaves on it. Even then it looked more like seaweed. And the word *Tupperware* still floated persistently to the surface like something dead showing up in the river.

'Going to a Tupperware party?'

Jason Kenny smirked as he walked past me down the aisle of the bus on his way to the back seat. He was in a group of boys, all ramming and shoving and trying to knock one other off course. I gripped my prop tighter when they went past.

'It's for my *skit*,' I said to Jason's back, but I don't know why I bothered.

I shuffled closer to the window. When we got down onto the flat the road was straight and long and you could see the amphitheatre rear up in the distance. There it was: that slab of stage, those shallow concrete steps. The Gothic arch, where our bus pulled up now. That arch stood like flotsam marooned by the tide. Just looking at it gave me the shivers.

In the car park the wind was blowing the right way for a change, so the smell of the mangroves folded back on itself. It was high tide and the waves had swallowed most of the shore. In places the water threatened to spill over onto the grass and it lapped at the edge of the oval. But that didn't stop the boys heading straight over with their football.

I was crossing the car park in the direction of the stage when Melanie Firth stepped in front of me with her friends and the three of them stood in a row, blocking my path.

'Give us a hand, would you?' I said, pushing my cardboard tree towards them.

Six eyeballs rolled slow. Four arms looped in chains.

'We're not here to give you a hand,' Melanie said.

Melanie Firth stood in the middle of the three so that both of her arms were linked through an elbow belonging to someone else. The backs of her hands met again at a place high on her stomach and they were pale and smooth, the skin taut over her beautiful bones.

'Then why are you here?' I asked.

'We heard a rumour,' Melanie said. 'And we want you to tell us if it's true.'

'How should I know?' I picked up my prop and started to move towards the stage.

'Because it's about your friend Cordelia Van Apfel. So we reckon you *will* know, and we reckon that you're going to tell us too.'

Had I heard that Cordie didn't break her arm falling out of that tree? That she jumped – it was *deliberate*, Melanie said. Trent Rainer saw the whole thing when he was doing the edges of the garden next door. Trent saw Cordie jump and he saw how she landed. Any reason she might try and land on her stomach?

'But she didn't,' I corrected. 'She landed on her arm. That's how she broke it.'

Didn't Melanie know anything?

'Yeah, but she only put her arm out at the very last second. She was trying to go belly-first. Trent said. He saw her do it.'

I hadn't heard that rumour, I told Melanie.

'You sure?' She smiled meanly and she gave me several seconds to think it over.

'And anyway, it's hardly a rumour when there was a witness and everything, so why are you asking me?' I said and I cursed her softly under my breath. But she heard it and it only made her smile even more.

'Go to hell,' she mimicked, and she laughed.

'Mr Avery said there is no hell,' Carly Sawtell told us. She was standing next to Melanie and she scratched the back of her calf with her other foot as she spoke, then wobbled and threatened to bring the chain down.

'When?' I challenged.

'At softball training.'

'As if.'

'He did.'

'What's hell got to do with softball anyway?'

But Carly Sawtell didn't know the answer to that. She'd been moved to the outfield by then, where Mr Avery's blaspheming didn't reach.

'So is it true or not?' Melanie said. She tapped her foot when she spoke and the girl on her left copied her, so then Carly Sawtell joined in, and all three of them tapped like the tapping was something catching.

I glanced around the oval for a teacher.

But after we'd arrived that morning a second busload had pulled up near the arch and more and more kids had been fed through its mouth and onto the oval and they'd spread out across the park until the oval was more movement than stillness, more blue uniforms than brown grass. I couldn't see a teacher anywhere.

'I dunno,' I said darkly. 'No one told me. Maybe you should ask Cordie yourself.'

'Maybe I will,' Melanie said loftily. 'Maybe you should ask her too. Maybe you should ask her why she'd want to do a thing like that.'

* * *

We missed our chance for a dress rehearsal that morning because we were sent back to school, prematurely, on the bus. All because the Year Six boys tried to make a campfire with a Bic lighter and a homework stencil and they burned a small island of charred grass beside the oval before anyone could stop them. After that, we were ordered back onto the bus and dress rehearsals were abandoned.

'You haven't seen our skit yet,' I pointed out to Miss Elith.

But Miss Elith knew that, thank you Tikka. And what's more, she wasn't happy about it. She didn't like the idea of us going on stage cold.

'I dunno, I reckon it'll be hot, Miss Elith,' I assured her, 'it's *blazing* out here today.'

But Miss Elith was cross that the dress rehearsal had been cancelled. And also she'd had enough talk of fires for one day, and it was time to get back on the bus.

* * *

After our failed dress rehearsal we went back to school and back to our classroom, where Mrs Laguna pulled the blinds down low. She turned on the fans and said we could do quiet reading, or quiet drawing, or quiet work with the Cuisenaire rods. Quiet seemed to be the operative word. We were too revved up about the Showstopper that evening to do any real work, Mrs Laguna said.

'Can I do a job for you, Mrs Laguna?' I stood by her desk and asked.

And Mrs Laguna sighed like she'd known the question was coming.

'Follow me,' she said. Mrs Laguna only had one job available for a sensible person that afternoon and that job was tidying up the storeroom where the art supplies were kept.

The storeroom was a small, airless annex tucked behind the blackboard at the front of our classroom. It stared out over the back fence of the school. And so that afternoon I sat happily in the storeroom, stacking pots and paints and brushes and tubes, and just generally being useful. There were half-a-dozen pigeonholes built into the wall of the storeroom, and each hole held a new mess for me to untangle. I arranged all the paints in ascending colour and sorted pelts of fuzzy fabric according to size and shade. There were Chinese takeaway containers filled with mismatched scraps of paper and tubs of fat-bottomed Perkins Paste with their insides oozing out. I even found a box of rosemary left over from Remembrance Day last month. Each piece was stabbed through with a safety pin so we could attach it to our uniforms. But the rosemary was brown and curled now, and the leaves looked like the claws of tiny dead birds sticking in the air. I left the rosemary and spent a long time separating the paddle-pop sticks from the pipe cleaners and bundling them up in rubber bands.

It took a while but eventually I got bored. And sweaty. And my legs started to ache.

I stood and stretched, and when I did I found a large tub of raw pasta shells hidden behind the wastepaper bin. We'd used that pasta back in term one when we'd made designs that we glued onto paper. Now, though, I opened up the tub and discovered there were still hundreds of pieces of pasta in there. All sorts, not just macaroni but bows and shells and half-moons and spirals, all brittle and smelling like dust. Some pieces had been dyed with food colouring and they were deep blues and greens, lurid yellows and reds. I lay on my stomach and fished through the tub, letting the shapes slide through my fingers like Bakelite jewels. I began sorting through them, making piles on the carpet. Blue tubes, red spirals, green bows. I separated the shells into two different sizes. Laid spaghetti lines all in a row. At one point, without thinking, I popped a piece into my mouth and it tasted like nothing and broke easily between my molars. Then I heard Mrs Laguna tell the class that they had ten minutes left until they had to pack up their desks for the day. I needed to start tidying up.

But instead of putting the pasta back in the tub I stayed where I was, flat on the floor, and began destroying the mounds of colours and shapes I had made. Next I smoothed the blue tubes into a line as flat as sky. I laid red spirals into a road – Blaxland Road – that long line that ran through our suburb, and I planted green bows on either side. The yellow bits could be houses and shops, I decided. I built the whole road and some of its offshoots before I started on Macedon Close. There was Mrs McCausley's place and the Van Apfels' house, standing sentry on either corner. Then lower down, our house backing onto the bush.

I'd built most of our side of the ridge before I sat up and saw what I couldn't see when I was lying on the ground. Inside the tub of pasta, a minuscule black leg. Or was it a snout? It was straight and stick-like, but flared at the end like some sort of sucker. Then I saw more and more suckers, more stick arms and stick legs. They were crawling, scrounging, slipping. It was swarming with *weevils*. They were down in the dregs, away from the light, where I hadn't seen them when I first found the tub. I watched as they climbed across each other, not caring where they trod. I yanked my hand back in horror, trying to shake off the germs. I wiped my fingers frantically on my tunic and ran to tell Mrs Laguna. I had never seen anything so gross.

Mrs Laguna was cranky when I told her what I'd found, but even more annoyed when she saw my suburb spread out across the carpet. 'You were supposed to be tidying up, Tikka. Not making more mess!' She swept away my suburb with the instep of her shoe, with all the force of a natural disaster. I helped Mrs Laguna scoop the pasta back into the tub and seal it up for the cleaners. But my skin crawled for the whole of my long walk home without Ruth.

* * *

The evening of the Showstopper was somehow hotter than ever. As if the dial had been turned up to ten. When we left the house and headed out to the car the sky burned with the kind of last-ditch heat that comes at sunset. My stomach churned in a way that it was impossible to tell if it was performance nerves or too much pineapple pizza. And when Dad backed up the drive, we seemed to be headed straight for the sun. Dry air blasted in my window and I sat back in disgust.

We had just straightened up, engine in gear, nose aimed out of Macedon Close, when Cordie came running towards us. She appeared at my open window and I pulled back in surprise. Sunshine made the whites of her eyes dance.

'Cordie!'

That same instant Mum yelled: 'Graham, stop!' And Dad fell on the brakes and the car jerked to a stop.

'Can I come in the car with youse?' Cordie said and her cast clunked against my car door.

'Christ, Cordelia! Where'd you spring from?' Dad said.

She thumbed towards her own car that was sitting in the Van Apfels' drive at the top of the cul-de-sac. There were bodies piled in it, though no noise was coming out. You could just about make out three blonde heads inside. Meanwhile, Mr Van Apfel stood half in and half out, one leg on the drive, the other swallowed by the car. He was smiling but his mouth was pulled tight at the corners.

'Please?' Cordie begged.

One word. But enough to answer our questions. One word to tell us the world. Things were not right in the Van Apfel household and Cordie was still doing all she could to get away.

'Are you still – Do we —' Laura didn't know how to pose the question in front of Mum and Dad. Instead she held up her purse to show she had her money with her as planned. She was all set to meet Hannah and Cordie in the clearing if they wanted. All the muscles were tensed in the side of her neck.

Dad said, 'Let me check with your parents, Cordie,' and he leaned on his windowsill to call out across the road. But

Mr Van Apfel yanked his head towards the back seat of his own car — *Get in* — before Dad got the chance to speak.

Cordie's face collapsed.

'It's okay, sweetheart,' Mum said, turning to face us in the back. 'We're all going to the same place. We'll see you again in five minutes at the show.'

Cordie nodded and waited until Mum turned around, and then she dropped a scrap of paper in my lap. It fluttered as it fell and landed right side up: *Go*.

Laura's head snapped to attention. 'So you're still going —' she started saying.

But Cordie was already gone. She turned and ran back up to the top of the street. At the car she hesitated as if daring her dad to say something.

Then she slipped inside with her sisters and they rearranged themselves on the back seat. As we drove away I stuck my head out the window in case any of the Van Apfel girls waved. But despite the heat, despite the fact that they had no airconditioning in their car, the windows were wound right to the top and there were no fingers waggling goodbye.

* * *

The car park was nearly full when we arrived in the valley. It would be showtime in a little less than an hour. Right when the dusk turned into the dark. The older girls had planned it well. Dad swung the car into one of the last empty spaces and I craned my neck to watch the Van Apfels arrive.

Their car stopped a few spaces up from ours. Laura and I got out and waited for the girls.

'We're going to go and get our seats in the amphitheatre while there's still some left,' Mum said to me. 'Big crowd tonight, Tik. You going to be okay?'

I nodded grimly.

'Break a leg,' Dad said. And I knew it was just theatre talk, but the last thing we needed was more broken bones.

My sister stood beside me, by the archway to the amphitheatre, while we watched the Van Apfels' sky-blue station wagon for a sign that the girls might emerge. Mrs Van Apfel got out first. Then Mr Van Apfel, then Hannah and Ruth. Hannah carried something under one arm, but from this distance it was impossible to say what. Cordie had been last in so she'd got the short straw: she'd been made to clamber over Ruth and forced to sit in the middle seat. Now she was the last one out. And when she appeared she looked too pale and too old, as if she'd travelled much further than just down the bends to the valley. She stood and moved over towards her sisters, and then the three of them shuffled across the car park, kicking up gravel and dust. Grey puffs of it hid their feet and half of their shins like they were already being erased. Their eyes were downcast as if searching for their feet. They trailed behind their parents.

When Mr and Mrs Van Apfel walked past Laura and me, Mrs Van Apfel nodded hello. Mr Van Apfel smiled broadly and passed me a pamphlet. *Salvation!* it guaranteed brightly.

'Thanks,' I replied and I slipped the flyer into my back pocket until I could work out what I was supposed to do with it.

'You could put some flyers on Mrs McCausley's table,' I said helpfully. 'Because she's setting up over there.'

I pointed to where Mrs McCausley had erected a fold-out table on the grass that stretched between the car park and the amphitheatre and where she was now handing out Tupperware brochures.

'Hers is for the new Airtight Alright range,' I explained because Mrs McCausley had told me earlier that week how the Showstopper was a sales opportunity. Just like she'd described how the new range came in four dishwasher-safe pastel colours.

'She'd let you share her table,' I assured Mr Van Apfel, ignoring the fact it was covered with candy-coloured plastic samples.

But Mr Van Apfel told me that what God promised didn't require a fold-out table on the grass, and to prove it he handed a flyer to Mr Gonski as he walked past.

'Like bloody election day,' Mr Gonski complained. 'At least when you vote they give you a sausage.'

Mr and Mrs Van Apfel continued walking towards the amphitheatre, a thick bundle of pamphlets tucked under Mr Van Apfel's arm.

The girls scuffed past in their parents' wake. Cordie held loosely to the back of Hannah's shirt with her cast arm, while her good arm dangled by her side. She wore her hair out and flipped over to one side in a style we hadn't seen before, but that everyone would copy by Monday.

'You busted?' Laura spoke low to her friend.

'Tell you later,' Hannah said urgently. She had a giant bag of popcorn tucked under one arm. The bag was made of plastic and it was comically large, almost a sack, so that the back end of the bag wobbled from side to side as Hannah walked, like a happy dog wagging its tail.

'What? It's for watching the show,' she said defensively when she saw me eyeing the bag. I noticed she spoke loudly enough so that her parents might hear.

'What happened after we left?' Laura said desperately.

But Hannah looked nervously at the backs of her parents. They were maybe ten steps ahead on the path.

'Where's your stuff?' Laura asked.

'Going without it. Just got the popcorn.'

'Still going?' Laura was shocked. Like she didn't have a scrap of paper in her pocket that instructed *Go* in Cordie's scrawled handwriting. As though Laura hadn't helped plan the whole thing, hadn't brought her purse along. The reality of running away was hitting home.

'We're going all right,' Cordie said fiercely.

'And Ruth?'

'*All of us*,' Ruth said.

'Not you,' Hannah hissed. 'It's not safe for *you*.' She said it too loudly then dropped her voice low. 'Not you, Ruth. You're not coming.'

'So how —' Laura started saying.

But Hannah interrupted. 'You gonna meet us or what?'

'Yeah.'

'Promise?' Hannah said urgently.

'Promise,' Laura said but she sounded uncertain. She inclined her head towards Mr and Mrs Van Apfel, who were almost at the amphitheatre steps. 'But they know you're going to run ...'

'They don't know *when*,' Hannah said. She spat the word out. 'They've got no idea it's tonight. Got our money?'

Laura patted her pocket to show that she did.

'Give it to them now,' I said to Laura.

My sister shook her head pityingly at me. 'Too risky,' she whispered because it was clear I didn't understand. But I wonder, looking back, if she wasn't deliberately missing her chances. And that by holding on to the money she was trying to keep hold of the girls.

'I'll still meet you at the clearing during the —'

Mr Van Apfel looked back at us sharply and Laura stopped mid-sentence. In her panic, she took a step back and Cordie's note fell from her pocket. It pinwheeled to the ground and landed on the grass, and for one awful instant nobody moved.

Then Mr Van Apfel motioned to the girls and they shuffled after him, and Laura bent down and cleaned up the note.

* * *

Backstage Miss Elith was in a tizz. But because it was an open-air amphitheatre, and because it was in the valley, 'backstage' was just the space behind the toilet block that stretched out and across the stumpy grass until it bumped up against the mangroves. *Whump*.

Mrs Van Apfel's curtains were used as blackout sheets that hung at the rear of the stage but they too looked hopelessly amateur. The curtains sagged in the top corner and they were too threadbare to hold back the sunset. You could see Miss Elith easily through the thin threads. Her jerky hands, her slumped shoulders. Her busy, big-curled head.

I peered past the curtain and saw she was wearing black backstage trousers and a T-shirt to match. *Showstopper* the shirt was trying to say in flamboyant lettering. But most of the letters were lost down the sides of Miss Elith's terrifying chest. *Ho-top* it said in her case.

There was a handful of chairs backstage, and a table covered in costumes and sheet music. Plus a tape deck, its useless cord snaking through the grass. No power in the pit of the valley. The dancers could only dance for as long as the fat batteries in the back of the tape deck lasted. (Luckily, a generator powered all of the lights.)

Mrs Walliams and the Senior Girls and Boys Choir were doing vocal warm-ups backstage, windmilling their arms as they sang. I watched as Mitchell Lorimer cracked Mitchell Ivamy across the back of the head with his windmill and then pretended to Mrs Walliams that it was an accident. Everywhere girls in leotards writhed, moving in synch with music that played only in their heads as they exorcised something trapped inside their Lycra. Instruments were tuned. They squeaked and honked. Someone practised the same four-note refrain over and over and still couldn't get it right.

But mostly kids played handball or Stuck in the Mud. Jacob Hunter had a Game Boy and there was a queue to watch him play. Jade Heddingly stood in line even though she had her own Game Boy at home.

I went to look at the audience sitting in the amphitheatre. The mums and dads and nannas and grandpas and neighbours and brothers and sisters. They pooled on the steps like the rainwater used to do, back in the days when it still rained. Some people had brought picnic blankets and some had brought food. They looked like they were settling in for the night. One family had cold sausages wrapped in foil and a whole loaf of bread, and they were taking slices fresh from the bag and passing sausage sandwiches along the line.

Mum, Dad and Laura were sitting near the back (an easy getaway for Laura later in the evening). The three of them were perched on our tartan picnic blanket, its pattern reassuringly familiar. The Rotary Club was here. So was Reverend Richmond, who insisted on being invited to everything but who always fell asleep long before it finished. I saw the Gonskis, in matching deckchairs strung with sunny yellow material. Pineapples doing the hula. Mrs McCausley sat off to one side, at a safe distance from the whole production, of which no doubt she didn't approve. In front of her a large family had brought their dog along, a lovely rusty-red one that lay still and satisfied in the last of the sunshine, but which perked up when its owners called: 'C'mere.' There were pairs of Year Six girls weaving through the crowd, rattling tin fundraiser cups. Sticking their noses in the air in the way Year Six girls do. Like it was the audience, not the river, causing the stink.

The fundraiser cups were red with handles and a slit in the top, and the girls stood, hand on hip, until people fed their spare change through the hole. Then they moved along to the next person in the row. I stood and watched the Year Sixes fleece the audience for a while. Until the sinking feeling in my stomach got too much for me and I took myself off to the river. By then the sunset was the same scarlet red as the fundraising cups. That horizon was an unholy red.

* * *

Down by the mangroves it was cool and still. I walked in as far as I could without getting my shoes wet, then I took them off and left them on a branch. I walked the rest of the way down to the water barefoot, and tiny bubbles foamed in the footprints I left.

Back in the amphitheatre someone spoke excitedly into a microphone but reception was bad in the valley. The words came out staccato sharp – some syllables evaporated altogether – as the sound system dropped in and out. After a while applause dribbled in through the trees and I realised they must have been starting. And even though my skit wasn't on until almost the end of the show my stomach started twisting itself into knots. I was on in the second half. After Caitlin Willesee with her ribbon and Jacob Hunter with his trombone. But before the Senior Girls and Boys Choir did their encore. That meant I could stay down in the mangroves a while longer and no one would notice. So I stayed and watched the tide arrive on tremulous waves. Then I went and collected my shoes off the branch where I'd left them and walked slowly back.

Miss Elith was sitting backstage with her nose practically pressed against the black backdrop curtain. She was rooted to her chair, her feet flat on the ground. Whatever catastrophe Miss Elith was expecting on stage, she was determined that she'd see it first.

'Tikka!' she said when I got close enough. 'Where have you been?'

She didn't wait for an answer. Instead she directed me to sit and wait with the rest of the second-half acts. She waved an arm in the direction of the row of chairs behind her without shifting her eyes from the stage.

'Actually, Miss Elith, I've got to go and get something for my skit. I left it with my sister in the audience ...'

It would be interval soon and I wanted to see Hannah and Cordie before they left. One last time. Just to say goodbye. And to check they had everything they'd need to run away and to ask when they thought they'd be back.

But Miss Elith said no. And that I'd have to do without it. And that it couldn't be that important if I forgot it in the first place. Then she watched me until I took my place in the queue, next to the members of the Senior Girls and Boys Choir.

It was almost dark by then and the lights at the oval had been switched on. They sent down eerie green beams. The amphitheatre stage was lit too. Only, from underneath. Like a torch underneath the performers' chins. The wind had picked up and it rippled across the river and the mudflats, carried mangrove stink across the oval. The smell settled in the dell of the concrete amphitheatre. It hung heavy over the stage.

'We thought you weren't coming,' accused Melanie Firth when I took my seat in the queue with my cast.

'Director's stuff,' I lied. As if Melanie would care.

Next to Melanie, Carly Sawtell was doing her best to look like a dingo in yellow flannelette pyjamas and yellow gardening gloves and a cut-up egg-carton nose. But the PJs were baggy in the seat and they'd started to pill, and the egg-carton pulp was going soft from over-handling. So mostly Carly looked like fuzzy custard instead of a wild dog.

Next to her, Sharrin Helpman and Jodi McNally were interchangeable in their matching blue school-sport tracksuits. Their toy handcuffs were the only sign to the audience that they should be seen as the police. In fact, the only believable part of our play was Melanie Firth as my daughter (she had enough contempt for me in real life that she could carry it off on stage). But for now the four of us sat silently next to the choir and watched the show from behind, through Mrs Van Apfel's thin blackout curtain.

'What are you singing?' I asked a girl from the choir.

'"I am Australian",' she said self-importantly.

They were hardly going to sing anything else.

Then Caitlin Willesee finished her ribbon dance and arrived backstage out of breath, her ribbon wound in a loose turquoise loop running from her thumb up to her elbow. Jacob Hunter and his trombone were up next. Sharp, raspy blasts all the way to Tipperary. But when he got to the end he started back at the beginning and I began to wonder whether the Van Apfel girls would even need my skit. They'd probably made it interstate on Jacob Hunter's trombone alone (could probably hear it over the border as well).

Then all too fast it was time to line up, side of stage. I felt sick but I couldn't say with what. Fear? Nerves? With anticipation? (With the knowledge that we'd never had a single successful run-through of my play and that no one, bar me, knew their lines?) Or just plain dread that Hannah and Cordie were going and that they were leaving the rest of us behind?

I shivered and Carly Sawtell saw me do it. 'Someone's walking over your grave,' she informed me.

Mr Avery emerged then, from the dark, from the wings. Waiting to shepherd us onto the stage. It was his job to usher everyone up the concrete steps and make sure that nobody tripped. And when he saw me reach for my prop – my cardboard tree, cut out of Tupperware shipping boxes – he smiled and pointed at its crepe-paper leaves.

'Ah, Birnam Wood comes to Dunsinane,' he said.

I nodded, even though I had no idea where Duns was or why you would go there again. And behind me Carly whispered: 'Weirdo. He must have learned that in jail.'

Then somebody started shoving and the line of performers lurched forward. It steadied itself, but only in the instant before we fell. In the audience a dog barked and someone called out: 'C'mere.' Then Mr Avery said: 'Right, Tikka, you're on.' The lights dimmed and I stepped onto the stage and took a deep breath.

CHAPTER SEVENTEEN

On stage I swam through the darkness with one hand outstretched until I brushed against the black backdrop sheet. I plonked my prop by its folds in the centre of the stage, but a southerly wind swirled and threatened to fell my tree. I could hear Melanie Firth whispering to Carly Sawtell. Then a new voice snaked under the veil of black cotton that hung at the rear of the stage.

The voice said the Showstopper concert had run over time so we'd have to cut our skit in half.

'*In half?*' I said incredulously. The whole idea was to provide a distraction, not to hurry the show to an end. 'Anyway, which half am I supposed to choose, Miss Elith? You can't have the ending without a beginning, and the audience needs an ending, you know.'

But Miss Elith didn't care. She had chairs to stack and lights to pack away for the hire company to collect. After 10 pm, you paid time and a half.

'Choose the beginning or the ending and stick to it,' Miss Elith said. Her voice was steely through the thin sheet. 'But we've only got time for one half, Tikka. I'm timing.' She disappeared again.

I hurried over to the wings of the stage to ask Mr Avery to turn on the lights. But side-of-stage was empty and Mr Avery was gone and the stage lights sprung on seemingly by themselves.

'We're starting in the middle,' I hissed to my cast as I jogged across the stage and positioned myself at the centre. 'Act two, page three. I've got the first line.' They'd have to take their cues from me.

I ran a critical eye over them. There was Melanie Firth, hand on hip, mouth in a pout. She was standing by a schoolbag, which was meant to represent a camping backpack but really she looked like she was waiting for the bus.

There were Sharrin Helpman and Jodi McNally, clutching the cuffs proudly between them like they were gripping the arms of a trophy.

Then there was Carly dressed as a dingo, not that anyone could tell. Her yellow flannelette pyjamas sagged gently at the knees. Her gardening gloves must have belonged to her mum because each digit ended long after Carly's fingers finished, and when she stopped moving the gloves beckoned bashfully.

I was still standing there surveying my cast, when the wind rushed in and shook the blackout curtain by its shoulders. It gusted across the stage and knocked my cardboard tree flat, its crepe-paper leaves lifeless, its *Tupperware* backside blazing at the night sky.

'Timber!' someone in the audience called out, and all around them people began to laugh. I dragged the tree upright. This was hardly the tone I was after. But as soon as I had the tree standing, it blew down again and the audience cheered like it was part of the show. 'Encore! Encore!' someone called from the darkness. 'Give her a go,' someone else said.

The laughing died down after that, but when it did I missed it. I felt horribly exposed in the silence and the glare. Worse though: Melanie Firth was still standing beside me on stage. To my left, where the light was most flattering.

She was supposed to leave the stage if we were starting halfway through. She shouldn't be here in this part of the play. 'Geddoff,' I urged her. My hand hung grimly by my side and I paddled it, waving her towards the wings.

But Melanie hadn't done a term of drama class for nothing. '*You* go if there's not enough time for everyone's lines,' she replied. 'My mum made this costume especially.'

'I can't,' I hissed, 'that doesn't make any sense. *You're* the one who disappears.'

'Gonna make me?' Melanie said softly. 'Huh? Are you, Tikka? Gunna sic your dog on me?'

Behind us, Carly Sawtell growled and that set off the dog in the audience. It barked excitedly, ready to defend its territory.

'Fine,' I muttered. If Melanie Firth wouldn't leave the stage, we'd just have to do our play around her. The audience was getting restless. I could hear them talking, and was that someone leaving the amphitheatre?

I stepped forward towards the edge of the stage and opened my mouth wide to the night. Elocution is everything, Miss

Elith always said. But when my words came out that night they were louder and fiercer than I expected. As if I'd called something up. My own inkan-nation.

'A dingo's got my baby!' I cried dramatically.

The audience gasped. C'mere barked warningly. Then someone who sounded suspiciously like Mrs McCausley complained: 'Is *this* what they teach them in schools these days?'

'My baby!' I said it again for effect. 'A dingo's stolen my baby!'

And even though what I was saying was blatantly untrue – for a start, Melanie was still standing there on stage. Also, she wasn't a baby – not even faintly my daughter – and our dingo looked more like a Muppet. And still it was enough. Just to invoke those five words was enough. The crowd sat in scandalised silence. No one moved until Carly Sawtell stepped forward in her yellow pyjamas and her egg-carton nose and raised her gardening-gloved hands indignantly to the crowd.

'No, I didn't! I didn't steal your baby. I never touched her!' she protested hotly. 'You never even gave me the chance!'

* * *

I was standing backstage several minutes later when Mr Avery showed up and began stacking chairs. He wasn't wearing a Showstopper T-shirt like all the other teachers. Just his normal short-sleeved shirt and his normal brown trousers, which he hitched up at the knees so he could perch awkwardly on a stack of chairs piled beside me.

'You okay, Tikka?'

'Yeah.'

'What was it you were trying to do up there?' he asked, but he didn't say it unkindly. Miss Elith had swooped on stage as soon as I had spoken. She'd flown fast and flown low, in her bat-winged Showstopper T-shirt. She was panting, even though the flight of stairs she'd scaled was hardly Kosciusko. Then she'd turned to the audience and she'd cancelled my skit. ('I'm sorry,' she explained, 'but I'm afraid we've run out of time. If you'd like to join me in welcoming the Senior Girls and Boys Choir back onto the stage …')

'It was just a skit,' I said feebly to Mr Avery.

Because how could I tell him I was only trying to help Hannah and Cordie?

'Did your parents know what it was about?'

They do now, I thought gravely. I hadn't seen my parents – they were still in the audience somewhere. And I wasn't in a hurry to find them.

'What did Miss Elith say?' Mr Avery asked.

'Miss Elith said I let myself down. And my cast. And also the school.'

Near the river a night-bird cried out sharply.

'And plus, it's not right to make art out of other people's tragedy.'

'It's not?'

'Just ask Miss Elith,' I said soberly.

Mr Avery was being so nice about the whole thing, I almost felt like telling him the truth. About how I knew the Chamberlain case was the wrong thing to choose, but I'd picked it deliberately as a diversion.

Then Jade Heddingly turned up and interrupted. She wanted to know why I hadn't told her about my skit. And I told Jade that I didn't really feel like talking about that right now and that I needed to go and find my sister.

But Jade was saying, *no.* Nobody was going anywhere.

No one was allowed to leave.

Then she said the words I'd been waiting to hear: 'Don't you know? The Van Apfel girls are gone.'

* * *

It took seventeen minutes for the first cop car to arrive after Mr and Mrs Van Apfel called the police. We know because Wade Nevrakis timed it on his watch. (Wade's watch had a sports-grade timer that was backlit pale green and could go underwater to thirty-five metres.) Seventeen minutes, plus almost an hour of deliberation first. *Do we call now? How do we know they're really missing?* Add to that the time it took for Mr Van Apfel to drive to Macedon Close and back just to check the girls hadn't walked home. All in all, it was an hour twenty-seven while we searched and we waited. Shone emergency torches scrounged from people's car boots along the black river.

An hour twenty-seven to work out what my sister understood in an instant: that something had gone very wrong.

'You should say,' I told Lor when the cop car arrived. (One flash of blue lights and I lost my nerve.) 'Tell them now. Say Hannah and Cordie aren't missing at all. Tell them they've just run away.'

Dad and I had been searching with one group to the east of the oval the whole time, while Mum and Laura's group scoured the west. Laura and I hadn't spoken – hadn't seen each other since I'd come off the stage – and it was suddenly important that my sister knew I'd held out.

'I haven't blown their cover,' I assured her. I could keep a secret as well as she could. I hadn't breathed a word to anyone the whole time we searched – not to the teachers, not to the parents. Not even to the choir fanning out among the mangroves, blossoming like a rash. They called the girls' names in two-part harmony: 'Hannah! Cordelia! *Ruth!*'

Because that was the other thing: Ruth was gone too. She had disappeared along with her sisters. 'Did you know about that?' I asked Laura when I saw her now. 'Did they say why they also took Ruth?'

But Laura looked stricken.

'I don't know where they are,' she said in a terrible whisper. '*Any of them*. They never showed up at the meeting spot like we'd planned, so I don't know where they are, or why they took Ruth.'

'It was because of my skit, wasn't it? Because it was cut short —' I started saying.

'What?' Laura snapped. 'They've *gone*, Tikka. They've really gone. I don't understand it.'

'So they went without you,' I said simply.

I wanted to point out that it wasn't nice, was it? When *you* were the one who was left out? And that maybe she'd think about *that* in the future, when she and Hannah and Cordie tried to exclude me from things.

'But they can't have. Can they?' Laura said desperately. 'They can't have gone without meeting me because they didn't have any money. Without that they can't get *anywhere*. They don't have anything with them – no food, no money, no nothing.'

'Maybe they snuck some supplies with them from home?'

'Did *you* see them carrying anything like that, when you saw them in the car park earlier?'

And I had to admit that I hadn't. Just that one bag of popcorn.

Behind us the amphitheatre was roped off with blue and white striped plastic tape. The police had wrapped it around tight, as though those slick stripes might keep anybody out. But Mrs Van Apfel's cotton curtain still flapped in the breeze, flaunting that police line.

'We should tell,' I said to Laura. 'We should tell the police. Or we should tell Mum and Dad and *they* can tell the police —'

'No!'

As Laura spoke a helicopter appeared like an insect on the horizon. It rose above the ridge line and lowered itself gingerly into the gully, the gusts from its rotors forming frothy peaks on the river.

'We won't tell,' she instructed. 'We *can't*.'

'Why can't we?' I asked fearfully.

'Because,' my sister snapped, as if she was irritated that it was left to her to tell me, 'Cordie's pregnant. That's why they're running away.'

'*Pregnant?*'

The ground seemed to tilt like a table being upended. I felt dizzy and reached for Laura's sleeve. Ahead of us, the search helicopter hung motionless in midair while the walls of the valley dipped and shifted all around it.

Cordie couldn't be pregnant.

'Who told you?' I demanded.

'Hannah said.'

'How does *she* know?'

'Cordie told her.'

'Is it true, but?'

'How should I know? I'm not a doctor.'

'Pregnant.' It felt weird just to make the word with my mouth. Cordie was pregnant? Was that even possible? She was just a kid. But even in my bewilderment, you had to admit there was a chance. With Cordie, anything was believable.

'So how will they —'

But Laura didn't know any of the details. All she knew was that Hannah was terrified their parents would discover. Who knew what they'd do then? And Cordie sure as hell wasn't hanging around to find out.

'But if Cordie — but if she really is —' I couldn't get the words out. 'She needs looking after. It's even *more* reason to tell!' I blurted.

'We can't,' Laura said. 'Imagine bringing her back to Mr and Mrs Van Apfel if she's pregnant. We can't tell anyone, Tik. You have to promise. *No one*, and especially not the police.'

'Why not the police?'

Laura looked at me like it was obvious. 'Cordie's a minor.'

'A what?'

'A minor,' Laura said sombrely. 'She's only thirteen, and if they find out she's pregnant, she could get arrested.'

So that's why we kept our friends' terrible secret. Because my sister said so. Because we didn't know any better.

And the whole time Laura spoke she clutched her purse under one arm, still full of cash for the girls. We were already implicated, that purse seemed to say, its sequins glinting in the searchlights.

'Besides,' Laura said, 'I reckon you've said enough for one night, don't you, Tik?'

She hitched her purse higher and nodded towards the stage, which was wrapped in plastic police tape.

* * *

It had been during the second half of the show, people said later. On the eastern side of the amphitheatre witnesses saw a large figure in the audience stand and move awkwardly along the row. Past the Gonskis, past the Tooleys, past the Townsends from number nine. Shuffling, smiling. Treading on toes. At the end of the row he stepped heavily off the concrete step, losing his balance momentarily. Then he righted himself and strode out across the grass in the direction of the gravel car park. The figure was tall and bulky. Big hands and wide shoulders. Had the goggle-eyed stare of a child. He paused behind a parked car, and then he opened the boot. Fossicked around, did a stocktake back there. And in the low glow of the interior car light, a person could just about say for certain that the large figure was Mr Van Apfel.

Several moments later a second figure emerged from the gloom at the side of the stage. This figure was almost as tall as the previous one but leaner, slighter in build. No Showstopper T-shirt. Instead he wore a short-sleeved collared shirt that mopped up sweat as it formed at the back of his neck.

Leaving his post at the side of stage, the figure walked in the opposite direction to the car park. He was headed towards the river. He walked slowly, inconspicuously. But as he passed the toilet block to the west of the stage, he stepped inside at the last instant. The toilets were badly lit (though the council was going to fix them just as soon as the funding came through). But in the moonlight and the glare coming off the Showstopper stage that figure looked a lot like Mr Avery. And as the Senior Girls and Boys Choir began to sing their encore ('I am Australian'), a dog barked abruptly in the amphitheatre and its owner called it: 'C'mere.' Then the barking got fainter, and the dog got smaller as he bounded off into the night.

* * *

'Brochures,' Mr Van Apfel told Detective Senior Constable Mundy when he was questioned. The neighbourhood was full of talk of Mr Van Apfel being interviewed at length, and on repeated occasions, over the coming weeks. 'I went to get more brochures for Hope Revival Centre's *Salvation!* service out of the boot of my car.

'I'd run out,' he added helplessly. 'I'd been handing them out all evening, before the show and then again during interval. I only had one stack left and I went to get more to hand out after the show, because I knew the encore was coming up.'

'I went to the toilet,' explained Mr Avery. He rubbed his hands up and down those hair-covered arms. 'I couldn't wait any longer. I'd been standing at the side of the stage helping students up and down the stairs all night.'

'You couldn't wait until the end of the show?' asked Detective Mundy sceptically. 'There were only a few minutes left.'

'I didn't know that. I thought that second-last act, that skit, would go for longer. And I hadn't had a break – there was no one there to relieve me.'

Mr Avery turned a painful, blotchy red. 'To relieve *my post*. Side of stage,' he clarified for Detective Mundy. 'There was no one to relieve my post.'

And it was true Mr Van Apfel had been distributing Hope Revival Centre *Salvation!* brochures that night. *Everyone* could attest to that. But why he chose that moment to go and get more when he could have gone during the interval or waited until after the show, well, Mr Van Apfel couldn't exactly say. Nor could he explain how he'd gone through so many brochures when, by his own estimate, he'd started out with more than five hundred.

'A run on salvation that night was there, mate?' Detective Mundy asked.

But Mr Van Apfel was hard-pressed to say. Just like he couldn't explain what took him so long at his car, or how he missed the whole rest of the show when there were still two (albeit short) acts to go. Or why there was a stack of his *Salvation!* brochures in the bin by the toilets. Did everyone in the audience throw theirs away?

In the same way, it was entirely plausible Mr Avery had gone to the toilet. Reasonable, you'd have to say. He'd been helping kids all night – all *Friday* night, when he could have been anywhere else. Only, nobody could verify they'd seen him at the toilets. And nobody saw him come back. In fact, no one had seen him for a good twenty minutes until he reappeared backstage stacking chairs.

The two of them – Mr Van Apfel and Mr Avery – were in syzygy as they moved around Coronation Park that evening. Like the sun and moon. Separate, and yet strangely aligned. And the way they told it to the police, it was as if they'd had no choice. Like their fates were sealed before they left the amphitheatre.

But almost immediately after both men disappeared from the amphitheatre the Van Apfel girls vanished as well. That left Mrs Van Apfel alone, peering into the dark. Scanning the packed amphitheatre for her three daughters.

'Don't go where I can't see you,' she'd directed them.

But they'd tripped over each other in their rush to get down the concrete steps, a stack of brochures tucked under Cordie's arm. They'd convinced Mrs Van Apfel to let them hand out the remaining *Salvation!* brochures to the captive audience.

'Make sure you wait for Ruth!'

It was the last instruction she ever gave them. The last thing they heard her say. And that was how Ruth came to be with them. Hannah and Cordie would have gone without her, if it were up to them.

* * *

After that first cop car pulled up, more and more cars arrived. Until the car park was jammed with cop cars. Swarming and wailing. Their lights making shadows that were slanting and strange.

'Blue light disco,' someone joked but nobody laughed, though at any other time we would have. And I realised I'd been holding Laura's hand so tight that I was nearly cutting off the circulation, and we had to swap sides so she could shake the blood back.

The police set up a command centre at the picnic sheds by the oval: they would organise the search from there. The sheds were in line with the amphitheatre and close to the river. The oval stretched out in between. Under the lights of the oval you could make out the picnic shed's red corrugated roof and the police crowded underneath the rusty ripples, talking and pointing and giving out orders. They held small torches that bobbed in the dark, and when the beams splashed onto the red metal roof they made bright tiny fires in the night.

It was just after 9 pm when Detective Senior Constable Justin Mundy arrived from the neighbouring district squad. He was wearing his football training gear because he played touch football in the off-season with the Minnows to try to keep himself fit. (The fish sticker on the back of his car was the giveaway. That thing had mean piranha-like fangs, unlike the Van Apfels' toothless ichthys.) Later we'd get Detective Senior Sergeant Craig Malone from the homicide squad in the city, who'd come with his own team, plus a team from the sex crimes unit. But until then we had to make do with Detective Senior Constable Mundy and our normal local area command.

The police took statements from everyone in the audience, who should have been watching the stage but seemed to have been looking everywhere else if their statements to the police were anything to go by. Mr Gonski said he saw the Van Apfel girls stand up and leave the amphitheatre during Jacob Hunter's trombone recital. Yes, he was sure, he said. He remembered exactly because he was tempted to leave at that point himself. Mrs McCausley had been sitting on the far left-hand side of the amphitheatre and the girls drifted close enough that she could hear their conversation. They were worried, she said, that they'd left it too late. *Too late for what?* Mrs McCausley hadn't heard. Reverend Richmond admitted he'd fallen asleep and so couldn't vouch for anything after the interval. But the family with the red dog had seen the girls leave. Their eldest boy even saw them again a second time, walking around the edge of the oval when he took the red dog – C'mere – to stretch his legs.

'Where were they headed?'

But the boy didn't know. He pointed vaguely to the river.

'They were handing out *Salvation!* brochures,' Mrs Van Apfel explained over and over to a stricken-looking young detective. He'd dressed in a hurry and the epaulette on one shoulder was undone and waved shyly every time the wind blew.

'I let them go,' Mrs Van Apfel said. 'The three of them went together. How could I know? Stay inside the amphitheatre, I said.'

While the cops did their interviews, the SES volunteers arrived, then the dog squad with their salt-and-pepper dogs. Then Dad said he thought it was time Lor and I went home with Mum, while he stayed to help with the search. The three of us left, and as we drove up and out of the valley, the moon sailed alongside us. Tethered like a balloon on a string.

* * *

In the following days they buzzed in like flies: the ground crews, the specialists, the teams from the city. Police divers surfaced and sank all along the river. Dropping like bait on a line.

By the cops' reckoning, more than four hundred people were within a one-kilometre radius of the amphitheatre on the night of the disappearance. They counted. Then they interviewed each one. Plotting movements, cross-checking stories. Asking the same questions over and over again.

What did we see? Could we remember any details? Were the girls happy? Were they in trouble at school? Could we think of a reason they might run away? Did we know of anywhere they might go? They wrote and recorded everything we said and then they filed it in their reports. They had more than twelve hundred information reports in the end, and more than two thousand documents all up. So many words, but none of them were enough. None of them brought those girls home.

Lor and I were interviewed three times during that period. Me once, Laura twice, each interview coming several days apart. I guess they wanted to speak with my sister more times because she was older.

Either that or I was the more convincing liar.

We didn't say anything about Hannah and Cordie's running-away plan. About Mr Van Apfel. Or about Mr Avery.

Not a word about Laura's cash, or my skit, or the fact Ruth was uninvited. We had more secrets than we had things to tell.

And on TV Lindy Chamberlain and her strappy sundress were replaced by photos of Hannah, Cordie and Ruth. They filled our screens each evening dressed in their ironed uniforms. Once they even appeared dressed as angels in Mrs Blunt's nativity play (though no mention of whether Cordie's costume included knickers or not).

Seeing them there, dressed for the nativity play, made me anxious about that script I'd kept for Cordie. The one for my Showstopper skit, back when I thought she might be in it.

That script was still stashed under my bed, with Cordie's name on the front, and all her unlearned lines highlighted pink. And the part I'd assigned her, before Melanie Firth got the job, was the character of Azaria. The one titled: 'Missing Girl'.

CHAPTER EIGHTEEN

They had Buckley's of knowing how long she'd been dead when they found her there by the river. Wedged into those boulders. Rammed right in like the valley wasn't low enough, like she'd tried to go deeper, tried to crawl right inside and be eaten alive.

Only thing: Ruth was dead.

They said when they saw her that her mouth was twisted into its usual curl. Said her head was tipped back, her jaw wide as a pair of cupped hands. Next they saw the flies, that brilliant roiling mess, shifting and dripping and liquid as the tide. They poured from her nose, clustered at her eyes. She could have been down there for days. She could have been dead the entire time we searched, at least that's what Wade Nevrakis said. And he was told it by his parents, who were there delivering sandwiches from their deli for all the searchers.

Kelly Ashwood spread it that when they found Ruth the black cockatoos already knew. In their bird way they'd sensed it, they'd come back for her. That's what Kelly Ashwood said. The cockatoos had already travelled up the valley that morning and then back down again, and now there they were, doing a third lap. Only this time they stopped when they got to the spot where Ruth lay dead and they wheeled and careened in a languid black loop, screeching their requiem from the sky.

It was the police from the local area command who found her stuffed in that rock. They saw her plait first. Poking out from between the rocks, looking like one of those woven markers wedged between the pages of her family's Bible. It *was* a Sunday afternoon after all.

CHAPTER NINETEEN

At first it seemed like Ruth would never get an autopsy, just like she would never get an eighth birthday. Only, the autopsy was denied because her parents didn't believe in them (and you couldn't say the same about birthdays).

But what I wanted to know was: why couldn't the hospital just *show* them? When I tracked Dad down to ask him, he was standing at the basin in the bathroom, shaving. He looked at me warily.

'Show them what, Tik?'

He held his razor in midair, paused on its way to his neck.

'An autopsy. If the Van Apfels don't believe in autopsies, why doesn't someone up at the hospital just show them one? You can't say you don't believe in autopsies if you've seen one for yourself.'

Dad smiled sadly and put his razor on the lip of the sink. He turned from the mirror to face me square before he answered me.

'It's not that the Van Apfels don't believe autopsies *exist*. They know they do. It's more that they don't agree with them. On religious grounds, you know? They don't believe that's what should happen to Ruth.'

I wanted to know what grounds *specifically* said that Ruth couldn't have one after everything else she'd been through. After everything she was going to miss out on now, why should she miss out on an autopsy too?

'I don't know *specifically*.' He smiled ruefully. 'But I'm sure the Van Apfels have got their reasons. Maybe they think it's desecration of the body God made. Or maybe they'd like to try and protect Ruth in some way they weren't able to do when she was still alive. But I really can't tell you for sure, Tik. It's not something I understand.

'The coroner has to consider the public interest too, though,' Dad went on. 'The coroner will think it through and then might decide that, for whatever reason, an autopsy isn't going to tell us anything helpful anyway. Often they can't determine the cause of death, especially if someone has been lying exposed for up to nine days like Ruth had. And you don't want to go through that for nothing.

'The Van Apfels have suffered a lot,' he added.

The mirror was fogging up and Dad's face was vanishing. The tap spat a rush of tears into the sink.

'Tikka,' Dad said, 'you know, this isn't really something for someone your age to have to worry about. It's not really something that you should —'

But I placed my hands over my ears. Hot tears brimmed in my eyes.

'Tell that to Ruth!' I shouted at him. 'Tell Ruth! She's not even my age and she's the one who needs an autopsy! She's *dead* and her parents won't even tell her why!'

I spun on my heel and ran to my room, and I slammed the door behind me. Then I turned and shouted at the closed door: 'And why am I the only one who can smell that river? Why can't any of you smell the stink?'

In the end the coroner *did* step in and overrule the Van Apfels' 'no autopsy' request. A coronial post-mortem was required but it didn't tell us much. Didn't tell us how Ruth turned up dead. The findings were inconclusive about exactly how she'd died and so we had no more answers than we'd had before.

But at least I felt slightly better for Ruth.

* * *

Ruth was put back in the ground on a Monday morning, eight days after her body was discovered, and seventeen since she first disappeared. Her funeral was held at the Hope Revival Centre, though there wasn't much reviving going on.

The Hope Revival Centre was where you could find Mr and Mrs Van Apfel most days by that stage, rather than at the police command post in the valley or at their house overlooking Macedon Close. They had attended the eight o'clock Rise Up service at the centre just the day before Ruth's funeral. 'Better to seek God's grace in here than go looking for it out there,' they reasoned for not joining the search for their remaining two daughters. And Mrs McCausley said: 'For heaven's sake, you won't find those girls in a church.'

But Ruth was there on Monday morning all right.

At her funeral, a photo of Ruth lay on top on her casket. Her plaits straight as two arrows, pointing south to the exits at the far end of the hall. She was buried, not cremated. Put back into the same earth the police had taken so much trouble to yank her from.

During the service they re-used the candles left over from the vigil we'd held, just over a week before, in the park. Mrs Lantana had overdone it at the time by collecting five thousand candles, and she had stored the leftovers in her garage, wedged down between the rat traps and a gone-soft carton of VB, before dragging them out for the funeral and stacking them in her reliable white station wagon. Then she ferried them to the church across the valley.

When we arrived at the funeral we were sent in two directions at the large double doors of the worship hall. There didn't seem to be any method to the division, only that the women ushering us in wanted the hall to be filled from the front on both sides. 'Like separating the sheep from the goats,' Mrs McCausley said when she was directed to sit next to me. My family and Mrs McCausley were on the opposite side of the aisle from Mr and Mrs Van Apfel, though it was impossible to say if that meant we were sheep or if it made us the goats.

There were no windows in the Hope Revival Centre worship hall. No natural light at all. Instead the ceiling was studded with rows of downlights that had been dimmed to the lowest possible setting, as if the congregation were sitting in a cinema waiting for the movie to begin. At the front of the hall was a colossal carpeted stage, complete with stage lights in unimaginable colours. Though they kept those rainbow lights switched off out of respect for Ruth. Or maybe Mr and Mrs Van Apfel requested to be kept in the dark.

There was a drum kit on stage, and a row of black microphones lay abandoned on the carpet. As if the band had gone backstage for a break and their encore would come after the service. Ruth's casket was centre stage. On top of the casket, next to a photo of Ruth, sat a yellow Care Bear, its daffodil down hacked into a spiked mohawk.

'*Cordie* did that,' I said in disgust, remembering the day she played hairdresser. Typical of her to try to steal centre stage when, for once, it was all about Ruth.

'Plus it stinks in here,' I muttered to Mrs McCausley.

'Lily-of-the-valley,' she explained, and she pointed to the flower displays up the front. Though mostly Ruth's funeral smelled like hankies and despair, and I couldn't wait to get outside.

Across the aisle from us Mr Van Apfel sat straight and stiff-backed throughout the funeral. Upright the entire time. While Mrs Van Apfel sat by his side and sobbed quietly, fatalistically because the worst had finally happened. Their chairs were separate from the rest of the congregation – they had their own self-made row – so that the two of them were closer to Ruth than anyone else in the hall, except for the pastor on stage.

And as the pastor started to speak – as he read a long and bewildering scripture that talked of angels and altars, of horseheads and bottomless pits ('*Let loose the angels bound in the river! One woe is past; and, behold there come two woes more hereafter …*'), as Funshine Bear smiled down benignly on the congregation from on top of Ruth's casket like some sort of

Pop Art deity, as the lilies began to wilt and brown at the edges in the stale airconditioned air – it was then that Mr Van Apfel turned to face the family and friends, the neighbours and teachers who sat massed and red-eyed behind him. He looked approvingly at the size of the congregation. Nodded at a few people. But in the instant before he turned back to Ruth, Mr Van Apfel caught my eye. *You know,* I thought. *You know your daughters planned to run away. And what's more, you know I do too.* Sweat prickled at the nape of my neck. But Mr Van Apfel smiled munificently at me for one moment. Then he turned back to his daughter's casket.

* * *

After the funeral Jade Heddingly pumped us for information while we stood in the foyer outside. Jade hadn't been allowed to attend the service on account of it being too distressing, her parents said. But that didn't stop her arksing us for all the gory details. 'Did you see her?' she wanted to know.

Mrs McCausley shook her head. 'Closed coffin, thank heavens. No one needed to see the poor girl.'

'What did they talk about?' Jade asked us then.

'The sermon was a strange thing on the Valley of Dry Bones,' Mrs McCausley said. 'All about putting tendons back on bones and bringing them back to life, as if *that* was helpful at this point.'

'Ezekiel 37,' I added for Jade's benefit.

And when Mrs McCausley saw that I recognised which chapter of the Bible it was from, well, she just about keeled over with surprise. I didn't tell her I only knew it from family Bible study at the Van Apfels' house. Because that was a lifetime ago. (Also, because it wasn't every day that you got to tell Mrs McCausley something she didn't already know.)

'I didn't recognise any of the music either,' she admitted to Jade. 'They weren't proper hymns; it was all pop music as far as I could tell.'

We stopped talking after that because the hearse was leaving and we all stood by the window to watch. I thought about Ruth, laid out in that casket. Sealed like a Tupperware box. And even after the sad sermon and the songs, all the photos of Ruth that had been shown in a PowerPoint presentation, the idea of her being kept safe inside that thing forever was the most heartbreaking part.

* * *

In the days and weeks after we buried Ruth, Mrs Van Apfel retreated inside their dark house at the top of the street. The house remained pristine; it was still scrupulously respectable. Only the pool turned a more insidious shade of green with neglect, while inside the spiral staircase continued to twist tight around the house's heart.

The Van Apfels didn't sell up and leave Macedon Close like we all thought they might. Nor did Mrs Van Apfel rejoin the search for Hannah and Cordie. She left it up to the experts to find no trace of her daughters. In fact, we never saw Mrs Van Apfel in the valley again after the day they discovered poor Ruth in that rock. She mostly stayed inside her house, or else she visited the Lord's. She clung to her Hope Revival commitments more than ever. Praise and Worship each Wednesday. Rise Up Sunday mornings. Embalming her soul in her schedule.

It was as if the red lines that she printed so carefully on her calendar were the only things holding her up. Mr Van Apfel, meanwhile, relied on a plastic outdoor chair he placed by the footpath that ran the width of his front yard.

He sat in that chair every morning and most afternoons. Like a dream. Throned on faded plastic. The chair was split up one leg but, somehow, still managed to hold his weight for all those hours every day. He sat there just watching, unless you got too close to him. Then he quoted Bible verses at you. It was like he was afraid he might vanish too if he wasn't out there in full view.

But we couldn't hold on to Mr Van Apfel any more than we could reach his wife, and bits of him fell away every day. In the months and years that passed he still quoted scripture at us if we strayed near his yard, but the verses were jumbled and half-hearted by that stage. And the funny part was, we got so used to him being there that after a while we stopped noticing him altogether. He still sat, but we stopped seeing.

And then it was complete: the Van Apfels had vanished in front of our eyes.

* * *

Though there was one night when Mr Van Apfel swam into clarity for us. When he emerged, clear and sharp-edged and engaged in a fury-filled tirade. He stood in the dark, at the bottleneck to our cul-de-sac, and rained down venom.

It was bin night that night, and red council-issue garbage bins lined the curb, interspersed with green garden-waste ones. Like Christmas decorations strung along the gutter. *Season's greetings! And a happy New Year!*

But as Mr Van Apfel wrestled with his bin, as he struggled to pull it into line, a garbage bag oozed out and over the lip of his bin and got caught on a plastic splinter. It punctured. And greasy chicken bones and limp lettuce leaves, piles of wadded-up tissues escaped and tumbled onto the road and lay in a heap at his feet.

And that was it. That was when we saw Mr Van Apfel fold.

He shouted at the bin – at his life – at the injustice of it all. Spilled rubbish was what it took in the end. He raged and he swore, without bothering to bend down and pick up the rubbish off the road.

He went on for minutes. He went on like that for so long that all around the cul-de-sac curious neighbours who'd been drawn to their windows by his shouts had enough time to leave their posts and go and mute their TVs and then return to their windows. To pull up a chair.

Meanwhile, in the street, black clouds gathered ominously, though in the night sky they were easy to miss. And anyway, who could take their eyes off Mr Van Apfel? His despair was mesmerising.

For an instant he paused. Drew a breath. Re-inflated. Looked like he was ready to begin again. Instead, he kicked his rubbish bin savagely and it wobbled capriciously. The thing teetered, and then righted itself.

The bin stayed standing but Mr Van Apfel crumpled. Collapsed in on himself like thin origami paper. He howled while he crouched there, alone in the dark. Then even the howling ended and there really was nothing.

Nothing, that is, except the soft sound of rain. It came strange and tentative at first. Like the rain itself wasn't sure it was falling. 'Dad, it's raining,' I said in awe. How long had it been? The two of us stood at the window in the lounge room and together we watched the rain.

It fell heavier, more certain, more convinced of itself. It flowed around the wheelie bins. It congealed with car oil on the road and ran down the slope in slick, warped rainbows.

And the whole time Mr Van Apfel stayed crouched in the dark, as if he couldn't feel the rain pelting him there. It made rivers down his cheeks and soaked his white collared shirt. Leaked through the patterned holes of his sanctimonious brogues. Until eventually the rain eased, and Mr Van Apfel stood up. He walked sulkily inside like a child.

* * *

A fortnight after Ruth turned up dead, the search for her sisters was scaled back. Not because we'd found them, but because we *hadn't*. (And Ruth didn't give much away.)

In its place a taskforce was set up to take over the investigation. This meant that our parents, the SES crews, and all those blue-capped cops under Senior Detective Constable Mundy's command were being replaced by a new set of experts.

It was left to Wade Nevrakis to tell us they were winding things up, and we knew Wade was telling the truth because we saw them drive out. We watched them as they went. The red sheds sat abandoned now the police command post was gone. Their rusty roofs glowed in the heat of the late afternoon, like embers not properly put out.

The case was being passed to a taskforce after just twenty-three days of intensive searching. Barely one week of searching per girl. (Slightly more for Ruth when you consider it took nine days to find her. But then, when they did, she was already dead.)

Mr Avery was dead too, by the time they discovered him. Hanging there in the shower. It happened eight months after the disappearance of the Van Apfel girls, which was both enough time for it to be considered a separate investigation and for the two to be forever linked in neighbourhood gossip.

It was his feet that gave him away. With their beautiful arches, their knobbly bones like contours on a map. He was hanging from the shower rail in his small rented bathroom, where he'd taken the time to slide the plastic curtain with its raindrop design carefully out of the way. August gusts through the window buffeted his body gently so it swung slightly. It shifted and stirred. While the curtain stayed slime-stuck against the wet tiles and *it* looked like the dead thing, not him.

He was dressed in his usual short-sleeved shirt and his brown, ironed trousers. His hairy hands hung outside his pockets. His tongue hung out too, and was stiff and dried out. As if he died trying to pass on what he knew.

Jim found him. Jim Jericho, who came in his Jim Jericho van. The one that said: *fix it* and *right price* and *mates' rates*. Jim had come round on his day off to fix a blocked pipe. Said the door was open. Said he just went on in.

Then Jim said: 'Jeez, mate, you couldn't believe it.'

And also: 'What a thing to find.'

Said a bloke would never get over seeing something like that. Not on a bloke's day off.

And whether Mr Avery's suicide was a sign of his guilt – of his complicity in the girls' disappearance somehow – was impossible to say. Not that that stopped people trying. Mrs McCausley said that it was conclusive evidence, his dead body there in the shower. She said that suicide equalled guilt and she'd suspected him all along. Ever since that day she first met him at the milk bar. And I didn't like to point out she *hadn't* actually met him then and, in actual fact, she'd missed him by minutes. Because a little thing like the truth never stopped Mrs McCausley: judge, jury and executioner.

Or maybe he was just sorry he hadn't done enough to save those girls, to save Cordie. We all knew what that felt like.

The police took Jim's statement. (Though Jim didn't know much more than us.) What Jim *did* know was how that thin curtain rail held up under the strain of the body, because Jim had fixed that rail himself. He'd made it secure back when Mr Avery first arrived and moved into that rental place.

Not long before Cordelia Van Apfel fell out of a tree.

CHAPTER TWENTY

On the Thursday after I saw Mrs McCausley at the SupaCentre I visited her for afternoon tea.

'You came before four?' She sounded suspicious when she answered the door, like she hadn't expected me to turn up on time.

'I give the kookaburras their dinner at four o'clock,' she explained as I stepped past the screen door and stood beside her in the hallway. 'But then I've already told you that, haven't I?'

I didn't know if it was a bad sign she'd repeated herself, or a good sign that at least she'd realised.

She led me down the darkened hallway before we emerged into her immaculate lounge room. The carpet was lush. Doilies fortified every surface. She indicated I should sit on the couch, but only where it was safeguarded by a crocheted blanket.

'I'll put the kettle on. Do you drink tea?'

'Lovely,' I assured her. And I sat on the couch and listened to Mrs McCausley move around in the kitchen while I took in the landscape paintings on the walls, the coffee table polished to shining, the porcelain dolls with lace bonnets shielding their dead glassy eyes and standing on a custom-made shelf beside the doorway. Her house was exactly as I remembered it. When Mrs McCausley returned she carried a tray filled with cups and saucers, a dainty dish of Scotch Finger biscuits. She placed it on the coffee table alongside a teapot that was wearing a knitted cosy.

'It's good of you to come and see me, Tikka,' she said, pouring the tea.

'Anything for a Scotch Finger, Mrs McCausley.'

Because there were worse reasons for visiting the house at the top of the street, even if Laura said she couldn't think of any.

'It's been a long time since you've been to visit me here.'

'A very long time,' I agreed. 'A while since I've been back to Macedon Close at all.'

'Ten years?' she asked.

'Maybe eight,' I admitted.

'There was no need for you to run away,' she said cryptically.

'How's your hip today?' I asked, changing the subject and helping myself to a biscuit. But Mrs McCausley's face fell at the mention of her hip.

'More to the point, how's *yours*?' She said it sharply, as if she was offended I'd asked such a personal question.

'My hip?' I was confused. 'But – but last time I saw you, you were telling me about your hip replacement.'

Mrs McCausley made a face that said she doubted that *very* much.

'Sorry, Mrs McCausley,' I said, 'I was only asking ...'

I trailed off because I was worried about upsetting her more. Could she *really* not remember that part of our conversation at the SupaCentre? Why would she think I'd make such a thing up?

After that the conversation drifted for a while. Her garden. My lab work. A new detective series on the ABC. I hadn't seen it. It was worth staying in for, she advised. The violence didn't worry her too much, she said, though the plot sometimes seemed overly complicated.

I was almost at the point where I thought it was time to leave.

'Your kookaburras will be getting peckish,' I said, and she smirked.

There was nothing wrong with Mrs McCausley's brain when it came to the punchline.

'It *is* almost their teatime,' she said, glancing towards the sliding glass doors that led out onto the back deck, but there was no sign of her kookaburras yet. Though it was impossible to see all of the deck from where we sat in the lounge room, because the doors were framed with heavy brocade drapes that were embroidered with their own, more delicate birds.

'But you can't leave before I say what I wanted to tell you,' she said. Her voice had found some of its colour again since I made the crack about kookaburras. 'Not before I tell you what I saw.'

'What you saw?' I asked. I was surprised she'd remembered she was going to tell me anything, but I was careful not to show it.

'Yes,' she said. 'What I saw the night before the Van Apfel girls disappeared.'

My head snapped to attention. 'What did you say?'

'What I saw the night before the Van Apfel girls disappeared,' she repeated. 'I've never told anyone else.'

And so Mrs McCausley told me about a night almost exactly twenty years ago to the day. The night before the Showstopper. When the Van Apfel girls were still here, still living across the cul-de-sac.

Mrs McCausley had walked out into Macedon Close that night with a brochure about Tupperware's new Airtight Alright range in her left hand and a sample salad spinner in her right.

'What time was it?' I interrupted.

'Eight-thirty?' she guessed. 'After *A Country Practice*.'

Mrs McCausley never missed an episode of *A Country Practice*. Her timing could be trusted.

She had teetered across the bottleneck of the cul-de-sac in her high heels and clack-clacked up the Van Apfels' drive. She was there to sell a salad spinner to Mrs Van Apfel (even if Mrs Van Apfel didn't know it yet).

'A salad spinner with a retractable lid for easy storage and stacking,' she explained, slipping effortlessly into her sales patter and shedding twenty years in the process. Mrs McCausley had been keeping Mrs Van Apfel in Tupperware for years. And while she never stretched to offering her neighbour an actual discount, Mrs McCausley was quick to point out that all Tupperware products came with a thirty-day return policy if you were in any way disappointed. (Which was more generous than it sounded when you took into account that disappointment was a very real risk when you were selling to Mrs Van Apfel.)

That night, however, Mrs Van Apfel had to wait for the chance to be disappointed and Mrs McCausley had to wait for her sale. Because as she approached the Van Apfel house, her Airtight Alright salad spinner tucked under her arm, Mrs McCausley heard raised voices coming from inside the house.

'"Sinful" this, and "penitence" that. To tell you the truth, I was embarrassed by what I heard,' Mrs McCausley said.

But not *so* embarrassed that it stopped her from climbing the three steps up and onto the verandah, where she had a clear view into the downstairs lounge room, and then from standing, unseen, on the Van Apfels' doorstep without ever ringing the bell.

From there Mrs McCausley could see straight inside to where Mr Van Apfel sat in his father's armchair, his feet planted on the old man's rug. In front of him Hannah and Cordie stood together in the middle of the room, copping the full force of his rage. In one hand he held a toothpick, which he pointed as he spoke, stabbing each word forcefully into the air. He had a small army of toothpicks in a container on the table beside him. 'A Tupperware tubful,' Mrs McCausley noted.

'They'd had roast beef for dinner,' Mrs McCausley remembered. 'I could smell it through an upstairs window. My Ralph used to insist on roast beef once a week.

'Half a teaspoon of baking soda to make the vegetables shine. *That's* the secret,' she confided.

'Where was Ruth?' I said. 'Could you see her too?'

She told me Ruth had stood shame-faced in the doorway.

'The doorway to the garage?'

No, Ruth was standing in the doorway that led off to the other parts of the house – to the downstairs bedrooms, the laundry, the study, to those spiral stairs. Mrs McCausley could also hear someone upstairs in the kitchen, clattering china plates into cupboards with enough force to make her disgust known, but not so hard she might chip a dish.

'Cordelia was the only one of those girls doing any talking,' Mrs McCausley reported. 'Their father, of course, hardly came up for air. But Cordelia gave it back to him at every chance she got. She wasn't going to take it lying down.'

'Take what? What wasn't she going to take?' I asked, my heart thumping.

'Oh, I couldn't hear any actual *words*.' Mrs McCausley looked askance at the question and for a moment I was worried I had broken the spell and that she would lose the thread of her story. But then she continued: 'Not *her* words anyway. Mr Van Apfel's were much easier to pick up. I could make out at least half of what he was saying.'

How long had Mrs McCausley stood there in the darkening day and listened to Mr Van Apfel shout at his daughters? Difficult to say, she told me.

(How long had she spent watching the drama unfold through the lounge-room window while elsewhere, in neighbouring houses, people sat and watched TV. And on those screens, at the end of television tubes, lay cul-de-sacs just like ours where people were fighting and kissing and eating. Putting china plates back into cupboards. Were being sinful in all the same unremarkable ways as his daughters, if only Mr Van Apfel had seen.)

'I was there long enough to witness Mr Van Apfel really lose his temper,' Mrs McCausley answered.

'He lost his temper?'

'Did he ever,' she said with marked disapproval. 'Ranting and slamming his fists down on the armrests of that lovely chair his wife had had reupholstered ... You know the one, she'd had it done in William Morris Tudor Rose,' she said emphatically.

'Not really.'

'You do. The green one.'

'And?' I urged. 'What happened then?'

But Mrs McCausley wasn't sure she should say.

'It's a bit late for that now,' I pointed out to her, and she agreed and looked relieved to continue.

Mr Van Apfel had stood then, backhanding the coffee table as he rose out of his seat and spraying a sea of toothpicks across the floors, where they covered the carpet and fell under his chair. Got lost in the fringe of the rug.

He spoke, but the words that came out were not words Mrs McCausley knew. And as he talked, his eyelids fluttered and his eyes rolled to the back of his skull, as if he preferred *that* view to the one that was there in front of him.

'Airdiddia diddia diddia,' he hissed. 'Hereisshisshia sshisshia sshisha. Airdiddia diddia.'

'What did it mean?' I asked.

'Oh heavens, I don't know! He was talking in tongues!' Mrs McCausley said. 'I'm only telling you what I heard. He stopped after a while and gave a stunned sort of blink, and in the kitchen the clattering stopped too.'

'And then?'

And then Mr Van Apfel strode across the room to where Hannah and Cordie were standing so close to one another that the backs of their hands were touching, their pinkie fingers curled together tightly. Hannah said something that Mrs McCausley couldn't hear, and her father dismissed it coolly.

'Shut up,' he said. 'The Lord knows your soul.'

Then he lunged forward and grabbed a fistful of Cordie's fine hair. He twisted it and her head twisted too. She gasped and closed her eyes in pain.

'Don't!' mouthed Ruth, still standing the doorway.

Hannah appeared to swear softly, her eyes on the faded rug at their feet. But her father ignored her, yanking Cordie's head, dragging her downwards by the hair. She grimaced and put out an arm to try to push him away, but her hand fell hopelessly short.

'Kneel!' he barked at her then and he pulled her onto the floor. She stumbled and got herself onto her bare knees, leaning towards him to try to ease the pressure on her scalp, but he saw what she was doing and twisted her hair tighter and she sobbed, her eyes still squeezed shut.

'Lord-Jesus-Lamb-of-God-Prince-of-Peace,' the words dripped off his tongue. 'You are the way, the truth and the light, no one comes to the Father but through you. No one knows the way but through you. No one sees the truth but through you.'

Each time he said 'you' he wrenched Cordie's head closer to the muscles of his leg.

'No one sees the light but through you,' he said. '*Say it!*'

And Cordie appeared to echo his words, her face twisted as she spoke.

'Amen,' came Mrs Van Apfel's voice from the doorway. Her eyes were closed too and she swayed slightly as she listened to her husband's words.

Mr Van Apfel still gripped Cordie's hair, and she must have spoken then because he bent low so his face was near hers. He brushed his cheek against hers, and when Mrs McCausley told me I could feel, just as Cordie would have felt, the beginnings of tomorrow's bristles brush against my cheek. Smelled that sour beef stink on his breath. His face creased and he eased his grip on her hair and let it fall from his hand so he could run the back of one finger lovingly down the bridge of her nose. His gift from God. Cordeli. *Aaah.*

He leaned in closer and whispered something into Cordie's ear, but she shook her head and seemed to refuse to say it. In the doorway Mrs Van Apfel repeated 'Amen' while her husband ranted about shame.

'And "deep pits"? Something about "deep pits" I couldn't catch,' Mrs McCausley admitted. 'And: "The wicked flee when no one is chasing them." I remember that line because he said it so loud and so many times. I'm surprised you didn't hear it from your place.'

'Flee?' I said urgently. 'What, like run away?'

So *this* was Mr Van Apfel's retribution then. How he'd made them pay over their running-away plan. No wonder Cordie was so desperate to try to get away. To try to travel in our car the next day to the Showstopper.

'Are you sure that's what he said? Flee?' I asked. 'That's important!'

'Of course I'm sure,' Mrs McCausley said. 'My hearing is perfect, you know.' As if the whole street didn't know she always watched her TV with the volume dialled right up to twelve.

Still, if Mrs McCausley was to be believed, in the next instant, when Cordie looked at her dad contemptuously, refusing to say what he was asking of her, Mr Van Apfel reached out again and this time gripped a handful of her hair in his fist. He twisted it and Cordie's eyes widened in pain but her lips pressed tighter together.

'No, Daddy!' Hannah urged.

But Mr Van Apfel ignored her and ripped the entire fistful from Cordie's head and stood holding it like a tail.

'Her hair?' I was aghast.

'Right off her head,' Mrs McCausley confirmed. Then she leaned in and lowered her voice as if this were the scandalous part: 'I *screamed*, it was so horrific.'

'You screamed?' I asked.

'Yes,' she admitted.

'Loud?'

'Loud enough,' she said.

Which was how, while Cordie knelt in stunned silence, staring at her hair in her dad's hand; while Ruth stood in the doorway next to her mum and sobbed self-pityingly, Hannah raised her arm and pointed towards the lounge-room window.

'Mrs McCausley,' she simply said.

And they all turned to face Mrs McCausley standing there on the verandah, her face frozen in horror. Her high-heeled feet were rooted to the coir-wire doormat, her hand clamped over her mouth. For a moment she had the decency to look flustered at being caught out. Then she lowered her hand and raised an eyebrow archly. She pursed her disapproving lips and lifted her sample to the glass. 'Salad spinner?'

'What did they say?' I asked.

'Oh, Mr Van Apfel was his usual charming self. Invited me in. Acted like it never happened. In fact, he was so relaxed I started to wonder whether I'd dreamed the whole thing. Except for the hair that was still in his fist.'

'It was still in his fist?'

'The whole time we spoke.'

'Oh my God, that's shameless!'

'You think I was going to lecture Mr Van Apfel about shame?'

'But what about the girls? Where were they?' I said. 'What about Mrs Van Apfel?'

'The girls disappeared upstairs as far as I could tell. Though Mrs Van Apfel stuck around. She bought a salad spinner but she didn't like the colour. She was never very easily pleased.'

'You still sold them Tupperware?'

'What was I supposed to do?'

Mrs McCausley was starting to clear away our afternoon tea now that her story was done. She looked her age again without the wind of scandal in her sails.

'But – but why didn't you say anything?' I said as she placed fine bone china, pretty floral cups and saucers and leftover Scotch Finger biscuits carefully back onto the tray. 'Why didn't you tell the police? Why didn't you report it during the investigation? *Or even report it now?*'

'Why don't you?' she replied evenly. 'Now that I've told you about it.'

(Though I was hardly going to start talking *now*.)

She paused as if considering whether to say the next bit, then she smiled conspiratorially at me.

'Anyway,' she said, 'no one would believe me any more. They all think I've lost my marbles.'

CHAPTER TWENTY-ONE

In the dinge and dark inside the garage it was hard to make out Dad's features. He was bent low, feeling around for the handle on the boot of his car, and I could hear his breathing. It was even and impossibly patient. After a long pause the lock clicked open and the rear door raised up, its interior light shining down on him like a dim, slim rectangular halo.

'This is it,' he said. 'A job lot.'

Inside the back of his four-wheel drive there were boxes stacked to the roof. Brown, no-nonsense cardboard cubes with *Foodbank* stamped on the side. We were here to transfer the boxes onto the floor of our garage so that someone else – some fellow volunteer at the local Foodbank – could come and move the boxes into the back of their four-wheel drive and then ferry them back to the warehouse in a long and convoluted chain of events I couldn't even begin to follow.

'You reckon you're up to it?' Dad asked.

'You reckon we might turn on a brighter light before we start?' I replied.

I walked over to the far wall and flicked the switch, and the overhead fluorescent tube blinked once, twice before springing into life. Dad looked thinner from here. He was well into his sixties now, and even though he still had plenty of hair, it stood up in soft, feathery tufts that were completely white. He ran his hands through it now.

'Is there an order to the boxes?' I asked as I walked back over to the car.

There wasn't. Each one was filled with the same tins of food. The same baked beans and kidney beans and pale peas and sliced beetroot. I spied a tin of condensed milk through a gap in the cardboard.

'You used to let us drink condensed milk. Do you remember that?'

'Did I?' Dad said with feigned ignorance. 'That can't be right.'

We began unloading, and the tins rattled satisfyingly inside their cardboard homes as we stacked them along the garage wall. It was hot work and after a while sweat trickled down the length of my neck.

'Visited your mate Mrs McCausley yesterday, did you, Tik?' Dad asked as we stacked. Mum must have mentioned I'd been there.

I nodded. 'Mrs McCausley says everyone thinks she's going senile, but she seemed okay to me.

'She can remember things with the most amazing detail,' I went on. 'Like ...' I hesitated. 'Like, she remembers being at the Van Apfel house on the night before the girls disappeared.'

I let that hang for a moment, but Dad continued shifting boxes with a deliberate air of equanimity. He wasn't going to be drawn into this conversation if he could help it.

'She said it was pretty heated over there that night. You know, Mr Van Apfel was being violent and stuff ...'

I watched as Dad dragged the next box across the carpet in the back of the car and then pivoted it onto the edge of the boot, ready to lift. He turned to face me and indicated I should grab the other end of the box. Together we lowered it to the floor.

'Violent,' he said after a long silence. 'Is that right? Mrs McCausley told you that?'

'Yeah, she did.'

'And what else did Mrs McCausley have to say?' There was no hiding the irritation in his voice.

'She's wasn't gossiping,' I assured him, because I knew what Dad thought of Mrs McCausley. 'What she was telling me could be important, Dad. She said Mr Van Apfel was shouting at Cordie, and then she saw him rip out a handful of her hair.'

Dad said nothing, only shook his head. But whether he was disapproving of Mr Van Apfel or Mrs McCausley – or of me, for dredging things up again – was impossible to tell.

'Can you get on the other end of this?' he said eventually, and we lifted and then lowered another Foodbank box.

I'd started talking now and I had that old feeling, the one I got a lot when I was a kid. The sense that something had been unplugged somewhere deep in my chest. I felt it dislodge so the words could come tumbling out.

'They were planning to run away, you know,' I told Dad. 'Hannah and Cordie and Ruth. They were planning to run away from home on the night they disappeared, and Mr Van Apfel knew about it.'

I paused.

'Hannah and I knew about it too,' I said.

'I know,' Dad replied.

'*You know?*'

'I do.'

Dad had been levering a box against the lip of the car but now he tipped it back into the boot to wait to be unloaded. He could see there was no avoiding this conversation now.

'Laura already told your mother. She spoke to her not long after she was diagnosed. Amazing what comes out of the woodwork when you're faced with a cancer diagnosis,' he said.

'What did Laura say?' I was floored.

'Exactly what you just told me. She said that the girls were going to try and run away that night, and that you two knew about it. Though to be honest, your mum and I suspected something was going on at the time. You five girls were thick as thieves, and we figured if there was any funny business going on, then you and your sister probably knew about it.'

'So why didn't you make us tell you? Or tell the police?'

'Ah well, we trusted you.' He laughed gently and brushed grit from his hands. 'You were good kids, Tik. You and your sister. We knew the pair of you had enough sense to speak up if it was something worth speaking up about.'

'But we didn't!' I protested. 'We didn't tell anyone and we should have! The police should have known, and if they had – if Laura and I had told them – then maybe they might have … I don't know, maybe they would have done things differently.'

'I'm sure they would have,' Dad said.

'But then, that's enough reason to … That makes it our fault that they didn't …' I could feel tears prickling in my eyes and I blinked them back.

Dad had stopped dusting his hands by now and he simply held up one hand in the same way he used to silence his students in class.

'Tikka, enough.'

It was ridiculous, but just seeing that familiar gesture, that palm, more creased than ever these days, was enough to make me stop.

'I don't know that speaking up would have made much difference, champ. Sounds to me like those girls were pretty determined to get away.'

Somewhere down the street someone started revving a car engine in sharp, angry bursts.

'There were a lot of people who should have been in the queue to talk to the police ahead of you, Tik,' Dad said. 'Mrs McCausley, for a start, if she knew so much. Why didn't she say anything to the cops? Or why didn't Mr and Mrs Van Apfel? I'm guessing Mrs Van Apfel got wind of the girls' plan to run away if her husband knew about it. Someone might argue that they should have been telling the police.'

He grimaced, and for a moment I wondered if all this lifting and carrying boxes was too much for his back these days.

'There were a lot of adults who didn't do the right thing by those girls. Your mother and I, we could have stepped in. Done more. Said something.' He gave a helpless sort of shrug. 'We could have questioned you and Laura harder. Sometimes I wonder. But you were only kids, and it was hard enough watching you lose your friends. You and Lor were a mess.'

I looked past Dad as he spoke, and I tried not to think about what it felt like back then, when our grief was so horribly raw. Instead I focused on the wall of cardboard boxes that were slowly piling up against of the brickwork of the garage. They made a second wall there, a cardboard-carton wall like the inner bailey of a fort. A fort of brown Foodbank boxes.

Dad turned his attention back to the remaining boxes in the car. Outside the engine noise died down and in the silence I could hear Dad's breathing again, though it was more laboured now. He slid another box towards us and tilted it, ready to lift. I took the weight on the other side.

'Anyway, Mrs McCausley didn't know about the girls' plan to run away,' I said as we lifted the box into the air. 'Only Mr Van Apfel and Mr Avery knew.'

Between us we'd lowered the box we were holding almost to the floor, but now Dad let it drop onto the concrete with a bang. Inside tins rattled like teeth.

'Mr Avery? The schoolteacher? *He knew?*'

'Uh, apparently.' I was surprised by the force of Dad's words. 'Cordie told him,' I said. 'At least, she said she did.'

I thought back to the fight Cordie and Hannah had had on the way home from school the day Cordie had bragged to Mr Avery about their secret plan. 'So what?' she said scornfully.

'He was interested. He's always interested in what I've got to say.' She'd stopped in the street to snap her sock elastic tight, and then she'd rolled the sock suggestively down her calf until it formed a thick sausage around her ankle.

'So Mr Avery knew Cordelia was planning to run away?' Dad said.

'Cordie said he did.'

'Did he know when?'

'When they planned to leave? I think so. Yeah, he did. Because he told Cordie it was a shame he was working backstage at the Showstopper that night so he wouldn't get to say a proper goodbye. Whatever that meant.'

Dad said nothing.

'What? Dad, what? What do you think it means? Do you think that would have been enough for the police to get him on? Because if you think it means he was guilty of something then we could —'

I stopped when I saw Dad's stony expression. He nudged a box tetchily with his toe.

'Do you know what it means, Tik?' he said eventually. 'It means nothing. We're talking about something that happened twenty years ago, to a group of people who are all long gone. Mr and Mrs Van Apfel. Mr Avery. In some form or another, all three of your friends. None of them are here, so you're not going to change anything now.'

'That's not true,' I said hotly. 'It affected everyone. *It still does.* You said yourself you wish you'd done more. You knew there was something bad happening at the Van Apfels' place, you had your suspicions, you and Mum, and you didn't do anything to stop it. How can you say that doesn't matter now?'

I could tell, even before I'd finished speaking, that I'd overstepped the mark, and now I felt a childish pang of shame. In the street outside the engine sounds started thrumming again, and the two of us stood, unspeaking, and listened as the revving sounds were joined by tyre squeal and whoever it was test-drove their handiwork in noisy circles around the cul-de-sac.

'Of course I wish I'd done more, Tik,' Dad said after a pause.

He turned back to the car then and slid another Foodbank box towards his chest.

Did I know, he said, almost as an afterthought, about the time he tried to talk to Mrs Van Apfel? When he went over and stood on the doorstep of the Van Apfel house after Hayley Stinson's sleepover party and asked Mrs Van Apfel what she knew about the schoolteacher and her daughter? Enquired how things were at home.

'What did she say?'

Dad couldn't remember exactly. Or if he could, he wasn't telling me.

'I don't remember getting very far,' he said 'But then, no one ever did with Carol. Not that I'm saying that what we did was enough. But jeez, Tik, telling yourself "if only" for the rest of your days sounds like hell to me.'

And at the mention of the word 'hell', Cordie's singsong voice was in my ear: *Mr Avery said there is no hell.*

Maybe Mr Avery was right and hell wasn't a destination, it was just some state we exiled ourselves to when we couldn't bear where we really were. Maybe Mr Avery was right, and maybe Dad was too and none of it mattered in this instant, inside the garage at home, with Dad working quietly beside me and the dust motes swirling around us, catching the sunlight that streamed in through a gap in the door.

Dad slid the last box towards us and we lowered it onto the floor.

'Cup of tea?' Dad suggested, and I nodded and followed him out into the late afternoon sunshine.

'You never know, Tik,' Dad said as we walked across the front lawn to the house. 'It's not something I ever seriously entertained until I found out what they'd had planned, but maybe Hannah and Cordie got away safely in the end.'

He held the screen door open for me.

CHAPTER TWENTY-TWO

After Ruth's funeral my world split in two. There was before and there was ever after. Left behind were the school plays, all those trips to the milk bar. Abandoned handstand competitions in the pool. Over there, in the past, on the far side of the abyss, neighbours still passed potato salad recipes and power tools across their brushwood fences while they talked about how it never rained. There, kids still played Knock 'n' Run like no one could explain the empty space that stood, wiping its feet, when the neighbours opened their front doors. They still collected cicada shells, those crunchy coffins that got left behind long after the insects went winging away. Greengrocers and Redeyes. Shrill Yellow Mondays. Black Princes, fresh from being buried in the earth. And at number one Macedon Close, on the corner, opposite the Van Apfels, Mrs McCausley still supervised the comings and goings of everyone in the street through the gap in her pinch-pleat curtains.

On that side was my childhood. Over here: a different animal. Here, I stood by the sign to our street every day before school. But Ruth never arrived, asking what I had for recess. And so each morning I walked to school on my own.

Plans were made to hold a memorial service for Hannah and Cordie – a combined one – at the Hope Revival Centre, like Ruth's. Only no one wanted to be the person to say it was time to go ahead with the service, even though the police search had been called off and the taskforce had taken over the investigation.

'Wait another week if you're not ready,' the pastor advised. He was the same pastor who had presided over Ruth's service. 'Jesus is cool with patience,' he said.

And so while songs were chosen and Bible readings were selected, while the order of service was word-processed and formatted and saved on a floppy disk, nobody had the heart to go and press 'print'. (They couldn't anyway, without a date for the front.)

Hannah and Cordie's memorial service was put on hold for the whole of that summer. It wouldn't have been the same anyway. It wouldn't have been like Ruth's. Not without any bodies.

And not while there was still a chance the two of them were alive.

The thing about Ruth's funeral was it was so appallingly *final*. Ruth was gone, forever after.

* * *

One afternoon, after Ruth's service and while we waited for Hannah and Cordie's, Laura and I saw Mrs Van Apfel in the bush. 'What's she doing down there, you reckon?' I said to Laura. 'Putting food out for the birds?'

The two of us stood side by side, safe on the back deck at home, looking out over the scrub on our side of the valley.

'That's not bird feed, Tik.' My sister spoke cautiously. The two of us had been sizing up each other's grief for weeks. Observing it, stepping around it, recalibrating it by the hour. Treading warily with one another ever since the Showstopper.

'What then?' I asked her.

We watched as Mrs Van Apfel walked through the bush on the fringe of the fire trail. She stuck to the scrub where the shadows were longer. On her left, our line of houses discreetly turned their backs. To her right the valley fell away to the river. She walked purposefully, methodically, her head bent towards the dirt. Tracing a deliberate path through the dappled sunshine. Every few metres she stopped and stooped to the ground and left something in the dirt, and the only thing to say that the whole thing wasn't a dream was the breeze that made goosebumps on my arms.

'She's laying crosses,' Laura said.

Palm crosses they were. Bent out of dried, twisted fronds. They were homemade, but they'd been folded tightly, pressed together with care. Mrs Van Apfel tried to stand them up but the soil was too shallow so she left them lying in the dirt.

'But why?' I asked Laura. 'How does she know Hannah and Cordie are dead?'

'Don't say that!' my sister said.

'What, "dead"?'

'Don't say it, okay?' Laura said again. 'Crosses don't mean anyone's dead.'

She was right, I supposed. At Easter, didn't they mean new life?

'What do these ones mean then?' I asked.

'Maybe it's her way of praying.'

Then I had a thought: 'Or maybe she's leaving them like breadcrumbs for Hannah and Cordie to follow her home.'

CHAPTER TWENTY-THREE

As for Ruth, can't you see her? Hope Revivalist to the end. Can't you picture her in the instant she abandoned their plan? Abandoned their plan and abandoned her sisters. When she headed back to the amphitheatre on her own.

'It's a sin!' she would have hollered when they refused to go home. 'It's a sin to run away, and I'm not gonna go with you!'

I must have imagined it a thousand times. When she left Hannah and Cordie, when she slipped and she fell. When she disappeared down that crack, in the rock, by the river.

You can see how easily it happened.

* * *

Already that night Ruth is *tired*. And she's got *sore feet* in her jelly shoes. She is hungry, hungry, hungry the whole time they walk.

'I want to go *ho-ome*,' she whinges mournfully.

And Hannah snaps: 'We're not going home. Not unless you get us caught, that is.'

Because that's the real danger at the rate Ruth is walking. Their parents will work out they're missing soon, and then there'll be hell to pay. Hannah knows. But Ruth is slow. She plods and stumbles. She's scared of the dark.

Though mostly she moans and wants to go back. And Cordie turns and places one hand on her hip where her T-shirt is tied in a knot. 'So go back,' she says coolly. 'You weren't supposed to come in the first place, you know.' And Ruth scowls and stops to pick a stick out of her shoe. It's impossible being seven when your sisters are thirteen and fourteen. Impossible to keep up. Impossible to be taken seriously.

'She can't go on her own,' Hannah points out to Cordie. (See how she acts like Ruth's already not there?) 'She'd never find her way back. No way she would. And what if something happens to her?'

'Yes, I would! I would find my way back, Hannah!'

Ruth's even more determined now. She'll prove she can do it. She'll show Cordie, and she'll show Hannah too. (Though it *is* very dark, and she hasn't been concentrating on the route Hannah has taken to get them this far.)

'And then you'd blab,' Cordie says meanly. 'You'll tell everyone where we've gone so they come straight after us.'

And Ruth can't argue with that — they all know it's true. She can't be trusted to keep her mouth shut.

And that's the other thing: Ruth's starving-hungry mouth. Ruth needs almost constant feeding. Ruth knows it, and

Cordie knows it, and Hannah's aware of it most of all. She's worried that, without Laura's money, it's going to be hard enough to try to feed herself and Cordie, let alone fill Ruth's stomach too.

But there hadn't been time to meet Laura in the clearing like they'd arranged. (Mr Van Apfel had hung around too long for that.) They'd been lucky to get away from the Showstopper at all. Hannah's not so naïve she can't see that.

But now they have Ruth slowing them down. Ruth with no sense of urgency. Ruth who wants to go back so badly she drags her feet in the dirt.

'Wouldja hurry up?'

'Slowcoach.'

'I'm going home!' Ruth announces, as if the words have been waiting there, simmering just below the surface all along.

Then she stomps back down the slope in her pink plastic jelly shoes, her chin tipped defiantly to the sky, and she vanishes into the scrub, plait swinging, fists balled, sending up startled birds like flares.

She'll find her way back. She'll show her sisters. All she has to do is head downhill and she'll come to the river. But she's further south than she thought, and it's very dark now and she can't see the amphitheatre across the water. Can't make out the oval, or the footbridge to take her there. She'll get higher, that's what she'll do. That way, she'll get a better look at where she is. At where she needs to get to.

I imagine her climbing grimly up and onto the boulders by the river, her stubby nails scraping against the sandstone. The rocks are jagged and high and she moves awkwardly. Crabwalks across their moss-kissed surface. Until she slips and suddenly she's falling, she's slipping between the rocks, and the night swims high above her and the walls of the valley loom like a lid, and she's home. She is home.

Ruth's done with running away.

CHAPTER TWENTY-FOUR

The hospital where Laura went for chemotherapy was not in a single suburb. Instead it sprawled between two towns, dwarfing the weatherboard homes and Californian bungalows that survived all around it. As if the whole huge facility had been dumped in the wrong place. Unceremoniously, beside the highway.

'You didn't think we'd get here so early, did you?' I asked.

Laura and I sat in her car outside the hospital. She was in the passenger seat for once.

'I didn't think we'd get here at *all*,' she said. 'Not the way you took on that truck changing lanes on the bridge.'

I grinned. I'd had to slide the driver's seat forward in order to reach the pedals that morning. My sister had four and half centimetres on me. Three weeks I'd waited before I was allowed to drive her car, and now I'd gone and mucked up her seat settings.

We were waiting to go inside for chemotherapy. I'd been by her side for the past two days too. (Though Mum said she'd do the next shift so I could stay home and pack. I was flying back to Baltimore on the weekend.)

It was blisteringly hot in the car, even with the windows down, and even in the deep shade of a Moreton Bay fig that sheltered half-a-dozen parked cars under its canopy. That tree must have reached twenty metres into the air. The car park was littered with fermenting purple-speckled figs. Its roots ruptured the asphalt with their collarbones.

'You too hot?' I asked Laura. 'I can switch on the airconditioning.'

I was sticking to the vinyl seat with sweat. But Laura was curled up with a fleecy jacket laid over her like a robe. It made her look strangely regal.

'No aircon. Please,' she said. 'I need to soak up the heat.'

She wouldn't be able to get warm once the chemo kicked in. She said it was like the cold got into her bones.

So we stayed in the car – in the heat – with the windows wound down, though I would have much preferred to wait inside the hospital. In there it smelled of sickness but at least there was airconditioning and filtered spring water in the cooler.

'When's Jade Heddingly's engagement party?' I asked to distract Laura. She looked ashen wrapped in that jacket.

'The Saturday after you fly out,' she said. 'Shame you can't come, you'd know just about everyone there.'

'Bad timing,' I said, pulling a face, though we both knew I was lying.

'Your mate Mrs McCausley will be there. And the Townsends from number nine, and the Tooleys. The Gonskis can't make it – they're away in Bali. Did I tell you Anna has a sarong shop over there now?'

I shielded my eyes from the sun as Laura told me a long story I couldn't follow, about Anna Gonski's sarong shop and the tax breaks they got, about how they spent each winter in Seminyak.

'And who's Jade marrying again?' I asked when she'd finished explaining. I was fairly sure Mum had told me, but I hadn't been paying much attention to all the talk about Jade's wedding.

And my sister gave me a look that said: *was I serious?*

'She's marrying Jacob.'

'Jacob who?'

'You know. Jacob Hunter.'

'What? The kid with the trombone?'

'Yeah. He's in the New South Wales Police Band now.'

'That's a long way from Tipperary.'

But if Laura remembered, she wasn't playing along.

Jade was having seven bridesmaids, Laura told me, including Hayley Stinson from swimming club. 'It's going to be a massive wedding,' she commented, and we sat and considered this in the heat and the quiet.

'Hey, what about Reverend Richmond?' I asked. 'Will he do the ceremony?'

I thought about the way he always wanted to be invited. And the way he could be counted on to fall asleep mid-event. Laura looked surprised. 'Reverend Richmond is dead. He died more than a year ago.'

She smiled wryly, and for the first time all morning. 'He died in his sleep.'

Mr and Mrs Van Apfel were dead too, though I knew that, of course. They'd died almost ten years ago, within weeks of one another. Laura had assured me at the time that it wasn't uncommon. 'Lots of married couples die close together, one after the other. We see it in the hospital all the time.'

'But surely that's only couples who are really old?' I'd said. 'The Van Apfels were only in their sixties, weren't they?'

Mr Van Apfel had died from an undetected pulmonary embolism – a blood clot that travelled to his lung. But when it came to Mrs Van Apfel, no one ever found out. An ambulance turned up, just weeks after Mr Van Apfel's death, and took her body away.

'And we only know that because Trent Rainer saw them wheel her out with a sheet pulled up over her face. It was in the middle of the day,' Laura had said. 'We were all at work.'

'Did Trent ask them what had happened?'

'He said there wasn't a chance.'

Their house was sold a few months later. And then resold at fairly regular intervals after that.

The silver frame of the car window glinted in the heat. Sparks of sunlight flickered along the ledge. Beyond the window, giant fig leaves shifted gently in the wind and showed their rust-brown underbellies.

'You're still going back to Baltimore then?' Laura asked, even though she knew the answer.

'I am,' I said. 'Three and a half weeks was the longest I could get off work. Although ...'

'Although?'

I glanced at her, at her jacket laid across her like a rug, its fleecy collar pulled right up to her chin. At the way the cuffs flopped, empty-handed, over the sides of her seat. She had dark circles under her eyes.

'Although, I don't know if I'll go back to my old job,' I said cautiously. 'I was thinking, I don't know … I guess I was thinking I might even go back and do some more study,' I said shyly. 'I was thinking, maybe medicine. Then paediatrics or something.'

'Paediatrics?'

'Maybe.'

Laura looked thoughtful.

'You'd be good at that, Tik.'

I waited for the punchline but it never came. Instead she looked at me sincerely, then she worked up a smile. 'You would. You'd be a natural.'

'You reckon?' I was elated. 'I've only just started thinking about it since I got back.'

Then she smirked. 'You've always been good at getting along with kids. It's like you're already down on their level.'

I grinned like a loser. She rolled her eyes and it only made me grin more. I wasn't stupid enough to go looking for Laura's approval these days, but it was still wonderful to stumble across it.

'Do you think you're nearly ready to go inside?' I asked then.

Ahead of us the hospital looked like an enormous cool, white Esky.

'In a minute,' she said, and she tipped her head back against the headrest and closed her eyes against the glare. For a moment

I thought she was going to try to sleep, then she started speaking again, more deliberately this time.

'You know,' she started slowly, 'how you asked me the other week if I thought we did the right thing by not telling anyone that Hannah and Cordie planned to run away? And did I ever worry we might have got it all wrong?'

I waited.

'I *do* worry,' she admitted. 'I don't know if what we did was right. In fact, the longer I think about it, the less certain I feel.'

Her eyes opened momentarily and she squinted in the sunshine. Then she closed them again without waiting to gauge my response. I saw then that this was a conversation she'd been working up to for a while. Maybe the whole time I'd been here.

'I always thought,' she went on, 'that if our *intentions* were good … Like, by keeping their secret I was doing the right thing by Hannah.'

'But now?'

She hesitated. 'Now I don't know if intentions count for much, Tik.'

'I never thought they did,' I conceded.

Out the window I watched the fig leaves stir in the wind. They flipped from green to rust-brown and back again, revealing their dark undersides. Seeing their two-tone leaves made me think of the pipis we used to collect in the clearing in the valley as kids. Those pipis were pale on the outside, while inside their shells they were a beautiful glossy lilac. It was because of their colour that we collected them, and we would arrange them in intricate patterns, purple side up, back in our valley of dry bones.

'So what do we do?' Laura asked, and for a moment I thought it was some sort of reverse psychology. So I'd be the one to do the reassuring for once.

'What do we do?' I echoed.

'Yeah,' she said quietly, and I realised she was serious. That I wasn't the only one who'd been lost in the years since our friends went missing. When they failed to turn up among the dry bones. So many things we used to dig up that weren't ours to touch. There were so many things in this life better left untouched.

'I guess we stick together,' I said eventually, because at least that seemed possible. Was the only thing that made any sense. 'We stick together, the same way we've always done, Lor.'

Across the car park a cleaner stepped outside for a smoke. He leaned heavily against the brick wall. When he exhaled blue smoke above his head in a funnel, the air around him quivered like water.

For so long we'd been haunted by those girls. Since the moment they first disappeared. We were the ones left behind, Laura and I. Defined by what was long gone. And if not that, then what? Who should we be?

I watched the cleaner exhale, then I let out a breath.

'And we let go,' I said hesitantly.

'We let *them* go,' Laura agreed.

I nodded. They only ever wanted to run.

And my sister looked satisfied then, like she'd heard what she was after. I watched the muscles in her neck relax.

The two of us got out of the car – Laura slowly, gingerly, with one arm placed across my shoulders. We started walking towards the hospital entrance together. Her arm felt good where it was, slung across my shoulders. I raised my hip slightly on her side to take more of her weight.

My sister still smelled so familiar to me.

CHAPTER TWENTY-FIVE

I was thirty-one that summer I came back to see my sister. Plain thirty-one – no need for the one-sixth these days. In a few years I'd be as old as Hannah, Cordie and Ruth *all combined*: fourteen plus thirteen plus seven. I was planning to live for another thirty-one years as well. Then another thirty-one after that. I might live nine lives in total for the Van Apfels' short ones.

But that's assuming Hannah and Cordie weren't out there somewhere, racking up birthdays themselves.

* * *

Before I flew back to Baltimore I decided to spend a day walking around the city. Start down near the quay and walk along the foreshore. Watch the moss-green ferries pulling away from the quay. It took less than an hour to drive from Macedon Close to the heart of the city. And that's where I saw her. *There.* In an underground car park of all places. As though she'd never left the east coast at all. Hadn't vanished along with her sisters.

She was standing waiting for the lift to arrive so she could ascend to street level. While I cruised past in my car searching for a parking spot, and instead found Cordie Van Apfel in my rear-view mirror.

That blonde hair, those bare arms. Her hips broader now. It was Cordie, all right. Corporate Cordie. With her handbag and her laptop bag in matching black leather. Her dress was a deep russet red. But even without the red dress, Cordie was enough to make you stop. The curve of each calf. The sway of her back. The way she jabbed at the lift buttons even though the arrows were already lit up, and then adjusted her dress expectantly in the reflection of the doors. She couldn't have been more Cordie-like if she tried.

But this was more than Cordie-like. This *was* Cordie, I was sure. And I wanted to pull over and leap out of my car and tell her to wait for me. To shout: 'Cordie! Just wait! Cordie, I'm coming!'

To ask her where on earth she'd been.

But there were cars backed up behind me, snaking away in the dark. There was no room to leave the queue and so instead I guided my car around the corner, down the ramp, and onto an identical level below. I flung my car into a parking spot and wrenched the keys out of the ignition. I was barefoot and my shoes were wedged under my seat but I was faster without them, I reasoned. I ran to the fire stairs and took them two at a time and the concrete was cold under my feet.

When I reached street level I paused on the footpath. For an instant I was dazzled by the day. Then I saw Cordie in the crowd at the end of the block, waiting for the traffic lights to change.

'Cordie!' I shouted. 'Cordie, wait!'

I began to run again. Started to weave in and out of the crowd, and there were elbows and shopping bags and shouted phone conversations. Across the street a jackhammer kicked off. I ran towards the intersection at the end of the block, and the traffic lights changed and Cordie surged across the street.

'Cordie, wait!' I yelled. 'It's *Tikka*! It's me!'

But the pedestrian light flashed red and the traffic resumed and Cordie was gone, swanning up the next block.

At the corner I hesitated. I could still see Cordie across the street. I could still see her and she still looked the same. She had one arm held high across her stomach at a right angle to keep her laptop bag from slipping, the same way she used to keep her cast arm safe. Her blonde hair was brighter, more artificial than it used to be, but I still longed to reach out and touch it. To tug it. To make her turn around. A taxi sped around the corner in front of me. Then another. Then a courier bike. The coast was clear and I darted across the road, and a car blasted its horn at my back.

Up on the footpath I was on the same side as Cordie now, and I started to run again. My soles were burning. Lungs on fire. I held one arm out in front of me as I jostled through the crowd.

Ahead of me her blonde head bobbed along the street. Strands of her hair blew backwards as she strode, like fingers beckoning me on. But the footpath was so congested and I was losing ground. She seemed to drift further away with each step I took.

In the gulf that stretched out between us now, a group of tourists swarmed towards me. They must have been retirement age and yet they travelled along the street in pairs like schoolchildren. They pointed at street signs and graffiti, talking excitedly in a language I didn't recognise. I watched as one woman in the group smiled beatifically at a pigeon on the footpath. Someone else took a photo of my bare feet with their phone.

Their tour guide walked at the back of the pack, his plastic lanyard swinging around his neck, his flagpole hoisted high into the air. At the top of the pole a small flag whipped and rippled in the breeze.

'Are you okay?' The tour guide eyed me suspiciously. He wasn't really asking, more pointing out the fact I was standing, wild-eyed and barefoot, in the middle of the footpath. I shook my head as the last of his group filed past.

'No – yes,' I corrected myself. 'Yes, I'm all right.'

He nodded and then continued ushering his tour group along the street while I stood watching.

I am all right, I thought, even though my heart felt like it might beat right out of my chest. Maybe it was all of those stairs I ran up, but the street seemed to swim dizzyingly.

On the breeze I caught the sharp smell of brine off the harbour and suddenly I was back – I was back in the valley with the stench of the river in my nostrils, and Cordie was there in her Daisy Duke shorts. A quizzical look on her face.

Why, she wanted to know, wouldn't I just let her run? Why did I insist on pulling her back, tugging her sleeve, dragging her home? *Hadn't I seen how bad that turned out for Ruth?*

I understood as I heard her voice in my mind that the only reason I kept seeing her was because I wanted to see her. Because even after all this time it made more sense than her simply being 'gone'. But sense wasn't the thing or, at least, it wasn't enough. All the new truths, the amassed facts (*Who heard what? Who was where?*). All our secrets we'd kept subterranean for so long. None of these things explained what really happened to those girls.

Van Apfel. From the apple. From the tree of knowledge.

I could see now: no one ever truly knows.

'I'm all right,' I said again. Only when I said it this time I turned my head away from the tour group and I spoke the words softly, whispered them to the woman in the red dress who was disappearing up the street. For a moment I thought I saw her hesitate like she might look around, but she didn't. She continued walking up the block.

And it was a relief then, to turn away and start walking in the opposite direction, away from that blonde head and back towards the car park I'd come from. I'd retrace my steps, and retrieve my bag and my shoes from under my seat so I could head out into the day for a second time.

And I guess the woman from the car park – the one who'd adjusted her red dress in the lift reflection – made her way to the far intersection. Who knows, maybe she crossed again and rounded a corner, before being swallowed up by the crowd.

Before she vanished back into thin air.

EPILOGUE

Imagine it. *Dream it,* the way that I've dreamed it so many times. Three shadows fill my dreams, fluid and small, and pulling away from the amphitheatre. See how they peel off and spread out like drips down a pane of glass. By the time they reach the brick toilet block on the left-hand side of the stage, they have fallen back into step and they move as one undiluted being. Always was, always is, and always bringing up the rear. In this dream, there are no other shadowy figures. Just the three of them. That unholy trinity.

Cordie leads.

In the impossible dark, she steers her sisters close enough to the toilet block that they can hear someone inside. Movement. The clink of a metal belt buckle. She draws the three of them past the light outside the entrance, sidestepping its stippled glare. Then she veers around the back and dumps a stack of brochures in the rubbish bin before she disappears from sight.

She is headed towards the river.

They walk in formation as they approach the oval: Cordie, then Hannah, then Ruth. Hannah's almost a head taller than their sloe-eyed leader and she stoops anxiously, unsure what to do with the view. Under one arm, a bag of XXL buttered popcorn sags sadly inside its plastic like a netted animal.

Cordie wears a T-shirt and shorts. Converse sneakers on her feet. Her hair still flipped over to one side. She's complemented the outfit with a locket that until just yesterday contained a good-luck tuft of Madonna's ginger fur but now holds sacred mouse fluff instead.

A shiver ripples along their line and Ruth hurries to catch it. She's not missing out on a thing. Though she's hungry already, and her pockets are empty, and please God, popcorn aside, let Hannah have packed snacks.

At the oval the lights glow a strange samphire green as though the world is submerged in the river. A dog barks and it bolts out of nowhere and onto the oval, and the girls stumble back in alarm, as if the two things are connected by a thin strand of wire so that the dog breaking free and running onto the pitch pushes the girls back into the shadows.

'It's C'mere!' Cordie laughs at herself in the dark. 'Look! It's only C'mere.'

They watch the red dog as it runs in circles, deer-leaping, high-stepping. Mouth stretched in a tongue-lolling grin. While in the distance a trombone *prwrrp-prwrrp-prwrrp*s comically. That kelpie's come with his own brass band.

'C'mere's come to say goodbye,' Cordie says wistfully. 'Wish we could give him a pat.'

Instead they keep moving, towards the mangroves, towards the river. Towards the footbridge that crosses the water.

They're careful where they walk – they stick to the shadows. They stay outside the boundary markings spray-painted onto the oval, then they weave through the ghost gums that lead to the river. In and out, in and out. Here and gone. And the leaves gleam like silver in the startling moonlight. They ripple like the scales of a fish.

But the river itself – that black slash of water – is deathly unmoving tonight. It's slack water, and Hannah knows the tide will rise further, the current will push closer before the tide turns later this evening. But right now it's still, and the whole world's stopped turning, except for three ghosts who skitter along the shoreline casting strange shadows. Long-limbed streaks. Night-birds dancing in the dark.

Meanwhile, back at the amphitheatre the trombone gives its final, triumphant blast and the audience breaks into applause. The girls stop. Hold their breath.

They peer into the summery gloom.

Then the stage lights go up and the audience settles down, and they know there's more Showstopper to come.

'What is it, you reckon?'

'Dunno. There's not enough of them for it to be the choir.'

Hannah squints at the figures standing on stage.

'Who cares?' Cordie says dreamily, because nothing matters now that they're gone. She wraps her arms around her midriff and hugs herself, grinning.

Back at the oval, C'mere is agitated. The dog can sense a charge in the air. He twists and flips, runs in frenzied circles. Won't c'mere or c'mhome when he's called.

And the girls run on, in the mangroves and the moonlight. In the miasmic dark. They're still coming, still running. They're living and breathing. Still tracing the vein of the river. As they run their footprints sink into the sand and the silt, and they dare the rising tide to erase them.